little
BIRD

A DARK MAFIA ROMANCE

USA TODAY BESTSELLING AUTHOR

KALLY ASH

Little Bird

Cover design by Sly Fox Cover Design

Edited by Swish Design & Editing

Proofread by Swish Design & Editing

For you know who...

Everything the light touches... is our kingdom. But a King's time as ruler rises and falls like the sun. One day, the sun will set on my time here, and will rise with you as the new king.

MUFASA

Fuck the sun.

BANE RIVERA

1

Bane

IT'S GOOD TO BE FUCKING KING.

King of pussy.

King of coke.

Lord and ruler of the finest goddamn gentleman's club in the whole of California.

From my vantage in the upstairs office, I looked down upon my dominion, feeling all fucking *Lion King*.

Everything the light touches...

Fuck, James Earl Jones was the man.

I'd worked fucking hard for all of this, firstly by graduating business school while working my ass off with drug baron, Marco Mancini. I'd lined my pockets with his cash before finally disposing of him.

Hey, a guy like me can't have fucking competition, right?

The bastard had to have seen it coming. He'd groomed me since I was a thirteen-year-old pickpocket on the streets of

Venice Beach. First, he had me acting like a gopher before I'd begged him for more. I'd literally *begged* him to sell coke, and the sick fuck had given me exactly what I'd wanted—the keys to the damn castle.

Long live the new king.

I drained the last of my drink, my gaze bouncing around the converted warehouse. The place had been stripped and refitted, doing away with all that industrial chic shit and adding a touch of class.

The Dollhouse was my pride and joy.

Fifty thousand square feet of pussy, kink, and debauchery.

So much pussy.

"Hey, daddy," someone said behind me. I glanced over my shoulder at Kandy, with a 'K,' naturally. Her real name was Cecile, and she was a law student trying to pay her way through college. I made it a point to learn everything I could about my employees because I never knew when that shit could be of use to me. For example, Kandy with a 'K' had a long-term boyfriend who was cheating on her, although fuck knew why. Kandy was smoking hot, and if I didn't have the rule of not fucking the dancers, you can bet your ass I'd have her bent over my desk right now.

Readjusting my dick, I turned around to look at her. Dressed in black lingerie that covered just enough to get men to dig into their pockets for Benjamins and fuck-me heels that made her athletic calves look killer, she stood there holding a glass of amber liquid.

I folded my arms over my chest. "What's up, baby?"

"I thought you might need a top-up," she replied in a smoky voice, gesturing to my now empty glass on the sideboard in front of the window. I crooked my finger at her, and she came fucking running. As she handed me the whisky, she asked in a purr, "Anything else I can do for you?" Her hand found my semi-hard dick, and she started to rub. I even let her for a minute. I mean, I didn't touch the drugs I sold, but blowjobs were something else. Being surrounded by beautiful fucking women with their barely-there lingerie-clad bodies did something to man's self-control. And by did something, I meant it strained it to fucking shit.

I watched her intensely as she stroked me, but I wouldn't let her do much more than that. I might have been a criminal, but I still had standards.

Don't let pussy distract you.

Don't snort the product.

Call your sister weekly.

See? Easy.

"You like that, daddy?"

"Don't call me that," I replied. "I'm not your fucking daddy. You're not on right now."

Kandy pouted but didn't stop rubbing my dick. With a wicked smile I'd seen her use on so many clients, she began undoing the zipper on my black slacks, but I grabbed her wrist to stop her.

Shaking my head, I pulled her hand away. "You know the rules, baby," I said the words softly, but I wanted to scream them. For years, my Dolls have been trying to get a piece of me. It had gotten to the point where I was now the ultimate challenge. Who could fuck Bane Rivera and survive?

What can I say? I have a fucking reputation for dirty fucking sex that the women always came back for.

"Get back on that dance floor and earn your tips." Gesturing to the drink, I added, "Thanks for this."

I watched as Kandy sashayed the fuck out of my office, closing the door softly behind her. Turning back around, I waited until I saw her descend the stairs tucked beside the bar, then went back to what I was doing.

And what was I doing? I was waiting for one of my fucking dealers to turn up with a fucking good explanation. He'd been light on his drop earlier in the day, the kind of money that made me pay attention.

There was another knock on the door, this one firm and unyielding. *Dagger.*

"Come in," I barked.

Dagger, my right-hand man, stepped into the room. His short, dark hair was wet, so he'd just come from dispensing some punishment for me. *Good man.* "Did you get him?"

"Yeah, he's out here pissing his pants for you."

A smile pulled at the corners of my mouth. "Just the way I like it. Send the fuck in."

Dagger grunted and stepped outside. A moment later, a guy named Hawk Montana was shoved into the room with such force that he tripped over his own feet and ended up sprawled out in front of me.

How fucking fitting.

When he tried to get up, I shoved my three-thousand-dollar Italian loafer between his shoulder blades and pushed him back down. I didn't think the guy would have been inclined to stay if it weren't for the sound of Dagger shoving a magazine into his new toy—a Heckler & Koch MP5K—before hovering the loud and fatal end over Hawk's head.

"Where's my money?" I asked in a bored drawl. Really, I had better fucking things to do with my time.

"It was all there," Hawk replied. "I counted it. Twice."

"Then I'd say you need to go back to school, Hawk, because it wasn't all there. *I* counted it twice, and you were at least fifty grand short."

All the color drained from Hawk's face as sweat started to form on his brow. "*Fifty* grand?"

I held out my hand to him, all five fingers up like good little soldiers. "This many, times ten, asshole, unless you can't count those up without the help of a calculator."

"I counted it twice," he muttered, more to himself than to me. "Jesus, Bane, I'm sorry. It was all there when I dropped it off. I swear!"

I looked over at Dagger, who shrugged.

Now, I wasn't a fucking monster. I wasn't going to kill the fucker yet, but I was going to give him one more chance.

"How about I make you a deal, Hawk." I crouched in front of him. "I give you two weeks to come up with the cash you owe me, and you deliver it to me like a good little boy. If you can't do that, then I'm afraid our working relationship is over… as is your heart's relationship with beating in your chest."

I stood, jerking my chin at Dagger. My man placed the submachine gun on my desk and hauled the other man up. When I was face to face with him, I said, "And to make sure you understand just how serious I am, you now have one week to get me my cash."

Hawk's eyes widened until I could see the whites all the way around. Good. He needed to be scared because what I had planned for him was going to go down as one of my messiest retributions in history.

People didn't steal from me.

Ever.

"Rough him up a little before sending him on his way," I said to Dagger as I turned back to the large picture window. I listened as Hawk was hauled away, mumbling something about how a week wasn't enough time and how he'd counted the money twice.

Honestly, I didn't give a fuck about the money. Fifty grand was a fucking drop in the ocean compared to everything else. I was punishing the guy on principle. I refused to let anyone screw me out of my money.

No. Fucking. Way.

Reaching down, I rearranged my dick in my pants, then threw back what was left in the glass. I may not fuck my dancers, but it didn't mean I couldn't enjoy the fuck out of them when I felt like it.

Surveying the floor, I spotted a Doll who would do for tonight. Normally, I would've called her up here, but I was feeling restless so I hoofed it down the stairs and out onto the opulent floor of The Dollhouse. The décor was decorated in rich reds and glittering golds. The walls were black, the poles and stages where my Dolls danced were polished to within an inch of their lives. Plush red velvet couches and dark brown leather chesterfield armchairs were scattered around, all oriented to get the best view of the Dolls while they worked.

This place was a classy establishment, one that also required a six-figure membership to attend. I had to have a way to keep the riff-raff out, and the men—plus some women—with enough green to back their penchant for fuckery were the ones I wanted.

My Ferragamos thumped over the dark-stained hardwood floors as I made my way over to Syndy. She looked up from the man she was talking to—a long-time patron who I knew had a wife and three kids at home.

"Mr. Gregory, so nice to see you again."

"Mr. Rivera," he greeted. "I was just telling Syndy here how much I enjoy blowjobs with my scotch."

"Don't we all?" I replied with a smile. Turning my gaze to my dancer briefly, I looked at her lush mouth, and my dick got harder. "If you wouldn't mind, I need Syndy for a moment."

Dick Gregory waved his hand in a *by all means* sort of way. As soon as the woman was gone, another one of the girls would take her place. When the owner of the fastest-growing tech company was on the floor, my Dolls knew how to work.

I placed a hand on the small of Syndy's back as I guided her off the floor and to one of the playrooms out the back.

"You said you wanted to talk to me?" she asked, somewhat confused by the change in direction.

"I want to see you, but it isn't for talking," I growled, sliding my hand down her to her bare ass and tightening my fingers.

Syndy's eyes lit up. "Yes, daddy."

She didn't know that the only fucking she was going to get was her mouth, but I let her believe she had finally tamed the illusive Bane Rivera. I checked each room as we walked past, finding the first three occupied. Swiping my access card at the reader by the door, I dragged her into number four. Locking the door behind us, I took a seat on the leather armchair in the center of the room, my knees spread wide. On the wall to my right was a cupboard with BDSM toys that got regular use by the patrons, but Syn wouldn't need them tonight. All I wanted was her mouth, her tongue, her teeth.

Syn stared at me with lust-soaked eyes for a moment, then

when I undid my zipper, freeing my cock, she fell to her fucking knees like this was church, and I was offering her absolution for all her sins.

"Just a blowjob, Syn."

She tried to hide the disappointment from her face, but I saw it etched there in all its crestfallen glory. She'd get over it, especially if Dick Gregory were still there when I was done with her. I sat back and watched as she gripped my cock at the base and ran her hand up and down it a few times, pumping and watching me through half-lidded eyes.

When she stuck out her pink tongue and licked the crown, I groaned but didn't shut my eyes. I watched every fucking second, not because I wasn't enjoying it—I fucking was—but because I didn't trust anyone. If I had my eyes open, I couldn't fucking get fucked over. This rule applied to business and pleasure. I wasn't even sure when I let my guard down anymore. Years of survival and the climb to the top had taught me that, and it was the one lesson I never forgot.

Syn took my entire length into her mouth, her tongue swirled around me as she moved up to the tip, her teeth dragging over the veins on the underside. She purred, the vibrations shooting straight through me like she knew they would. I let her play with me for a while, going at her own pace, before grabbing the back of her head and wrapping her ponytail around my fist. From there, I held her head immobile while I fucked her warm, wet, willing mouth. I shoved into her until I hit the back of her throat. Syn didn't have a gag reflex, which was one of the reasons I used her.

She took everything I gave her, saliva dripping from her well-used mouth, falling on her breasts still being held in check by her balconette bra. She groaned as her orgasm approached, her hand burrowing deep into her lace panties. She played with herself as I fucked her mouth, her eyes staying open, staying fixed on my face. When she came, though, she squeezed them shut, her body shivering with pleasure. Her moans became long and drawn out, and although I could normally last hours getting my dick sucked, tonight I didn't want to waste time.

As the vibrations in her throat ricocheted through my shaft, I felt my balls tighten. I was going to come. I pumped more furiously into her mouth, my grip tightening until I finally stopped and came at the back of her throat with a loud breath hissed through my teeth. Syn swallowed me down, her throat working, the compression of my dick squeezing the last little bit from me.

I released her hair slowly, running my fingers down to her jaw, then dragging my thumb across her pink, swollen bottom lip. She sucked the digit into her mouth, swirling her tongue around it.

"When are you going to fuck me, Mr. Rivera?" she asked in a low, rough voice.

I stroked her mouth again before shoving my semi-hard dick back into my slacks and standing to zip them. "Never, baby. I don't fuck my employees."

She got to her feet smoothly. "I'll quit right now if that's what it takes."

Wrapping my arm around her waist, I leaned in and kissed her cheek gently. "No, you won't. You need this job too fucking much, and I'm a bastard."

"You're a bastard who knows how to fuck, though."

How the fuck did she know? There were rumors floating around about me, sure. I'd heard many of them and quashed most of them too, so I raised an eyebrow at her. "You're fucking right I know how to fuck, but that doesn't mean I'll ever fuck one of my Dolls. I don't shit where I eat." And with that, I left the private room and returned to my office to get on with business.

2

Wren

I JOLTED AWAY IN MY BED, BLINKING IN THE DARKENED room. What had woken me? Turning, I glanced at the clock, trying to focus my blurry eyes on the digits on the digital readout. Was that one o'clock—*in the morning?*

Bang, bang, bang!

Someone was at the door.

Opening up the drawer on my side table, I pulled out my Beretta 92FS and got out of bed. It was still in the high nineties in my non-air-conditioned apartment, so I'd slept in a shirt and panties. But this was Boyle Heights, and there was no way in hell I was answering my apartment door in the middle of the fucking night without a weapon in my hands—modesty was simply optional at this point.

Bang, bang, bang!

"Jesus! Wren, let me in."

At the sound of my brother's voice, I flipped on the living

room lights, undid all three deadbolts, then the slide lock before opening the door. Hawk was weaving on my doorstep, his face a bloody mess, one of his eyes swollen shut.

"What the fuck, Hawk?" I guided him inside, re-shut things, and forced him to sit on my worn-out couch. The furniture groaned around him, but it didn't fall apart—this time. He still hadn't answered me, so I walked into the kitchen to grab some ice before hitting the bathroom for the first-aid kit.

When I came back, he was laid out on the faded yellow couch, an arm laid gently over his face. "What happened?" I asked, easing onto my knees beside him.

He moved his arm, so he could open his one good eye and look at me. "I fucked up, Wren."

My stomach clenched. "Fucked up, how?"

Hawk was forever getting into trouble. He had been ever since we were kids, and because I felt responsible for him, I'd always done what I could to get him out of it. I feared the day he turned up with a problem I couldn't fix, though. Every time the problem got bigger, the stakes got higher.

"Fucked up how, Hawk?"

He blinked and sucked in a breath through his mouth. His nose was probably broken if the angle was anything to go by. "I've been selling drugs."

"What about RadioShack? I thought you had a job. Why would you need to sell drugs?"

He stared at me with such pity, but I wasn't the one bleeding and bruised on the couch. "I lost that job a few months back."

I wanted to punch him in the face, but I held myself back. Besides, I was pretty sure he was feeling sorry enough for himself right now. "Why didn't you tell me? Why didn't you tell me you needed cash, too?"

"I can't sponge off you for the rest of my life, sis."

If it were a choice between sponging off me and dealing drugs, I would've taken on the financial burden. Although, I wasn't sure how much more my failing dog grooming business could take. "No, Hawk. Jesus. I can't believe you did that."

He shrugged, then winced like he'd forgotten he'd had the shit beat out of him. "It's done now, but I owe the boss."

"How much do you owe?" I was afraid to ask, but I had to know how hot the water was here. When he didn't answer right away, I pressed, "Hawk, I swear to fucking God if you don't tell me—"

"Fifty grand." He stared at me, begging me to understand even though I had no idea what the particulars were this time around. My brother had always been the kind of kid to bet over his head. Most times, his bluffs worked, and he walked away with more cash in his pocket than he'd had in the previous months. I always thought his luck would run out eventually, though.

It turned out this was that time.

Jacking up onto my feet, I cut a tight line in front of him, grinding my molars as I tried to think about how I could secure fifty grand for him. There was no way I wouldn't help bail him out, but the *how* was a fucking mystery. I barely scraped together enough for the rent on my shop and apartment on a weekly basis. My savings account was in the negative the last time I looked.

"When do you have to have it by?"

"I was given a week."

A week to find fifty grand? I'd already refinanced the shop, so Lord knew the banks weren't going to help me out. I glared at him, hands on my hips, and I adopted the true ticked-off-bigger-sister position.

Who the fuck had he done a deal with? I waved my hands in front of me, silencing my already silent conversation. No, I didn't want to know details.

Hawk's business was his business—until he made it *my* business.

Mother*fucker*.

"Who did you steal from?"

"Bane Rivera." At my questioning look, he added, "He owns that gentleman's club, The Dollhouse, over in West Hollywood."

I had heard of The Dollhouse, I'd also heard about the reputation of its owner. Bane Rivera had been voted most eligible bachelor three years running. I was not ashamed to say that I'd picked up those copies of the magazines and stared at him, taking in his dark hair, dark eyes, and scruffy jaw. He looked like pure sex on the pages, but a man like that didn't rise to the top without getting his hands dirty somewhere along the way.

"Well, I'll just go down there and talk to him."

Stupid. *Stupid* idea, but I was grasping at straws here.

"You can't do that," my brother said weakly.

I huffed and lowered myself back to the floor in front of the couch. "You lost the right to tell me what to do when you barged in here, bloody and broken, and owing the richest man in California fifty grand." I opened the gauze pack and Bactine and began to clean Hawk's injuries. As I sponged the blood away from his face, I realized the wounds were mostly superficial. The bruising would be a bitch, though.

By the time I was done, Hawk was asleep—although fitfully—on my couch. I laid a light blanket over him, then dumped the used medical supplies into the trash in the kitchen. It was edging up to two o'clock in the morning, and I knew I wouldn't be able to get back to sleep—not with the news of my brother's troubles on my mind.

Marching into my bedroom, I changed into some jean shorts and threw on a tank top. I didn't bother with a bra given that I didn't intend to stay at The Dollhouse all that long. Going to see Rivera might be the worst decision I'd ever made, but it was also the only one I could make. After this, though, I swore my brother was on his own.

Sliding my bare feet into my Vans, I grabbed my car keys from the hook by the door and shut the apartment quietly behind me. Traffic was light as I drove to West Hollywood. Even in the dark, I could see the wealth and affluence of the people who lived here. We hadn't always been poor. At one stage, my dad had had a thriving printing business, but then he began to gamble. It was only small bets here and there to start with, but as soon as my mom died, he upped the stakes and spiraled into a pit that he had no hope of climbing out of. He died penniless, leaving Hawk and me to scrape and scramble our way through this life. Neither of us had gone to college. Neither of us had wanted to. We'd grown up quick, and survival was the name of the game.

The game had left Hawk bitter and stupid.

It left me cautious yet independent, stubborn, and fucking unwilling to be taken advantage of.

"Holy shit," I muttered when I pulled up to the curb outside The Dollhouse. The entire building was at least three stories high, the red-brick industrial exterior making it look like it belonged somewhere down by the docks. There were no windows, no tacky neon signs—no signs at all. It was like it was just known as the premier gentlemen's club in LA by sheer will alone.

As I parked the car and shut off the engine, I had a brief moment of hesitation.

What the fuck was I doing here?

What did I hope to achieve?

Well, whatever it was going to achieve, I had no choice. Hawk had made sure of that.

Getting out of my car, I pulled down the legs of my shorts that had ridden up a little, shut the door, and locked the car. As I cast a glance at my early-model Toyota, I doubted anyone would try to boost it, but I also couldn't afford to replace it. I walked up to the bouncer at the door, who stared at me like I was the wrong kind of person to walk in here.

"Dolls enter through the back," he told me.

"Dolls? What? No, I'm here to talk to Bane Rivera."

His eyes found mine again. "Dolls enter through the back." His tone was sharp, and I bobbed my head because maybe this wasn't going to be as bad as I thought it was. I ducked down a driveaway running beside the building, coming to a large steel door. The words STAFF ONLY were scrawled across it in block letters. Raising my fist, I knocked.

It opened with a buzz, and I stepped into what looked like a very long hallway. There were half a dozen doors on either side, but they were all unmarked. The low buzz of people talking and the seductive beat of throbbing music and drinks being poured filtered through from the door to my left, so I opened it and stepped into a room of black, gold, and dark red. A shiver tracked over me as I was hypnotized by the low-lighting, the music, the women dancing in their eight-inch pleasers on raised platforms. This place was pure sex.

Walking over to the bar, I caught a lingerie-clad woman's attention and called her over.

"What can I get you, sweetheart?" she asked in a sexy drawl.

I almost ordered a drink, but then I remembered why I was here. "I need to speak to Bane Rivera."

The bartender jerked her chin up at a wall of glass hovering over the bar. "He's in his office," she said in a completely normal voice.

Well, clearly, I did not deserve the sex-kitten routine. Glancing around, I tried to find my way up there.

"Take the door tucked away around the end of the bar," the same bartender said.

I nodded in thanks, finding the door and opening it. Butterflies turned into an all-out assault on my stomach, so I pressed my hand to the space just below my navel. I was nervous as fuck, but I had to do this. When I reached the six-foot by five-foot landing at the top of the stairs, I stared at the door and blew out a breath.

Fuck. It was now or never.

I knocked and prayed I could get my brother out of this.

3

Bane

I LOOKED UP FROM MY WORK WHEN THERE WAS A knock on the door. It was almost three in the morning, and I wondered who it would be. "Enter," I said, returning my eyes to my desk.

I looked up again once the door had closed, taking in the blonde-haired beauty who had just stumbled into my office. Her blue eyes widened a little when she saw me, but her gaze didn't drop.

"Who the fuck are you?" I barked. And how the fuck had she gotten in here? Where the fuck was Dagger? Turning my head, I saw him down in the club, chatting to one of the waitresses. Fuck.

"Who are you?" I asked again when the woman remained silent.

Tilting her chin up in defiance, she glared at me. "My name is Wren Montana," she said, her voice strong. "I believe you know my brother, Hawk."

"Hawk Montana," I replied with a sneer. "The bastard who thought he could steal from me."

She bobbed her head. "I'm not here to condone what he's done, but I am here to ask you if there was some other way he could get that money to you. Fifty grand is not an easy sum to find."

"It would be if he hadn't stolen it from me in the first place." I settled back farther in my chair, molding into the soft, supple leather. "Did he ask you to come here?"

"No."

"So, what… you thought you'd just try your luck and ask me to let his indiscretion go?"

For the first time since she came in here, she ducked her eyes. "Yes."

I let my gaze travel down her body. She was dressed in a thin tank top that showed off a set of breasts I wouldn't have minded titty-fucking. Her waist was narrow, her hips flared. Her legs, though? Fuck me, I wanted them wrapped around my waist. Her little Daisy Dukes showcased them perfectly.

Standing, I rearranged my erection and stalked toward her. She tipped her chin up in defiance as I did, and I got a little harder.

Circling her, I ran the tip of my finger down her arm, then around to her back. When it inched onto her ass, she spun around to slap me, but I caught her hand before it could land. Our faces were mere inches apart, and I could smell the scent of her shampoo. Fire erupted in those blue eyes of hers.

"I'm not one of your whores," she hissed. "So don't touch me without my permission."

I let her wrist go and stepped away. She had fire. I liked fire.

My dick especially liked fire. "Well, Little Bird, now I know what you're made of."

"Fuck you," she snarled.

I laughed darkly. "Oh, I intend to at some point." I didn't date. I had no time to date. I barely got time to fuck women I wanted to fuck given that my time was split between the club and my drug operation.

But Wren Montana—I wanted to fuck her.

I wanted to see how deep that fire went.

I wanted to see if she would let me break her, then beg me for more.

"What do you want, Little Bird?" I asked, liking the way my new nickname sounded each time I said it.

"I want you to forget about the money my brother owes you."

I shook my head and perched on the edge of my walnut desk. Skimming my fingers along the edge, I thought about what Wren would look like bent over it, her knuckles clenched white as she held on tight while I fucked her raw. Her eyes darted down to my hips, then back up again, and I smirked. "I can't forget what he owes me. Nobody steals from me, and nobody can escape the punishment either."

All of a sudden, tears welled in her crystal-clear eyes, and my heart fucking lurched in my chest. I didn't suffer blubbering emotional women. Even if one of my Dolls comes to me with a tear-worthy issue, I took care of their problem expeditiously but left all the emotional shit kicked to the curb. Tears on Wren, though—*fuck*, I was in trouble.

"Please. He doesn't have the money. *I* don't even have the money—"

I held my hand up for her to stop. "He asked you for help?"

"He's my baby brother. There's nothing I wouldn't do for him."
Man, that was so fucked up. It was the man's duty to look after
his sister, not the other way around. Locking down my emotions,
I said to her, "He has a week to get me my fifty thousand."

"And what happens if he doesn't?" The steel was back in her
voice even though tears sat silver and voluminous in her eyes.
"What then, huh? Will you beat him again or worse?"

"Or worse," I replied darkly, without a touch of remorse.
"Nobody steals from me. Nobody gets to think they've pulled
one over on me. *Nobody* survives this breach of trust."

Roughly, she swiped the tears from her eyes and straightened
her shoulders. Fuck, she even thrust her chest out a little, drawing
my attention to her breasts. The air-conditioner kicked in then,
sweeping the room with a gust of arctic air and causing her
nipples to pebble. *No fucking bra.* I fucking liked this woman.

"You're a goddamn mobster." She hurled the words at me like
they were daggers instead of syllables.

Pushing up off the desk, I got to within an inch of her body,
her breasts almost brushing against my pecs. "You're fucking
right. I am. Now, get that fine ass of yours out of here, Little
Bird, before I bend you over my knee and spank that defiance
out of you."

I braced for the slap. I was not prepared for the lust that
surfaced in her gaze. So she liked it rough, did she? I filed that
little nugget of information away for later because I knew there
would be a later. Any woman who could stand up to me, defy me
like that, was a woman I wanted to get to know.

She retreated on shaking legs, throwing one last filthy glare over
her shoulder at me just before she shut the door. I ran a hand
through my hair and blew out a breath. Turning to the window,

I watched as Wren walked toward the entrance to the club. Her head was held high, her walk confident.

Fuck, I wanted to break her.

Behind me, the office door opened. "Who was that, boss?" Dagger asked. "A new Doll?"

I rounded on the guy, barely containing the anger I had at him for not being at the door to stop her from coming in. But then I thought about it. If he'd stopped her, I wouldn't have had the pleasure of meeting her. So instead of chewing the bastard out, I smiled at him. "She was Hawk Montana's big sister."

Dagger's expression didn't change. It hardly did. The only emotions I'd ever seen on his face before were blank and blank. There wasn't a damn thing I could tell him to do that he wouldn't see through.

"What did she want?"

"She wanted me to forget about the fifty thousand he owes."

"In exchange for what?"

"Nothing. She came in here with no fucking bargaining chip *at all*." Which either meant she was incredibly smart or incredibly stupid. Stupidity didn't seem to fit Wren. There was calculation in her eyes, an old knowledge that understood how this world worked. "I want you to find out what you can about her."

"You got it." He glanced at his watch. "Closing time soon."

I did the same time check. So it was. Three o'clock rolls around quickly.

"Get that information. I want to pay her a visit tomorrow."

"Yes, boss."

Dagger left, and I returned to my desk. I would see my Little Bird again, and I would take what I wanted from her without any complaint.

4

Wren

I NUDGED HAWK WITH MY FOOT. HE GROANED AND rolled away, giving me his back.

"Wake the fuck up, Hawk," I snarled. I was running on only four hours of sleep, thanks to his barging into my apartment beaten and bloody. Then, there was my visit to Bane. The man who was even sexier in person.

Before I got sucked into those thoughts, I walked into the kitchen to get some coffee. I made enough for both of us, taking the cup into the living room. Hawk had gotten himself vertical, which was a good start.

"Drink this," I told him, shoving the coffee under his nose.

He grabbed the cup with both hands and took a shallow sip. He looked at me over the rim. "What am I going to do, Wren?"

"Fucked if I know," I replied, running a hand through my hair, shoving it out of my face. I watched his expression crumple. "What did you do with the money?"

His eyes darted away from my face, his tell showing me everything I needed to know. "You lifted it, didn't you? You fucking idiot." I stood up to pace. "Did you think he wouldn't notice?"

"Snake never did," he replied in a petulant tone.

Ah, so here it was. This had worked in the past with another dealer, so Hawk figured why wouldn't it work again?

"Snake is a drug-addled junky peddling cut-to-shit heroin. Like he gives a fuck about making green. All he's interested in is making sure he has his own supply taken care of."

Hawk rested his elbows on his knees. "I know it was stupid, Wren. I *know* I fucked up. But there has to be a way, right? You can ask the bank for a loan? Use the shop as collateral?"

I turned to stare at him. What the fuck was he thinking? "My business is on the verge of collapse, Hawk. How in the hell do you think I'm supposed to get that kind of cash?" I was glad I was holding the coffee in my hand because if I didn't, I was going to punch him in the fucking face.

"Fuck."

"You're not fucking wrong, Hawk. Jesus!" I stalked back and forth for a little longer, trying to get all my jumbled thoughts into some sort of order. What were we going to do? Bane Rivera didn't look like the kind of man who would simply let my brother off with a slap on the wrist. More like a bullet in the head. There had to be a way to get him to back off, to extend the timeline. I paused in my pacing and took a sip of my coffee.

What if I offered to pay him off in installments? It would be tight, but I could afford a couple of hundred a month. At that rate, though, I would be paying Rivera off for nearly thirty years. That was if the guy went for the idea. I didn't hold out much hope.

"Argh, I can't even fucking look at you right now, Hawk." Taking my coffee cup with me, I stalked into my bedroom and slammed the door. I couldn't afford to focus any more of my energy on this. I still had to go into the shop and earn money. I had to pretend that things were okay, that my brother hadn't messed up in the biggest way possible.

Draining the last of my cup, I placed it on my dresser, then pulled on a pair of black leggings and a hot pink polo shirt with my business name and logo on the breast. I'd opened Bubbly Paws a couple of years ago hoping to cash in on the craze of people treating their dogs more like humans. It turned out my hunch had been right, but about a year ago, another dog grooming salon had opened, and, for some reason, I was slowly losing my patronage to them.

Without sufficient cash flow to throw into advertising, I was left having to suck it the fuck up. I didn't hold out hope for an improvement any time soon, but I wasn't a quitter, so I'd see it through. I shoved my feet into my Vans, then went into the bathroom to brush my teeth and do my hair.

I'd just placed my hairbrush down when my phone rang.

Putting it on speaker, I said, "Tell me you're coming over with copious amounts of alcohol tonight," I said to my best friend, Darcy.

"I'll do you one better. We're going out tonight."

I stared at the phone. "Going out?"

"Yeah, you know, getting a few drinks, maybe getting you a few numbers? Please tell me you haven't forgotten what fun is. I worked really hard to get you to lighten up."

"I know what going out is, Dee, but tonight? I thought it was date night for you and Baron on Fridays."

"Baron has to work late."

Baron was her husband of five years and the only man Darcy had ever loved. They'd been high school sweethearts, and they were so perfect for each other it made me sick to my stomach.

"Come on, Wren. You're my only single friend. You're my only excuse to go out anymore."

Rifling through my makeup bag, I pulled out my foundation and shook the bottle. "I don't want to be used, Darcy."

She laughed. "You'll be using me. I'm the best fucking wing-woman you've ever had."

I snorted, applying my foundation efficiently. "We can have one drink."

"Yes! I knew I'd wear you down."

"Where do you want to go?"

"Temptation in West Hollywood."

I whistled through my teeth. "I hope you know someone who knows someone who knows someone because getting on that list is hard."

"Oh, we're on the list, babe. Don't you worry."

Applying some mascara, I asked, "How in the hell did you manage that?"

"Baron manages their books. All he had to do was ask."

Fuck, I knew I liked Baron for a reason. "What time should I meet you?"

"Nine?"

"Done. I'll see you then." I hung up and finished applying a clear gloss to my lips. Taking one final look at my reflection, I decided it was as good as it was going to get. Besides, I was going to get splashed by shaking dogs all day, anyway. I looked as tired as I felt, but I wasn't going to earn money without actually heading to work. I could worry about Hawk later. Hell, maybe this would be the wake-up call he needed to start getting his shit together.

Grabbing the keys from the hook by the door, I said over my shoulder, "Lock up the windows and door when you leave, please, and for fuck's sake, don't go getting yourself into any deeper shit."

When I got downstairs, I turned to the right to walk the two blocks to my dog grooming shop. From memory, I had at least ten dogs coming in for a wash and another three for clipping. Then when I was done, I could look forward to going out with Darcy.

As I rounded the corner onto the street of my shop, I stopped dead and blinked. Bane Rivera was standing against the front window dressed in an expensive black suit and crisp white shirt. Sunglasses shaded his eyes, but I knew the moment when he saw me. I could feel his gaze on me like it was a visible caress. I began walking again, approaching him with my keys out.

"What are you doing here?" I pushed the key into the front lock and opened the door, not waiting to see if he would follow.

As I flipped on the lights, he sauntered into my shop, looking all sorts of misplaced while I turned off the security alarm.

"So this is where you work, huh?" he asked, amusement coloring his tone.

"If you're here to make fun of this place, you can fuck right off now." I went to move around the counter to drop my bag, but Bane stopped me by wrapping his fingers around my wrist. I glared at the offending digits then back at him. "Are you sure that's what you want to do?"

His mouth turned up into a cocky smile. Like he was used to getting everything he wanted. Like the world would drop its panties for him. And why was I thinking about dropping my panties in his presence?

"What would you do to me if it is?" His question was a bare rumble of a purr, a buzz deep down low in his chest. I stared up into his dark eyes, my gaze tracking from his mouth to the tattoos on the side of his neck, back to his eyes.

I swallowed, praying my voice sounded strong when I answered, "I don't know."

His brows rose. "You don't know?" Jerking me closer, I was forced to drop my bag and place my hands on his chest to stop me from crashing into him. He wrapped his arms around me, pinning my arms to my sides. Dipping his head to my ear, he whispered, "Don't tease me, Little Bird. You will not enjoy the punishment, although I know I will."

Shoving free of his arms, I tried to get my breathing back under control. My brain was firing a thousand different thoughts in a thousand different directions. Slowly, I scooped up my bag and walked behind the counter. I took a few minutes more than necessary to stow it, and by the look on his face when I stood back up again, he knew. He knew he'd messed with my equilibrium.

"What do you want?" I asked again.

"You."

I blinked, sure my hearing was on the fritz. "Me?"

He leaned against the counter, folding his arms across his chest. The movement revealed the gold Piaget watch on his wrist, which winked in the overhead lighting. "Last night, you came to beg me to let your brother's debt go. Not once did you

offer me an alternative to the money."
I frowned. "Alternative?"
"An alternative." Reaching into his pocket, he pulled out a business card and handed it to me. I took it, finally glancing down at the thick stock. It was black with his name embossed on one side and a number in gold on the other.
"What's this?"
"An offer."
My heart lurched into my throat as the implications of what he was saying hit me with all the finesse of a semi-trailer careening out of control. "You want me to work for you?"
"Clever girl," he murmured, his eyelids lowering. "Come and work for me, Little Bird, and I'll wipe that debt of Hawk's away. Forever."
I rubbed my thumb over his embossed name, committing the shape of the letters to memory. This was one of those times in your life that changed shit forever. "And if I say no?"
Straightening, he stalked toward me behind the counter. I backed up a step, slamming into the wall. Bane crowded me against it, caging me in with his hands on either side of my head. He leaned in close, placed his nose at my neck, and inhaled. Then his words, words that trickled like a lover's promise, found their way into my ear. "You love your brother too much to say no."
My chest pumped as I tried to drag more air into my lungs. All I caught was the scent of his cologne—something deliciously spicy and dark. I swallowed raggedly, tilting my face up to meet his. "No," I said the word with as much conviction as I could muster, but given his proximity, I was struggling to even perform the most basic functions like breathing and blinking. There was something so magnetic about him. He was savagery contained in

a suit, an animal tamed only because he was in public. I had no doubt that when it came to sex, he would own my body. And I would give it to him.

He must've seen that realization in my eyes. Flexing his hips into mine, I had to bite my lip as his erection pressed into my pelvis. "Still thinking about me bending you over my knee?"

"No," I whispered.

He clicked his tongue. "When you submit to me, Little Bird, I will make your ass red raw, and you will love every second of it."

"I highly doubt that." My words came out weaker than I'd anticipated, but Bane was twisting everything around in my head. I'd never had such a visceral reaction to a man before.

"Think about my offer, Wren Montana." He stepped away from me and left the shop. I stared at the door, unable to catch my breath.

Holy shit.

Holy *shit*.

Diving into my bag, I called Darcy.

She picked up on the second ring. "Babe?"

"Hey. Ah… you're never going to believe what just happened."

There was a thump like Darcy had put something down— probably her coffee cup. "Spill it."

"I just got offered a job."

"A job? Why would you need a job? You have a job. A job where?" Her questions came out rapid-fire, just like they always did when she was multitasking.

"What else are you doing?"

"Huh? Oh, trying to type out this report for my boss."

I picked up the card and looked at it again. "I'll call you back then."

"Pfft… no, babe. We're talking now. I got this."

I smiled. Darcy always knew when I needed her the most, and right now I needed her. And not because of Bane coming in here and offering me a way out of Hawk's mess, but for everything life had ever thrown at me. "It's a long story."

"Stop stalling and tell me already."

I inhaled deeply, then let the breath out slowly. I had about twenty minutes before my first appointment would arrive. "All right, here's the long and the short of it, Hawk was an asshole and did something stupid. Now, that something stupid has come back to bite him in the ass."

"Ooo, I love it when you're all cryptic, but knowing your brother as I do, he probably pissed off the wrong person. And now you feel obligated to help him because he's your baby brother, and that's what you do. Am I right?"

Fuck, she was so right about that. "Pretty much."

"Also knowing you, you also know how to fix it."

My heart lurched in my chest because I hadn't known how to fix it, but as I looked down at the black card on my counter, maybe I did. The question was, what else was it going to cost me?

5

Bane

WRAPPING MY HAND AROUND SYN'S LONG HAIR, I forced her down farther onto my dick bobbing in and out of her mouth. Seeing Wren and not being able to touch her like I wanted to had left my dick hard—too fucking hard to think about anything else. I had to have an outlet for that frustration. Otherwise, nothing would get done for the rest of the day.

She gripped my thighs, digging her false nails into the muscle. I sucked in a hiss and pumped harder, hitting the back of her throat over and over again. She groaned her appreciation of the rough treatment, so I upped the tempo. Slamming into her, I tilted my head and let my gaze drift to her breasts bouncing from inside the cup of her bra. She was in red today, the color clashing with her bottle-colored hair.

As soon as she tugged on my balls, they tightened with a release. With a roar, I slammed into her once more, spilling down her throat. She swallowed me down, sucking and licking and looking for more. She let go of my cock with an audible pop, and it came to settle against my lower belly, glistening with her saliva.

Running my thumb over her bottom lip, I murmured, "You love cock, don't you?"

She nodded. "More than anything." She stood smoothly, her spike heels evenly distributing her weight. "Need anything else from me?" she asked, running her hands suggestively over her breasts and down into her panties. "You got me all wet."

"Go find someone to fuck, then," I told her dismissively, tucking myself back into my pants. "I'm busy."

I didn't bother to watch Syn leave. Instead, I returned my attention to the screen of my computer monitor and tried to ignore all thoughts of Wren Montana. It was completely useless. Wren was so firmly stuck in my frontal lobe that I'd thought about nothing else since last night.

That was the reason for the visit this morning.

That was the reason I gave her my card and offered her a job.

It probably wasn't the job she would be expecting as I had no desire to share her with any other man. The woman was a fucking hellcat. I liked spirit, especially when that spirit was directed at something meaningful. So many times, women were just bitches for the sake of being bitches, but with Wren, I could see what drove her—family and a sense of responsibility.

I saw the same in myself.

Picking up my phone, I dialed my sister, Bianca.

"Baby brother," she answered breathlessly. "To what do I owe the pleasure."

Rubbing my eyes with my thumb and forefinger, I groaned out, "Please tell me you didn't answer the phone while you were having sex."

She snorted. "No. I'm out for a run with Valentine," she replied.

I sat a little straighter in my chair. Valentine was her four-month-old daughter. "Should you be doing that?" I barked, then reined that anger back in. Bianca had never reacted well to anger, but I wasn't asking out of anger. It was concern. Bianca had had a difficult pregnancy, topped off with a fucking difficult labor that had left her in the hospital for about a week longer than necessary after giving birth.

"Yes, brother, I'm fine," she replied in a bored voice. "The doc gave me the all-clear. All he said was I had to take it easy."

"And you goddamn will." I looked up when Dagger came into the office, and I put my finger up to show him to wait a minute. "How's my favorite niece anyway?"

"She's good... misses her uncle, though. When are you coming over for a visit?"

"I don't know." I stared absently at the club through the window. Being that it was lunchtime on a Friday, it was slow right now, but in another couple of hours, members would be foaming at the mouth to get in. The working week was over, and they were looking to blow off some fucking steam. "Work has been busy."

"How's the club doing?"

There was no derision in her voice when she asked. She knew that the club wasn't about being a chauvinist or a sex fiend, although I *was* a sex fiend too. She understood that I was a businessman first and foremost. She thought I only sold pussy. She didn't know about the drug business on the side, and that was the way it was going to stay.

"It's great. Profit margins are healthy. I might actually look at expanding like we talked about."

"That's amazing, Bane. I'm really happy for you." There was a faint, tinny beep over the line, and Bianca said, "Shit, my heart rate's dropping. I'd better get going. Thanks for the call. When should I tell James we'll be expecting you?"

I clicked into my digital calendar. Weekends were out on account of that being the busiest time of the week, but we were closed on Monday for deep cleaning. "Monday for dinner."

"I'll make your favorite."

I chuckled. "Love you, sis."

"Love you, too, brother."

I ended the call and looked at Dagger. "We have a problem," he said.

I stood, buttoning my suit jacket. "We run out of condoms again?" I asked in a bored drawl. "Because that shit is way below my pay grade."

"One of our guys got hit."

I was instantly on alert, narrowing my eyes at him. "Got hit, how?"

Dagger's expression didn't change. *At all.* "Same as the last one."

My hands balled into fists of their own volition. "Fuck!" A month ago, we lost one of my dealers to what we thought was gang violence. He'd been shot in the chest when he'd opened his apartment door. His cash had been taken, but the drugs had been left, which was fucking strange since he had about ten thousand worth in his house. I didn't think anything of it. *Until now.*

Now, his execution made sense.

Stalking out from behind my desk, I began to pace. I was a

caged tiger ready to swipe at anything stupid enough to get close to the bars.

"We need to find these fuckers and get rid of them." Dagger watched me with his cold, dead eyes. "Do we have any leads?"

"Most logical choices are Manzetti or Sanderson."

I ground my teeth so hard my jaw ached. I refused to be taken out of the coke game by anyone. "Find out who it is, then bring me their goddamn head!"

Dagger said nothing, just turned around and left the office, leaving me with a fuck-ton of simmering rage. I was anticipating some retribution for cutting in on the East Coast drug trade, but I was thinking it would be more like my dealers getting beaten up or an easy warning. I expected to know where the threat was coming from, but this shit was fucked up.

I was in the fucking dark here.

I was not totally to blame, though. I'd known I was setting up a territory that fringed both Manzetti's and Sanderson's. I'd taken over their No Man's Land and filled it with my own coke, slightly undercutting the bastards on price to ensure it would take.

Mancini had always taught me to take what I wanted, then fight tooth and nail to keep it, and that was what I was goddamn doing.

6

Wren

GOD, I HOPED I KNEW WHAT I WAS DOING. THROUGH the windshield of my car, I looked up at The Dollhouse, feeling my stomach churn. I felt like I was making a deal with the Devil here, although if I were honest with myself, Bane Rivera was one fine-looking devil. Glancing at the black card on the passenger seat, I tried to recall what he'd told me on the phone this afternoon after I'd finished with my last client. He'd said I could come through the front, that the bouncer would wave me through.

As I worked through washing dogs and clipping claws, I had time to think about Bane's offer. He said he'd wipe Hawk's debt if I worked for him. He never said how long, though, or doing what, although I suspected I already knew, so I'd reasoned with myself that this was just a meeting to discuss the particulars. I had not said yes to this. I was not committing to working at a fucking gentlemen's club, no matter how exclusive it was.

Letting out one final breath, I got out of my car and locked it. I glanced around as I made my way to the front, feeling like everyone was staring at me.

"Can I help you, ma'am?" the bouncer asked, his bald head gleaming with sweat in the late evening heat that was still clinging to LA.

"Yes, my name is Wren—"

"Go on through," he said, cutting me off. "Mr. Rivera is expecting you."

"Th-thank you." I stepped through the door he held open for me and let out a sigh as the cool air swirled around my feet. The club looked much the same as before, the lux fabrics and the opulence an almost indecent assault on the senses, especially when it was pared with women dressed in lingerie dancing on raised platforms with poles, in cages, and on men's laps. I walked to the bar, then stopped. Bane never said to go to his office, and I figured barging in on him once was enough. I waited for him by the black-lacquered bar, my gaze bouncing around the room.

There were so many men here already, a lot of them sitting in quartets in comfortable-looking leather armchairs with high rolled arms. The women were perched either on their knees or on the arms of the chairs themselves, their long, lean legs draped over the men's laps. A lot of the women didn't look real to me. *How could someone look like that,* I wondered, *and how could they choose this as their career?*

"Little Bird."

Jumping, I turned to find Bane standing there in the same suit as I'd seen him in this morning, although he'd jettisoned the jacket. His shirt was open at the collar, revealing a tantalizing look at the tattoos that continued from his neck down onto his chest. His dark hair was fuck-me tousled, his dark eyes drinking me in.

"Jesus, you scared me," I told him.

He smirked.

The bastard.

"Would you like a drink?"

"Fuck, yes. Whisky on the rocks."

His smile widened a little more before he turned to the bartender waiting at his elbow. After he'd ordered our drinks, we waited in silence. Bane was staring at me, his gaze never staying in one place too long. It dropped from my face to my chest, then lower. I had no idea what he was expecting to see. I'd come straight from work, so I smelled of wet dog and was covered in hair. I'd toyed with the idea of getting changed, but I figured this wasn't actually going to take too long. I'd find out the details, then I'd leave.

"Let's go and sit down," he said, handing me my drink and gesturing to the main floor of the club. I let him lead the way, trying to ignore how great his ass looked in those slacks. He picked a couple of seats at the far end of the club as far away from the gyrating pole dancers as we could get.

"I thought you might want a little privacy," he told me in a dark voice that made my ovaries quiver a little bit.

I took a sip of my whisky, savoring the burn. "This won't take long."

With humor dancing in his eyes, he also took a sip from his glass before placing it onto the small table beside him. "I make it a point never to do things fast with a beautiful woman." He lounged back in the chair, his elbows on the high arms, his legs spread wide. I got a very vivid picture in my mind of what it would be like to be with a man like him, one that oozes dominance and power.

I cleared my throat. "We need to discuss the offer you made me this morning."

He steepled his fingers together in front of him. "And I am all—"

He was cut off when an artificial redhead in matching red lingerie flopped into his lap. "Hi, daddy," she purred, running her finger over his jaw like a lover would.

With far more gentleness than I expected, he eased her off his lap. "Get out of here, Syn. You can clearly see I'm in a meeting."

The woman, Syn, cast her eyes to me, her expression turning sour. "A new Doll?" she asked.

Bane stared at me, a smile on his sinful mouth. "Maybe. Now get the fuck out of here."

I watched the other woman go, then swallowed another mouthful of whisky. When I turned back, Bane was still staring at me, only all amusement was gone.

"What's a Doll?" I asked.

"What I call my dancers."

"Oh." Nervous energy fluttered around inside me, pinging against my skin and making me suddenly jumpy. Is that what Bane wanted me for? To be one of his Dolls? I looked around at the other women. They were all dressed in barely-there lingerie, their faces perfectly done, their hair immaculate. If his offer was for me to become one of his dancers, I wasn't sure I could.

"Should we get down to business then?" he asked smoothly.

Drawing in a shaky breath, I turned back to him. "Yes," I croaked. Jesus-fucking-Christ, what was I doing? I knew I was considering making a deal with the Devil, but could I lower my standards this much? I had no issues with sexuality. I had no issues with other women who wanted to express that sexuality, but the idea of becoming a dancer was throwing up roadblocks in my head. I couldn't do this—not even for Hawk.

I threw the last of my whisky down my throat and stood. "I'm sorry, Mr. Rivera, but I can't do this."

"Do what, exactly? We're having a drink."

I ran a hand through my hair, checking my ponytail was still in place. Of course, it was. It hadn't moved all day. Why the fuck was I stalling on this?

"I can't become one of your *Dolls*," I blurted out. "Hard limit."

His eyes became hooded. "I never mentioned anything about you becoming one of my Dolls." His words were controlled like rage was suddenly seeking to claw out of him. What had I said to make him react like that? "In fact, what I want from you, you probably won't want to give me because if you're offended by some women dancing in lingerie, you won't like what I was about to offer you."

Keeping Hawk's life firmly in my mind, I let out a breath. "What are you offering?" I asked in a whisper.

He gestured to the chair. "Sit down, and I'll tell you."

I stood there a moment longer, waging war with myself. I could do this. I could sit and hear the guy out. Moving back to the chair, I sat, bringing my legs up beneath me. "If you expect me to whore myself out, you've got another thing coming. Nothing is worth giving up my pride for that."

I glared at him, but what I'd said had clearly amused him.

"I don't want you to whore yourself out as one of my Dolls."

"What do you want me for then?"

"I want you to be my personal Doll."

A shot of lust ricocheted through my body at the same time as outrage did. Conflicted by the two strong emotions, I shut my eyes for a moment and breathed. "Your personal whore, you mean?" When I opened them again, his dark eyes were roving my body.

He shrugged unashamedly. "I don't care what you label it… I want you for myself."

"What if I told you I had a boyfriend? Would that offer still stand?"

His dark eyes clouded over a little as he leaned forward in his chair. "You don't have a boyfriend, Little Bird, so don't even fucking think about playing that card."

Although outrage still hummed through my body, I swallowed down the insults I wanted to hurl at him, remembering my brother's life could hinge on this. "How long?"

"Two weeks."

"And after two weeks, I'm free to leave, never to see you again?"

"If you can walk away from me at the end of those two weeks," he replied smugly.

I huffed a laugh and unfolded my legs, placing them onto the hardwood floor. "What would be involved with me being your Doll?"

"You will be available to me at all times."

Narrowing my eyes at him, I rolled that statement around in my head. Available to him at all times was a pretty broad request. "Available for what?"

He smiled, and my heart nearly jumped right out of my chest. It was terribly unfair that he was this good-looking. In fact, why would he even want to be seen with me? I smelled of wet dog and was covered in fur six days a week.

"This and that," he replied, taking another sip from his glass.

"This isn't how contracts work. You can't be vague or ambiguous. I will never agree to broad statements like 'available to you at all times' and 'this and that.' Sorry." I folded my arms defensively across my chest and stared at him.

"All right, Little Bird, do you want to know what I really want from you for two weeks? I want your complete submission in all things. Sex, yes, but I will make that very pleasurable for you, but in other ways, too. You will be there to accompany me to dinners and meetings when needed."

"Jesus," I muttered. This sounded a hell of a lot like *Pretty Woman*. Hey, at least we were in the right city, right? I stared at him, taking in every angle of his face, his jaw.

Two weeks.

Could I give up two weeks of my life in order to get Hawk off the hook?

"What about my brother?"

He spread his legs out a little wider, my eyes tracking the movement. "I'm not into men."

"No, I mean, what happens to his debt? Will it be wiped?"

"Of course."

"I want that written into the contract."

"Contract?"

"You think that all this won't be put into writing? I'm going to make damn sure it is, so we both know where we stand."

"No contracts," he said in a hard voice. "My word is my bond."

"Then, we don't have a deal," I told him, daring him to counter my threat with one of his own. When he didn't, I stood. He mirrored me, his expression vacillating between humor and frustration. He finally fixed it on indifference and held out his hand for me to shake.

"I'll let you think about this a little longer before you give me your answer."

What an asshole. Opening my mouth to argue, I shut it a minute later. I didn't need to waste time on this. It was not beneficial, and it would only serve to put me in a worse mood. He brought my hand to his mouth, brushing his lips against the back of it.

"I will be seeing you later, Wren. You can count on that."

As I stalked away, the only thought I had was that I would never sell myself to a man like that.

Not even for my brother.

7

Bane

JESUS-FUCKING-CHRIST, MY DICK WAS SO HARD. AS I watched Wren stalk away from me, I caught the looks from my patrons, from my Dolls. They'd never seen me with a woman like her before—one who had no idea about her sex appeal. Her sharp tongue and quick mind also turned me the fuck on.

"Want me to take care of that for you, daddy?" Syn asked, sashaying her way over to me. I knew the moment Wren left that she would swoop in.

Dropping to the floor between my legs, she reached up to rub my dick, but I stopped her, pressing my fingers into her wrist.

"No, Syn."

Fuck, this had happened before. I'd had Dolls getting possessive over me, and I'd had to get rid of them. I didn't belong to any woman, and as soon as they thought they did, they were gone too.

I stood, side-stepping Syn who was blinking at me like she couldn't believe I'd turned down a blowjob. I wouldn't have let her suck me in public, though. There were strict rules in the club, which included no sexual acts were to be performed on the general floor. That's what the private rooms were for. Syn was walking a fine line to think I would let that shit go.

When I was safely locked back in my office, I called Dagger, then got back to the paperwork that had been demanding my attention for the better half of this week.

TWO HOURS LATER, DAGGER STROLLED THROUGH THE door, his hair wet and his clothes clean.

"What did you find?"

"One of Sanderson's guys sniffing around on our turf."

"Did you question him?"

"Why do you think I got showered and changed?" he replied. Of course. Dagger wasn't known for his patience, and when information wasn't given quickly enough, he had a tendency to get out one of his knives to make the person more receptive to his desires.

I leaned back in my office chair and crossed my legs at the ankle. "Do we have anything yet?"

Dagger shook his head. "No. The guy was fucking keeping his thoughts to himself."

I didn't believe for one fucking minute that he didn't know *something*. "You need to fucking find out. There can't be any blowback onto the club."

"No problem." He turned to leave, but I stopped him. "Do you have someone on Wren?"

"Yeah."

"Tell them to call me when she goes anywhere other than her work and home."

Dagger pulled out his phone, his thick thumbs flying over the screen as he relayed the message. "Done. Anything else you need or am I good to walk the floor?"

"We're done."

He left me alone, and the silence was driving me fucking insane. I'd done all the paperwork, and the report from Dagger only made my skin fucking twitch. I needed a distraction, and the only one I could think of that I wanted was a little blonde with legs for-fucking-days. Snagging the jacket off the back of my chair, I slid into it then made my way downstairs.

It was edging onto eight o'clock in the evening, The Dollhouse was filling up nicely. I had all the Dolls working tonight because it was the best day for them to get tips. As I strolled past the bar, the bartender, Rachel, grabbed me.

"Got a minute to talk, boss?" she asked, shoving her black hair over her shoulder. She was wearing a black teddy today, and given the nature of pouring drinks, it was the only position in my club where I allowed that amount of clothing. When I'd first hired her a couple of years ago, she'd been adamant she wasn't going to toe the company line. After one night fully clothed, she soon figured out the tips were better the less she had on.

I checked my watch, but I had nowhere to be until I got a call from Dagger's guy. I was going to pay Wren a little visit tonight and prove to her that agreeing to my offer would be a pleasurable one. "Sure."

"I was wondering if I could work a few more shifts in the future." She dropped her gaze, and I looked a little harder at her face, at her body language. Her makeup was a little heavier tonight, and my hands balled into fists.

"Is your cunt of a boyfriend hitting you, Rach?"

She recoiled at my tone, touching the black eye hidden behind the foundation and whatever the fuck else she had on under there. "It was an accident."

"Jesus Christ," I bit out under my breath.

"I need to get more cash together to leave him. I swear he won't hit me again."

"And if he does?" I slung the words at her like acid. I never understood the mentality of a woman who stayed with an abusive partner. I might use women for sex, but I still respected them and their wishes. To hit one—especially one you professed to love—was a dog act.

"One of the other girls said I could go stay with her."

I bit the inside of my cheek. "Don't wait for him to hit you again. Pack your shit up when you get home and go stay with whoever the fuck said you could crash at theirs."

She nodded her head, her eyes downcast. "And the shifts?"

I resisted the urge to run my hands through my hair. "Of course, you can have more fucking shifts," I snarled.

"Thank you, Mr. Rivera," she mumbled and moved back to her post.

I stared at her in silence, wondering what the fuck would happen to her. Most people thought I didn't give a shit about women, but the ones who worked for me were under my protection. I would fucking destroy anyone who tried to hurt them.

With that knowledge weighing heavily on me, I walked through the front door and spoke to the bouncer.

"I'm going out for a few hours. Dagger is here if there's an issue."

"You got it, boss," the guy replied.

I was about to walk away when I stopped, driven to ask him, "You all right? Everything okay?"

His eyes flared in surprise. "Yeah, great. Thanks."

I nodded. "Good man. Call me if you need me."

I strolled away from the entrance of the club, sliding into the rear seat of the town car that was parked out in front. I was being driven back to my apartment when I got a phone call from a private number.

"Target is going out tonight."

"Where?" I demanded, gripping the phone more tightly.

"Temptation."

I hung up and told my driver, Andy, to hurry the fuck up.

8

Wren

SKIMMING MY HANDS DOWN THE STRETCHY ELECTRIC-blue fabric of the dress I was wearing, I looked at my reflection in the mirror. Even I had to admit that I looked great. I'd gone a little heavier on the eye makeup, lighter on the face, and painted my lips a bright red. Darcy was going to have a fucking aneurysm when she saw me.

With one final check of my reflection, I grabbed my phone and switched purses, making sure I had all the essentials, which included a condom. Because a girl never knew when she might need one. Plus, seeing Bane this evening had left me an aching mess despite the proposition he'd made.

Since coming home, that had been all I could think about, but even as I tried to come up with all the reasons why I shouldn't, I kept returning to the fact that Hawk would be off the hook after this. It wasn't a stay of execution, rather just a reprieve until he fucked things up again.

So when I looked at it that way, there was no point in even considering the offer, was there? Of course, I wasn't a cold-hearted bitch. I understood that Hawk would probably not be walking this earth anymore if I let Bane destroy him like he wanted to.

Slipping my feet into the only pair of heels I owned, I locked my apartment and walked outside to call an Uber. I only had to wait a few minutes before I was safely tucked into the back of an air-conditioned minivan driven by what looked like a soccer mom.

"I love that dress," she exclaimed as she navigated her way through the busy LA streets.

"Oh, thank you," I replied, pulling the hem down a little. It was funny—if I were wearing a pair of shorts, I wouldn't give a fuck how far they'd ridden up, but in a dress, it was a different story.

We ended up chatting the entire way to the nightclub, and when she pulled into the curb, she gave me a bottle of water and told me to keep hydrated. I got out, making sure everything was in place before strolling over to the bouncer and giving him my name.

"Welcome to Temptation," the bouncer said. "You're in the VIP section. The hostess will escort you to your table."

VIP? What the fuck?

I nodded mutely and walked inside, my breath leaving me in a whoosh. This place was amazing. The lighting was moody, the music moving through me in an almost erotic beat. A young woman with blonde hair met me just inside the front door. When I gave her my name, she guided me through the club to a VIP area cordoned off with a red velvet rope. Unclipping one end from the pole, she smiled at me as I walked in. Surely, there had to be some sort of mistake. Darcy had said Baron was only the accountant for this place. Somehow, I found it hard to believe that his position would warrant the VIP section.

I stood there for a moment, simply absorbing the club's mood and wondering where I could get a drink.

"Here," someone said behind me, holding the stem of a champagne flute. I looked down at the tattoo-covered hand and spun around.

"What are you doing here? Please don't tell me you own this club, too?"

He shook his head, his eyes giving nothing away, especially in the low light of the VIP section. "No, Evangeline wouldn't sell it to me," he replied easily. He gestured to the champagne again. "Drink?"

I reached out and took the glass from him, our fingers brushing briefly. A small growl escaped him, but I had no other gauge of his mood. Taking me by the elbow, he guided me to the long couches set against the back wall. We were hidden on three sides—the wall to our back and one side and a partition on the other side that opened onto the bar. Although I knew we didn't have real privacy, it certainly felt like we did.

Bane drew his attention back to me with his hand on my thigh, his thumb caressing the skin just above my knee. I stared at his tattooed hand with his long fingers. His hand was bigger than mine, my leg looking so small compared to him. If he wanted to, he could just sweep his hand up and under my dress. A little breath escaped me as I tried to ignore the fact that it was what I wanted him to do.

"What are you thinking about, Little Bird?" he asked close to my ear, his warm breath feathering against my skin like a lover's fingers.

I swallowed. Jesus, I felt hot all over but like my skin was too tight for my body at the same time. "I'm trying to figure out how Darcy got us into the VIP section."

His grip tightened on my thigh. "I thought you said you didn't have a boyfriend," he growled.

"I don't. Darcy is a woman and my best friend."

As soon as I said those words, he released the death grip and swept his hand a little higher. "Good. And in answer to your question, Darcy didn't get into the VIP section... I did. We have this entire place to ourselves."

I looked around the private space one more time. There was a door on the far wall, a picture of a man and woman split by a line on a plaque in the middle. Well, at least I knew where the bathroom was.

"How did you know I was coming here?"

"I have my ways." He picked up his glass of champagne and swallowed a large mouthful. I watched the way his throat bobbed as he swallowed down the gold liquid.

"Have you been tapping my phone?" Indignant didn't really start to explain the ferocity of my feelings. I could handle men who thought they needed to dominate a relationship, but I wasn't up for a stalker-grade man, especially not one like Bane Rivera. He had money and resources on his side.

A smile curved up the corner of his mouth. "No, Little Bird, I haven't been tapping your phone."

I felt like there was more to be outraged about here, but I decided not to push. Not now. I understood what he was doing. He was proving to me that he could insert himself in my life in any way he wanted.

"It's not going to work, you know."

His eyebrow quirked up, and he took another sip of his drink, watching me over the rim. "What's not going to work?"

My eyes darted to his lips, wondering if they tasted like champagne now. "You proving that you can be everywhere I am. It won't make me change my mind about the proposition."

"You're right." He shifted his body toward me, placing his face close to mine. "But my life would be a lot easier if you simply gave me what I want."

I shook my head. "How many women have you seduced into relationships with you this way?"

"None." His reply came out smoothly with not an ounce of deceit. "And I don't have relationships. I fuck."

He said the words with zero inflection like he didn't give a damn one way or the other. Placing my flute down, I stood. Bane looked up at me, his expression amused. If he was trying to push my buttons, top marks for him.

"Where are you going?"

"The bathroom," I replied, moving off toward the door at the back of the VIP area. I pushed inside to find that it was just one stall inside the room along with a marble sink and a small armchair upholstered in velvet. I turned to lock the outer door when Bane pushed inside, slamming the door shut behind him. He slid the lock into place with finality, and I glared at him.

"Do you mind?"

"Yeah, I do," he growled, coming at me like a starved man. Wrapping one arm around my waist, his hand went to my neck, holding me in place. A rush of excitement skittered through me, the warring emotions of fear and arousal wreaking havoc with my thoughts. Bane pushed his erection into my belly, making me moan.

"This is what you do to me, Wren." He flexed his hips again, rolling them with frustrating slowness. "Why do you have to torture me?"

Me torture *him*? My fingers tightened around the lapels of his jacket as he thrust against me again.

I was suddenly breathless as I realized this was exactly what I wanted.

I wanted him.

Unleashed.

Uncaged.

Savage.

Tilting my face up to his, I silently begged him for what I needed, for what only he could give me. With a growl that lit up every single one of my nerve endings, he kissed me. I was braced for the same kind of savagery that he seemed to operate on daily, so I was stunned when his lips and mouth were soft against mine. I was struggling to put together the rough, demanding Bane I'd seen and this version here with me now. He backed me into the bathroom countertop, lifting me one-handed over the edge. His other hand was still wrapped around the base of my neck, his fingers tight and demanding.

Pushing my knees apart, he stood between my legs, dominating my space. I ran my hands over his shoulders and down his back, fucking praying we got to do this again when we weren't fully dressed. I gasped when his fingers found the edge of my panties. He hooked them out of the way, sliding a finger straight into my drenched pussy.

He growled against my mouth, the sound vibrating through

me, pushing me higher.

"Fuck, your cunt is so wet."

"Yes," I moaned, lowering my head to kiss his neck. He tasted of that same cologne and something else. I couldn't place my finger on it, but I knew I would always remember him. Pumping the digit in and out, he slid in a second finger, curling on the upstroke. It felt like electricity was arcing through me, a live wire without grounding. I felt him everywhere. He was everywhere, from his fingers inside my pussy, his taste on my tongue, and the sound of his groans that ratcheted up, matching my moans. It was one erotic scene I had no hope of erasing because once this was done, I knew it would haunt me for the rest of my life.

Retracting his fingers, he forced my head back and pushed the digits that had been inside my pussy past my lips and teeth, making me taste myself. Greedily, I sucked myself off him, swirling my tongue around the digits. Bane's eyes darkened, and he pulled my mouth closer, replacing his fingers with his mouth. We kissed like we were about to be separated for a hundred years, both of us unable to stop.

"I want to see what that mouth of yours can do," he said in a graveled voice. "But I need my face down in your cunt even more."

A whimper escaped my throat. I was surprised I was enjoying this dirty talk so much. All my other sexual encounters had been as vanilla as you could get, but this—Bane—was something else.

Dropping to his knees, he shoved the bottom of my dress up, exposing my pussy to him. He tore at my panties, pulling the stitching free and dropping the pile of lace to the tile floor. He dove in without preamble, urging me closer to the edge of the counter to give him better access. Wrapping his hands under my ass, he held me teetering on the edge while he lapped, sucked, and licked at my pussy. Throwing my hands out, I held myself steady on the walls, my heels digging into his shoulders. Bane growled as he ate me, a starving man in front of a long-desired meal. I threaded my fingers through his hair, holding him against me, grinding my pussy against his stubble.

My orgasm caught me by surprise, making me thankful I was already sitting. I screamed out Bane's name, the syllable ebbing off into a low groan as he teased every single last orgasmic shudder from me.

I was panting when I finally came back online. I looked down at Bane as he wiped the back of his hand over his mouth, wiping away my arousal.

"Fuck, I need to do that again," he rumbled, leaning back in between my legs.

9

Bane

I WAS IN FUCKING HEAVEN.

Wren tasted like champagne, and I couldn't get enough. She was edging closer to her second orgasm after only rocking and shuddering through the first about five minutes ago. I was relentless as I attacked her cunt with my mouth. I needed it. I wanted it. I wanted her to be shoved so violently off the edge that I would be the only man alive who could give her this. I needed her addicted to me.

Her fingers tightened in my hair, her nails scraping against my scalp sending pulses of erotic pain through me. It seemed my Little Bird might enjoy the kind of sex I did if the way she took direction and then just as quickly took charge was any indication. The sounds of her whimpers spurred me on, drowning out every single fucking thing I had going on in my head. When I was with her, I forgot all about the club and the drugs and my dealers. All I could think about was Wren and whether I was making her feel good.

Her thighs started to quiver as her orgasm approached, and then at the right moment, I slid two fingers into her drenched opening and started to pump them.

In.

Out.

In.

Out.

Driving her higher.

Pushing her…

… to the edge of ecstasy.

"Bane," she whimpered, drawing out my name in one long, guttural moan. I flicked my tongue faster against her clit, curling my fingers inside her, teasing out her orgasm. Her inner walls began to pulse, squeezing, and I got a fucking fantastic idea of what it would feel like with my dick inside her.

Later.

That would come later.

Tonight was all about showing my Little Bird what she was missing out on. Her refusal to take up my offer had stunned me. I thought with her brother's life on the line, she would do whatever it took. I know if the situation had been reversed, I would've done it for Bianca. There had to be more to the story. More than what she was saying.

When her body finally stilled, I removed my fingers and brought them to my mouth. Her eyes flared with awareness as she watched, but everything about her was relaxed like I could do whatever I wanted to her right now, and she would accept it. Happily.

Her gaze tracked me as I rose to my feet, hungry for more. I straightened my jacket, pulling the sleeves of my cuffs down. I'd been so crazed by her in her tight fucking dress that I hadn't even had the forethought to take the damn thing off.

She slid off the countertop, shimmying her hips to get the fabric of her dress to smooth down. The movement did nothing but jack me up a little higher. Grabbing onto her hips, I spun her around, so she was facing the mirror. I ground my aching cock against her ass, smiling when her eyes shuttered closed. Pushing the hair from the side of her neck, I kissed her there, nipping gently with my teeth.

"Think about my offer, Wren."

Her eyes flared wide, then a frown formed on her face. "That was about the offer?"

The hurt in her question was like a gunshot to the chest. It *had* been about the offer, but it had also been because I couldn't keep my fucking hands to myself. I told her as much because I always believed honesty was the best policy, even if it hurt.

"I need it in writing, Bane."

We were back to that?

"No." If my word wasn't enough, a fucking piece of paper was a moot point.

Slowly, she turned back around to face me. "I need to know that Hawk's debts will be gone after these two weeks. I don't care about what happens between us…" I stiffened at her words, but she pushed on. "I don't need a Christian Grey-style contract where all the limits are set out."

"Good, because that was fucked up. It took all the mystery and fun out of their fucking."

Her eyes widened. "You've seen the movie?"

I grunted and folded my arms. "Read the books."

The smile that pulled up her lips made my heart stutter. It was amazing. Incandescent. And I had to get her to do that more often.

"My sister made me." Her smile widened, and I couldn't help but lean in to kiss her. "Stop grinning at me like that."

"You just caught me by surprise, Bane Rivera."

"Yeah, well, don't fucking say a word to anyone. I'll deny the shit out of it."

The mood that had been lightened suddenly dimmed. "But you're not going to be able to give me what I want, are you?" She looked at me with such sudden disappointment that the urge to move fucking heaven and earth for her gripped me.

No woman had made me feel like this before, not in such a short amount of time. I would do anything for my sister, but she was family. Wren was not. But fuck, I wanted her to be more than just something to play with for two weeks. It would be a start, though.

"It's too dangerous to have a piece of paper lying around with this sort of shit on it. If the cops got a look at it, I'm fucking done."

Fuck, there was that look again.

Wren wrapped her arms over her chest, her eyes downcast. "Then… there is *no deal*. I'll figure out another way to get you the money Hawk owes you." She walked past me, unlocking the door but not yet opening it. I turned my head to find her studying me, trying to see what, I didn't know. Wordlessly, she tugged on the handle and let herself out. As the door shut again, the sound of the music throbbing outside in the club was crushed like my fucking hopes that Wren would finally agree. I knew that if it were under any other circumstances, she wouldn't have me. She was too smart to get tangled up with someone like me, so this deal was all I had left.

This deal or I let her go.

But that was never going to fucking happen.

I rinsed my face of Wren's cum, then took my time drying it before walking back out into the VIP section. Wren was gone, not that I was surprised. She was a woman who had a fucking backbone, though, and each denial she gave me only made me want to chase her more.

"Bane," someone called. I looked over my shoulder to find Evangeline standing there. "Leaving so soon?"

I shrugged. "My business meeting didn't go as planned."

A small smile flexed the corners of her mouth. "Maybe you shouldn't conduct business in the private bathroom, then."

Fuck, of course, she knew. Evangeline was a ball-busting bitch, and one I considered a friend, but she saw everything.

"I'll take that under advisement." Turning, I left the club and stepped outside. My phone began to ring, so I pulled it from my pocket. It was Dagger.

"Yeah?"

"You need to get down here. Syn has lost the fucking plot."

Fuck. "On my way."

I looked up and down the street for my car, cursing when I saw Andy wasn't there. I told him to cut laps of the block since I hadn't intended to stay all that long tonight. As I swung back to look the other way, the town car appeared on the far side of the block. When it pulled up to the curb, I got in, told him where I needed to go, then sat back into the soft leather seat for the return trip.

When we arrived back at The Dollhouse, I strode through

the club and up into my office, ducking to the side when a paperweight came flying at my head. I dodged another projectile, then grabbed Syn around the waist, turning her around, so her back was to my front, and wrapping my other arm over her chest. Why the fuck hadn't Dagger done this already? I looked around and found him bleeding on the floor. His eyes were pain-fogged as he clutched at his thigh. Blood pooled on the floor beneath him, squeezed out from between his fingers.

"What the fuck happened?" I roared, trying like hell to contain Syn who was bucking against me wildly.

"She's fucked up," Dagger replied, hissing a little. "She came here looking for you. I told her you were out. She started yelling something about some bitch you were seen talking to earlier, then she hopped on the crazy fucking train and broke the brakes."

Goddammit. And this was exactly why I didn't fuck my Dolls. They think it means something it doesn't, or in this case, it created a delusion of fucking ownership.

"Like I fucking need this right now?" I barked at Dagger. It looked like he'd been stabbed in the thigh. Hauling Syn onto the floor, I straddled her waist and pinned her arms above her head. I didn't want to hurt her. Causing pain to women was not my thing, but if one were going to come at me with a paperweight and a fuckton of jealous energy, then I'd do what I had to.

"Wendy!" I barked, the use of her real name rather than her stage name snapping her out of her rage. She blinked at me, and the fight drained out of her. Tears welled, and she started to cry.

"Why, Bane?" she howled. "Why don't you want me?"

And there it was. The exact reason I didn't want her. She was too fucking emotional. Too demanding. Too needy. She was just *too much.*

"You know I don't date."

That statement dried up the waterworks. "I don't want to date you, Bane. I just want you to fuck me and only me."

I frowned. That sounded a hell of a lot like dating to me. Well, my brand of dating, at least. "You know that can't happen for exactly this reason." I gestured to my trashed office, to the rug Dagger was bleeding on, to the fucking man she'd stabbed. Syn was another brand of crazy altogether.

"But I love you."

"You don't love me. You only think you do."

"But I've given you two blowjobs in as many days."

Fuck, her logic was twisted. "Because you were there, Syn. Lips around my dick are all the same."

"But I love you," she whispered again. Like saying the words were going to make them any truer. "We're meant to be together."

I glanced over at Dagger and shook my head. With a wince, he nodded and tried to stand, but his leg buckled beneath his bulk.

"Stay the fuck down, you stupid bastard," I snarled before turning back to Syn. "I'm sorry, baby, but you're fired. Effective immediately."

The color drained from her face. "You can't fire me. You can't fire me..." On and on she went with the denial. I was afraid to let her up given the amount of crazy she'd displayed tonight, but Dagger wasn't in any state to move. Transferring Syn's wrists to one hand, I dug in my pocket for my phone.

"Rach," I said.

"Mr. Rivera?"

"Yeah, can you call the doc and get him to swing by. There's been a situation in my office."

"Do I need to send Tony up?"

"Nah, he's the only one on the door. Just call the doc." I hung up and tried to wrap my head around this shit. Syn was still blubbering about how she can't be out of a job and she loved me.

Dagger was taking it like a fucking man and not making much noise at all.

I was mourning the loss of my Wren high.

Yeah, tonight was a fucking disaster. I was a girl short and a bodyguard down. And the desire to claim my Little Bird was starting to become a relentless pounding in my skull.

10

Wren

I DREAMED OF HIM. OF BANE. OF HIM BENDING ME over the countertop in that private bathroom and slamming inside me. My dream-self screamed in pleasure at the invasion, at his ownership of me. I hadn't even seen his cock, but dream Wren had an incredibly active imagination. And a very generous one.

Rolling over in my bed, I let out a deep breath and kicked off the thin sheet that had been covering me. It was only seven in the morning, and it was already in the nineties. The only positive I could take from the situation was that it was Saturday and the last day of the working week.

Getting up, I showered and dressed in my uniform, already looking forward to finishing up this afternoon and doing nothing tonight. Going out last night had left me almost too exhausted to sleep, but with the vivid image of Bane's head between my thighs, my subconscious was clearly eager to get into the REM zone.

As I ate breakfast, I checked my phone. I had a couple of missed calls from Darcy which had come through after I'd crashed. Fuck, I was supposed to meet her last night. Instead of listening to the voice mails, I just hit dial.

"Oh, thank Christ you're not dead," she answered.

"Good morning to you, too."

"Don't give me that shit, Wren Montana. Where the fuck were you last night? You didn't call. Didn't text."

"I'm so sorry, babe. It's kind of a long story."

"Does it involve sex because you know that's the only acceptable excuse for me."

I sank into my couch, a bowl of cereal on the table in front of me. "Yes, it involves sex."

"All is forgiven, then," she said. "Proceed."

And I did. I told her how Bane had hijacked me at the front door by putting me on the VIP list. How he'd followed me into the bathroom then proceeded to give me two of the best orgasms of my life. I'd been so ashamed of myself when I left the bathroom that all I wanted to do was go home.

"Wren, babe, what are you going to do? I mean, I totally get why you wouldn't want to become Bane's private pussy, but isn't it a means to an end? Two weeks isn't that long, and then Hawk's debt will be gone."

"Maybe," I conceded. "Until he fucks up again. We both know he's going to."

"True… so what are you going to do?"

I ran a hand through my ponytail and dropped it onto my lap. "I don't know."

"Want me to come over tonight?"

I smiled. Darcy was the best friend a girl could have. "Nah, I'm okay. When I finish up work tonight, I'm going to soak in the tub, then watch some Netflix before bed."

"All right," she said reluctantly. "But if you change your mind and want me to come over, I will. Baron will totally understand."

"Thanks, babe. I better let you go. I'll talk to you later."

I hung up the phone, not feeling better at all. Maybe I was being stubborn in not accepting Bane's terms. He was right that a piece of paper could be dangerous for a man like him. It would look like he'd solicited sex, which in a way he was, but this was a personal contract.

And if I did do this, Hawk would be off the hook. I loved my brother, would do anything for him, but there had to be some limits. There had to be a line in the sand that I wasn't willing to cross. Bane Rivera might just be that line.

As I walked to the shop, I shot a text to my brother, asking if he had any luck raising the cash he owed to Bane. I answered his call a moment later.

"Hey, so I think I've found a way."

"A legal way?" I asked. My brother looked for loopholes like a lawyer did—with precision and dedication.

"It's horse racing… of course, it's legal."

I barely held in my groan. Of all the stupid, dumb-ass moves he could make.

"Hawk, for fuck's sake! Really? You're gambling to get money?"

"Well, if you know of a better way to clear my debt with Rivera, I am all ears."

I hadn't told him about the proposition. If he knew, he'd begged me to take it because he could be selfish like that. I understood fear was driving a lot of his words and behaviors, but I still felt that nagging sense of responsibility.

We'd been on our own since I was sixteen and Hawk was twelve. After bouncing from foster home to foster home together, I became emancipated at eighteen, got us an apartment, and took care of him ever since. That need to protect him was as strong as a mother's instinct, and I couldn't shake this ingrained need so easily.

I arrived at the shop, unlocked the door, and slipped inside. After shutting off the alarm, I told him, "I don't, but I'm going to go and talk to the bank to see if they'll offer me an emergency business loan."

He blew out a breath, then said the words I'd been waiting to hear from him. "I'm so fucking scared, Wren."

"I know. We'll figure it out, though." I glanced up as my nine o'clock client came in with her poodle. "I have to go, Hawk. I'll let you know how I go with the bank."

I FINALLY FLIPPED THE SIGN CLOSED ON THE SHOP FRONT and breathed a sigh of relief. I was officially in weekend territory, and I couldn't wait to get home. After scrubbing the place down and setting the alarm, I grabbed my bag, locked up the shop, and began the short walk home. I stopped in at the liquor store and picked up some wine, but as I walked past a display of champagne, I paused. A champagne kiss was all I could think about. That, along with the man who had given them to me.

"They're on sale right now," the clerk said, giving me a warm smile.

I returned it but shook my head. I couldn't afford champagne right now. I clutched my cheap bottle of red wine more tightly and brought it to the counter. "Maybe next time," I told him with a small shrug.

"Big plans for tonight?"

"I'm not sure. Unless you count a long soak in the tub and Netflix as big plans."

He grinned. "You sound just like my girlfriend. She does the same."

"Smart woman," I replied, digging into my purse for some cash. I scraped together the last of my money to pay for the booze, then said goodbye to the clerk.

When I got to my apartment, I unlocked the door, then went through the re-locking routine before placing the wine on the kitchen counter. I'd just toed off my Vans when there was a loud banging on my apartment door. Walking over, I yanked the thing open, staring at my brother who was breathing like a racehorse.

The irony was not lost on me.

He burst into my apartment, slamming the door shut behind him. I narrowed my eyes at him, bracing myself for the next words out of his motherfucking mouth. "I fucked up, Wren."

I was suddenly getting flashbacks to when he'd said those words to me only a few nights ago. "What the fuck have you done this time, Hawk?"

"I owe a bookie some money." I stared at him in disbelief, trying to file all his words into my mind in an orderly fashion. They made sense on their own, but thrown together, I couldn't quite grasp how fucking *stupid* he was being.

"You're kidding, right? Tell me you're fucking laughing at my expense."

He shook his head, his expression serious. "No, sis."

Rage bubbled up inside me, this dormant beast of emotions that Hawk seemed to tap into every time he did something like this. "Fuck! How much do you owe?"

He actually winced. "Twenty thousand."

I blinked. "If you owe Bane-fucking-Rivera fifty thousand dollars, why the *fuck* would you bet another twenty you don't even have?"

"I was desperate, okay. And it was a sure thing. Come on, you have to believe me."

"I do believe you. I believe you're a gigantic asshole who doesn't think about how this shit impacts his sister. What am I supposed to do with this information?"

He began to pace, spearing his fingers through his blond hair. "I don't know. I don't know," he muttered. "Did you speak to the bank about that loan?"

"Are you fucking serious, Hawk?" My voice had hit screeching levels, and I wasn't even apologizing for it.

"Well, have you? You could borrow enough to cover both debts."

Stalking into the kitchen, I pulled my emergency bottle of whisky from a top cupboard and slammed it down onto the Formica. "Fuck." I poured myself a shot of whiskey and swallowed it. Wincing at the burn, I yelled, "You do know how loans work, right? I have to pay all of this back, *plus interest*, and how am I supposed to achieve that if you're out there fucking making bets and being a general prick about things?"

He followed me into the kitchen, leaning against the counter. "There has to be a way."

I eyed him over the rim of my whiskey glass as I threw another shot back. "There is. It's called a dirt bed, and it'll be yours."

I hated that I had to threaten him like this, but he wouldn't learn. What did he think the bookie was going to do when he found out Hawk didn't have the money he owed, just pat him on the back and say better luck next time? I poured myself another shot, hissing through my teeth as the cheap alcohol burned my throat. I tried to come up with a plan that could work, but all I came up with was one that I didn't want to touch with a ten-foot pole.

I didn't want to touch it, but maybe I could stroke it just enough, so it'd back off.

Striding from the kitchen, I walked into my bedroom and swiped the black business card off my dresser. In the living room, I scooped up my phone and punched in the number on the back. As I put the device to my ear, I let out a breath and prayed I was doing the right thing.

There was a click, and then...

"Little Bird."

11

Bane

"LITTLE BIRD? ARE YOU THERE?" I CHECKED MY PHONE to make sure the connection hadn't cut off.

"I'm here," she said with an irritated sigh.

"To what do I owe the pleasure of a phone call?"

"I need a favor."

My eyes slid shut as the four sweetest words were uttered on the other end of the phone. "I'm listening."

"My asshole brother owes a bookie twenty grand after betting on a horse race. If he'd won, he was going to pay you back with that money."

"Let me guess, his horse didn't win."

"Not even fucking close," she replied. "Are you able to loan me the money to pay the bookie?"

I wanted to laugh out loud. This was all too fucking perfect. Wren's desperation was the thing to make her come running to me, looking for help. I leaned back in my office chair and placed my feet on the desk. "Hawk would owe me seventy thousand, then," I mused.

"I'm aware." Her words were curt like she was biting her tongue. She hated every minute of this. But me? I was fucking enjoying the hell out of it.

"I totally get it if you don't want to get in any deeper with—"

"Deal." When she said nothing in reply, I made sure the call was still connected. "Wren?"

There was the sound of a door closing. Then, "I'm here."

"Good. I'm coming over to discuss the terms." I hung up without waiting for her reply. She was in no position to argue with me, anyway. I had her just where I wanted her. Standing from my desk, I looked down on the club, seeing it all running as it should.

Dagger had half a dozen stitches in his thigh after Syn's attack, but he'd insisted on still working tonight. For that, I was grateful because I was about to do something I hadn't done since I opened The Dollhouse.

I was leaving early on a Saturday night.

Plucking my suit jacket off the back of my chair, I patted my pockets for my keys, then picked up my phone, dialing my driver.

"Be there in five," he replied and hung up.

Sliding the device into the breast pocket of my jacket, I left the office. When I walked past the bar, Rachel gave me a small smile. The bruising was getting worse, but that was a good sign. It meant she was healing.

"Have you moved out yet?" I demanded, taking her situation very fucking personally.

She bobbed her head as she focused on pouring a drink. "I'm

staying with Kandy for a while."

"Thank fuck. Let me know if you need help finding a new place. I own a couple of apartment buildings downtown." She stared at me like I was speaking in tongues. "You good?"

Clearing her throat, she croaked, "Yeah, I'm good. Thanks, boss."

I lifted my chin in Dagger's direction as I passed her, slowing when he paused his conversation with one of the dancers. "How's the leg?"

"Fine," he replied, raising his brows in question.

"Heading out for the night. Make sure everything runs smoothly. Call me if shit gets hectic."

"Will do."

I clapped him on the shoulder as I passed, then stepped out onto the street. My town car was right where it was supposed to be, and I gave Andy Wren's address.

She lived in a shitty part of town, and I would talk to her about setting her up elsewhere that had a lot more security. Knowing my Little Bird, she wouldn't fucking like it, but I took care of what was mine. Just thinking about how she'd fight me on it made my dick hard.

By the time we pulled up at the curb, I was aching for her cunt. That little taste I'd had at the club hadn't been enough. I wanted the whole damn meal this time. But before I could satisfy the darker side of me, we had a little business to take care of.

I took the stairs to her apartment, knocking on the door when I got there. A moment later, Wren pulled it open, and my brain kind of fritzed out. She was dressed in those fucking Daisy Dukes again, her lean tanned legs on display, and a loose white T-shirt that hung off one of her shoulders. Stepping away from the door, she let me in, her eyes on me the entire time.

I was glad to see the place was empty. I turned when she shut the door behind her, and she wrapped her arms around herself for a moment before letting them go loose at her sides.

"Drink?" she mumbled, already walking into the kitchen. I followed her in there, seeing a bottle of whisky on the counter beside a shot glass. "Sorry, I don't have any of that expensive shit you have at The Dollhouse," she said, gesturing to the whisky. "If I did, I wouldn't be shooting this fucking swill."

I watched as she poured herself a shot and threw it back.

"How much have you had to drink?" I asked, wrapping my hands around the bottle and placing the opening to my mouth. I kept my eyes on her as I took a large swallow, then lowered it.

"Not enough."

"Regretting your decision to call me?" I asked. I had to know where her head was at. I wasn't into coercing women. They had to want to do something, but I knew Wren's submission would be sweet.

"No. I'm fucking pissed off with Hawk for being so fucking thoughtless." She stared at me, and her gaze seemed to strip away everything I showed to the world. "Do you ever wonder why you fucking bother with family sometimes?"

"Never. Family is everything."

She huffed a laugh and took the bottle from my hand, pouring herself another drink. "What if the family you have is so fucking self-centered that they can't see that everything you do is for them?"

I thought about that for a moment, then replied, "Then maybe they don't deserve you."

She saluted me with a sardonic smile, then slammed back the

shot. Leaving the glass on the counter, she weaved past me on the way to the couch. Her living room was sparsely decorated, but there were a few personal touches here and there in the form of photographs of her and Hawk growing up.

"I love what you've done with the place," I drawled.

"Don't be an asshole," she snarled, jabbing her finger in my direction. "You're the one who invited himself over."

My dick twitched at her tone.

With a smirk, I slid out of my jacket and undid the cuffs and top button of my dress shirt. Wren watched me the entire time, her blue eyes darting from my hands to my throat to my cock straining against my slacks. She bit her bottom lip, then looked away.

"You can look, you know," I said as I settled onto the couch beside her. She swung her head back to look at me. "You should be able to look at what you cause."

Her mouth parted slightly before she shook herself. "Believe me, I know exactly what I cause."

There was a good foot between us on the couch, and it was a foot too wide as far as I was concerned. Taking her by surprise, I reached across and lifted her effortlessly, settling her on my knee. She wrapped one arm around my neck as she tried to get her balance back, and I shook my head when she tried to pull away. Curling my fingers around the base of her skull and the other on her upper thigh, I settled back, enjoying the way she felt. Although she had stiffened at the initial contact, she was slowly relaxing.

When I was sure she wouldn't bolt, I swept my hand on her thigh up a little higher, skimming the fingertips under the frayed hem of her shorts.

"We should discuss what's going to happen," she said softly. "If I agree to this."

If? Fuck, no.

I *needed* her to agree to this.

I *needed* that two weeks.

If she needed more convincing, then I would persuade her tonight because there was no way I was leaving without getting something for my good deed.

I could press her for that later.

For now...

"Yes." I always wanted to know what the terms were. I knew what I wanted. I knew what I was getting and what I had to give. "The original offer of Hawk's debt being wiped still stands."

She narrowed her eyes at me, her fingers stilling. "And the deal with the bookie?"

I was a bastard for twisting this. Fuck, I wanted to kiss her, to slide my tongue into her mouth and make her grind on my lap. "I'll get rid of the bookie, but I need something from you in return."

"What?"

"Tonight. You give me all of you tonight in whatever way I want, and I'll take that additional debt on."

She mulled that over for a beat. "I need to hear the conversation between you two for myself. I need to know."

Smart woman. I stood up quickly, taking her with me. She wrapped her legs around my waist, clinging to me. My dick jerked against her core, and her eyes slid shut. I felt around for my phone in my jacket pocket, then returned to the couch, settling us back down again. Wren's breathing had grown erratic in that short trip, the sound of her sharp panting making me fantasize about what she would sound like while I was pounding into her.

"What's his name?"

"Do you have everyone on speed dial?" she asked.

"His name."

"Frank White. Do you know him?"

I didn't bother to answer her question. I knew everyone, and everyone knew me. I pulled up Frank's number, hit dial, then put it on speaker so Wren could hear.

"Rivera, how's the pussy business," the guy answered after a couple of rings.

"Good. How's the bookie business?"

"Fucking fantastic. I had some asshole bet twenty thou on a race I'd fixed," he told me, laughing. I ground my teeth, working my jaw to stop myself from tearing the guy a new asshole.

"Yeah, about that guy… Hawk Montana is his name, right?"

There was the sound of fingers flying across a keyboard before he said, "Yeah. How'd you know?"

"I need you to wipe that debt."

"What the fuck, Rivera. I don't come into your business and tell you—"

I cut off his fucking tirade. "Frank, you'll get paid, but you won't be chasing Montana for it. I'll transfer the cash to you after I get off the phone."

"I don't know, Rivera…"

The fucker was fishing for more. With gritted teeth, I added, "I'll give you a one-month pass to The Dollhouse… unlimited access."

"Now, that's more like it," Frank replied. "Deal. Send me the money in the next ten. Otherwise, I'm sending my guy after

Montana in the morning like I was planning to."

I hung up, then clicked into my banking app. I had accounts everywhere, some legit, some not so legit, but they all worked for me. I transferred the twenty grand to Frank's account, then logged out.

A minute later, a text from Frank said he got the money, and he'll see me tomorrow night for his first day with my Dolls.

"Done," I told Wren. "I've held up my end of the bargain. Now it's your turn." I needed to be in her cunt tonight. Denial was only good for so long.

She worried her bottom lip with her teeth.

When I saw her hesitation, I added, "Think of this as a free pass. We're both simply getting what we want here. One night of pleasure, and if you don't want to take my offer after that, then I won't pursue you again. You can try to deny this attraction, Little Bird, but I know you want me to fuck you, and I can't go another day without tasting you again. Just let me bury myself in your cunt because that's all I've been able to think about since last night. Then tomorrow, we can figure out a way for you to see that my word is worth more than a piece of paper."

Her fingers tightened in my hair, where she was playing with it at the nape of my neck. Her gaze darted from my eyes to my mouth.

Yes, she wanted that too.

One night of my tongue in her sucking, licking, biting.

One night of my cock inside her.

Bringing her to fucking orgasm over and over again.

Without waiting for another word out of her mouth, I kissed her roughly, sliding my tongue into her waiting and willing mouth. She opened even more widely for me, allowing me inside her. I stroked at her tongue, eliciting soft moans from her throat. My heart hammered in my chest as I took what I wanted from her. And she gave it all. Freely.

Breaking away, I slid Wren from my lap and deposited her onto the couch roughly, watching the way her breasts bounced under her shirt with the force.

"Move to the other end," I commanded, pulling the tails of my shirt out of my slacks. I unbuttoned it quickly, then dropped it to the floor before working on my belt. Wren's eyes widened when she heard the sound of the buckle coming loose. I slid it free of the loops in my pants, folding the leather over on itself until I had a short whip of sorts. I slapped it against my palm, enjoying the way Wren's breathing increased.

"Like that, baby?" I asked, my voice low and graveled.

She moaned and bit her bottom lip. I groaned. There was no fucking way I could take my time with her. Next time, maybe, but tonight, I had to take her like I wanted. Rough. Savage. Unrelenting.

I unbuttoned my pants and stepped out of them.

Wren's gaze dropped to my bare cock already waiting for her. She swallowed and sat up, reaching for me. I shook my head, making her pause. Taking a seat on the couch, I motioned for her to get up.

"Strip for me."

She sank her teeth into her lip again as she thought about it. I was about to bark another command when she popped the button, slid the zipper down on her shorts, and hooked her thumbs into the waistband. She shimmied out of the denim, kicking them to the side. My eyes roamed all over her smooth thighs, but what I really needed to see was being hidden by the shirt. I glanced at her face.

Pulling the hem up over her head, she took off her shirt, leaving her in white lace panties and a matching bra. My dick jerked violently against my stomach, drawing her eyes. They widened a little, lust blowing out her pupils. I stroked myself while she watched, the desire for her plowing through me like a fucking freight train through a snowdrift. I don't think I've ever had a woman I wanted so much. Not like this.

"I want to see everything, Little Bird," I told her, my voice low and rough. Fuck, I needed to get myself back under control.

Reaching behind her, she unhooked her bra and shrugged it from her shoulders. I took in the beauty of her tits and knew that was where I wanted to dedicate some time. With my free hand, I motioned for her to lose the panties too. She did, and when she stood again, I drank in my fill.

Perfection.

Wren Montana was a fucking queen, and I wanted her to be mine.

12

Wren

AS I STOOD THERE NAKED BEFORE BANE, I WAS waiting for the shame to hit me. The guilt. The humiliation. I was braced for it all, but what I got instead flawed me. Lust pooled low in my body while desire set my blood to boiling. Jesus fuck, I knew I wanted Bane, but not like this. Not with this much strength.

He patted his bare knee, inviting me closer. I stepped free of my panties and walked closer. My veins singed with awareness, my pulse spiking when he reached for his folded belt.

"I think my Little Bird needs a spanking for taking so long to come to the right decision."

Instead of disgust rolling through me, it was desire. It was need. It was this overwhelming sense that I would like everything he would do to me tonight. And for the next two weeks.

"Lay across my lap with that fine ass of yours in the air."

Although self-conscious, I did as he asked, positioning myself across his knees with my face against the edge of the cushion. He ran his hands over my ass, dedicating time to each cheek as he massaged them.

"I'm going to enjoy making your ass red," he murmured, spanking me softly with a cupped hand before massaging it away. I moaned a little at the sensation, at the sting that seemed to register in my brain as pleasure rather than pain. "Hmmm, you like having my hand on your ass?" he asked in a deep rumble.

I tried to nod. I think I did.

His hand landed on my ass again, harder this time. Almost immediately, he massaged away the sting leaving me aching and needy. I moaned again, the couch cushion catching the erotic sound and stealing it away. He turned his attention to my other cheek, slapping it, then teasing away the pain.

I sucked in a gasp when I felt something cold trail up the back of my thigh. I began to squirm, but Bane pressed on my lower back, stilling me.

"I won't hurt you, Little Bird," he told me. "I'll make this feel fucking fantastic."

Swallowing, I nodded and shut my eyes. The question about whether I'd done the right thing was lapping in my head. That hard, cold thing trailed up the inside of my thigh, brushing against my pussy, and I cried out. I realized it was his folded-over belt. He was hardly touching me with it, but after warming me up with spanking, my entire body was electrified, waiting for his next touch.

He dragged the belt up over one of my ass cheeks, then pulled it away. I moaned at the loss, surprised that I liked it so much. Was that fucked up? A hiss was suddenly escaping my lips as the belt came down on my ass with a crack, the new sensation lighting me from the inside out. A low, appreciative moan bubbled up from Bane's throat as he struck me again. The soft leather was warming slowly, taking away that first shock of sensation.

I arched my back as Bane's fingers teased at the entrance of my pussy. He pushed a finger inside me, rubbing my juices over my clit. I could already feel an orgasm coming. With the combination of submission and spanking, I was primed for him, primed for the pleasure he could give me.

"So wet," he murmured. He circled my clit, spreading liquid warmth all over me. Against my lower belly, I felt his cock hardening even further. If this was erotic torture to me, I could only imagine what it was doing to him. He plunged two fingers inside me, pumping them with new fervor. His control must've snapped, not that I was complaining. I clutched at the couch cushion beneath me as he finger fucked me to an orgasm that left me blind.

"Oh, fuck!" I screamed as the pleasure washed over me in a wave so big I feared Bane had ruined me for every other potential future sex partner. Bane spanked me as that wave crested, shoving it firmly into tsunami territory. I came with such fury, such wanton abandon. Writhing, bucking, thrashing, I came so hard and with such force that I could hardly catch my breath. When I could finally breathe again when the pleasure had ebbed away from my body, I turned my face so I could see him.

Bane had the fingers he'd had in my pussy in his mouth, sucking them clean. I groaned again. He was going to kill me. He was such a filthy man, but I found myself enjoying every damn second.

"You taste like champagne to me, Little Bird," he rumbled. "I don't need to ask if you enjoyed that because clearly you did."

I nodded. "Good, because I plan on spanking you as often as I can."

A shiver climbed over me, settling against my skin. Smoothing his hand over my ass, the nerve endings skittered in his wake. Who knew touch could be so powerful?

"I'd planned on taking more time with you at my place this first time, but I won't complain. Having you here like this is fucking enough. Come and straddle my waist."

Getting up, I did as he asked, throwing one leg over his hips and settling against him. His cock was a hot rigid length between my pussy lips, rubbing my clit in the most delicious way. I squirmed against him, a gasp escaping my lips. Bane stared at my chest, his dark gaze drinking in my breasts with an almost reverent expression. He pinched one nipple, rolling the bud between his thumb and forefinger. The pressure was just this side of pain, and I flexed my hips against him, rubbing my pussy against his cock. I smiled when he groaned, so I did it again.

Bane brought his other hand to my breast and tweaked the nipple before taking them in each of his hands and squeezing gently. When he lowered his mouth to one of my breasts, a long shudder pushed past my lips. His tongue was like velvet against my skin, his teeth like a dagger. The mixture of pleasure and pain he seemed to bring to everything in the way he touched me ratcheted up my lust to a new level. He switched sides, sucking my other nipple into his mouth.

Biting.

Licking.

Sucking.

Driving me fucking insane.

Threading my fingers through his hair, I held him to me, pressing his face closer to my body. He thrust up, the ridges of his dick hitting my clit was an almost euphoric high. My head dropped back as I moaned. I doubt I'd ever been this turned on by a man in my life.

"Fuck," Bane muttered harshly, pulling away. His expression was wild, like he didn't know what to do with all the sensations. "I want to fuck these beautiful tits, but I have to be inside you more."

I whimpered at the visceral image he managed to paint in one breath. He stood me up, so he could grab something from his pants pocket. A condom. Then he sat back down and ripped open the foil wrapper. I was rapt as I watched him slide the latex down his shift, groaning a little when he pulled at his cock.

He reached for me, splitting my thighs on either side of his body. His cock brushed against my entrance, the blunt head seeking entry. I held myself above him for a moment, just staring into his dark, fathomless eyes.

"I want to watch your face while I fuck you," he said, kissing me hard and slamming inside me at the same time. I cried at the beautiful invasion, and the pure rightness of him being inside me eclipsed all thoughts that what I'd agreed to do with him was wrong. Bane-fucking-Rivera could fuck me anytime he wanted, and I would happily get lost in him.

He moved slowly at first, teasing the edges of my sanity with his slow, steady rhythm. A deep pull of need had settled into my belly, though, a well of pleasure only he could tap, and I begged him to do just that. I kissed him, his tongue plunging into my mouth, dominating my senses. When we broke for breath, his gaze went to my breasts.

"Touch yourself," he commanded softly.

I reached for my breasts, cupping them softly, then rubbing my thumbs over my nipples. Bane placed his lips where one of my hands had just been, sucking me into his mouth and biting down. I moaned, my body flooding with warmth. Thrusting more deeply, I held back the scream as he hit deep inside me, pushing me past pleasure and into a pain that slowly melted away into just more intense pleasure.

Releasing my breast, he sat back. "Get yourself off while I watch. I want to feel you come on my dick at least a dozen times tonight."

A dozen? Biting my lip, I snaked my hand down between our bodies and flicked the tip of my finger over the sensitive flesh. My orgasm struck like lightning, the combination of his bossy commands, his thrusting cock, and my desire to please him, rendering me a victim to my hedonism.

I screamed his name before finally burying my head in the crook of his neck and shuddering through the rest of my orgasm. Bane continued to pump inside me, driving himself deeper, taking over me. I let him. It was good to forget that I was the responsible one, the one who had to look out for my baby brother.

Bane suddenly pulled out and flipped us, so I was kneeling on the couch while he fucked me from behind. I clutched at the back of the frame of the couch, my breasts bouncing with the force of his strokes. Increasing his pace a little, I shut my eyes, absorbing the thrusts, absorbing the way he was claiming me.

HOURS LATER, WE WERE ON THE FLOOR. BANE WAS going down on me again, the sight of his hands wrapped around my thighs was more than my sex-addled brain could really handle. He'd made good on his promise of orgasms, and he was going for the twelfth now, only I wasn't sure my oversensitive body could do it. I felt raw—well-used but not misused. Bane was very considerate of my comfort the entire time, but he was driven with unrelenting focus now.

I squeezed my eyes shut as another orgasm crept over me. It wasn't that crashing wave anymore. Rather, it was a slow build-up that teased at the orgasm, peeling away layers of it until I was left with no choice but to face it.

When I eventually stilled, and my breathing had finally eased, Bane slid back inside my body, my inner walls clenching in welcome. Placing his forearms on either side of my head, he fucked me missionary style, his dark eyes on my face. We were both covered in sweat and cum—mine, not his—but I'd never been happier to be where I was. Bane's strokes were slow now. Gone was that urgency of before, and in its place was a gentleness I had only glimpsed briefly from him.

"Come one last time for me, baby," he grunted. "Come with me."

His words were the trigger. My body did not feel like my own, and I screamed his name as I came for the final time. Bane's body went rigid as he chased me over the edge. His roar echoed around the room, his orgasm pouring on and on. When he finally stopped thrusting into me, he rolled over onto his back and took me with him. Sprawled across his chest, I lay there, panting, sweating, unable to move.

"Holy fuck," I whispered against his chest.

He chuckled. "I'll take that as a compliment." Pushing my ponytail out of his face, he forced me to look at him. "I want every man to know how I fucked you raw."

His dirty words sent a thrill through me, and although my mind was willing, perhaps my body wasn't. I shut my eyes as sleep tried to claim me. Bane shuffled me off to the side, where I curled up on the rug, content to just stay there.

"Shower first," he said, scooping me up easily. "Then bed."

"To sleep?" I asked, peering at him, at the strong line of his jaw and the beard that was just the other side of a five o'clock shadow. He eyed me with a smirk.

"I thought I could get another taste of your cunt first." I squeezed my legs shut involuntarily, and he chuckled. "Maybe not. I've worn you out."

"Are you always so… thorough?"

He paused, his eyes growing dark for a moment before setting me down on the bathroom counter and turning on the shower. When it was clear he wasn't going to answer that question, I let him wash us both before sliding into bed.

Rolling over onto my side, I shoved the sheet back off me, but Bane had other ideas. He wrapped himself around me, his leg over mine, his arm over my chest to cup one of my breasts. Just as I drifted off, I got the distinct impression Bane Rivera wouldn't make it easy for me to leave, either now or in the future.

13

Bane

IT HAD BEEN THIRTY HOURS SINCE WREN FINALLY GAVE me what I wanted. Thirty hours of me getting fucking hard at work just thinking about her. I was ready to have her again, but the deal we had was one night only, and I had to make her see I was her only choice.

I picked up my phone and dialed Bianca.

"Don't tell me you're canceling," she said by way of greeting.

"Fuck, no, I'm still coming, Bianca."

"Oh," she replied, stunned. "What's the reason for the call, then?"

"Can't a brother call his sister more than once a week?"

In the background, Valentine started to fuss. I glanced at the clock. It was just after eleven, so she must be getting ready to nap. "You can," she replied, shushing Valentine softly. "But I guess you caught me by surprise. So, we're still on?"

"Yeah, but I wanted to see if I could bring someone."

There was a long pause before my sister demanded, "Are you seeing someone? You've never seen someone. Who is she? What's her name?"

"Pump the breaks, Bianca. Fuck."

"Sorry, but it's true. You haven't dated… like ever."

Propping my feet up on the desk, I thought about that statement. It was true, I'd never had a proper relationship. I fucked around when I was at school and all through college, but I could never bring myself to settling down with just one woman. "I'm aware of my track record with women."

"So, who's the lucky lady?"

I reached for my whisky and swallowed what was left in the glass. "Her name's Wren."

"Wren," she cooed. "Tell me more."

"What more is there to tell?"

"Loads, Bane. Seriously. You'll bring her, then?"

"Yeah." The thought of Wren meeting Bianca actually made me smile a little. They were similar in many ways, and in others, completely different, so we were either going to have fucking fireworks or a fucking campfire where we all sang *Kumbaya* together. "We'll see you at seven."

I hung up the phone then drained my drink. The Dollhouse was closed due to it being a Monday, but I always seemed to come in anyway. Call it habit or call it fucking pathetic, but I lived and breathed this club. Grabbing the bottle of whisky, I poured myself another and sat back in my office chair. I hadn't told Wren about dinner tonight. But she would come, I knew she would.

"Fuck." I stood, rearranging my erection that was insistently pressing against my zipper. I had to do something with this energy battering my body. Otherwise, I was liable to skip dinner and just take Wren back to my apartment to fuck. Pocketing my phone, I stalked from my office to downstairs, where the cleaning crew was working hard. A couple of them nodded to me as I passed, then I was stepping outside.

My car was by the curb, and I got in.

"Where to, boss?" Andy asked.

"Take me to the gym. I need to beat the shit out of something."

We drove in silence, and by the time we pulled up at the boxing gym, I was ready to knock someone the fuck out. So much energy was under my skin, making me fucking jumpy.

"I'll be about an hour. Come back then," I told Andy, then walked into the grimy gym. After getting changed, I shut my locker, wrapped my hands, and pulled on my gloves. I went to one of the bags first, hitting it with a combination of jabs, hooks, and uppercuts until my upper body was screaming.

There were other patrons in there, but none of them paid me any attention. At the back of the room, two men circled each other in the ring. I let myself go on the bag, letting out all my frustrations in the hope that when I finally saw Wren again, I wouldn't unleash my dark side on her too strongly. There was no way I could avoid showing it to her, but I had to do it slowly.

With each combination I worked through, I thought about my little problem with my dealers, wondering what I could do to find out more. Dagger had exhausted his contacts, but I still had one more ace up my sleeve. Bianca's husband was a cop in LA. Surely, he'd know something about dealers being shot at. I made a point to ask him tonight.

By the time I was done, sweat had poured off me. Outside, it was in the nineties, but in here, it was nudging one hundred.

Pulling off my gloves and the wraps, I drank an entire bottle of water, then threw it into the trash. Back at my locker, I grabbed what I needed for a shower, then moved to change rooms taking a peek at my phone while I was at it. It was only a little after twelve.

After showering quickly, I then went back outside. Andy drove me back to my apartment, where I would stay for the rest of the day.

Just as I opened my apartment door, my phone rang.

"Boss?" Dagger said when I answered.

"What is it?"

"Another one of our guys has been taken out."

Squeezing my eyes shut, I let out a deep breath. "When? Who?"

"That kid, Santiago. In his apartment. Cops are crawling over the area right now, but I managed to get the drugs out before they got there."

"Fuck!"

"What do you want to do?"

I ran a hand through my hair, thinking about my options. We still didn't know who it was, and going around killing either Manzetti's or Sanderson's men was a bad fucking idea. We needed concrete proof of this.

"I'm going to get in contact with a potential source and find out what the fuck is going on." I hung up the phone, then stalked to the wet bar. After pouring myself a drink, I drained the amber liquid. What the fuck was happening? One of those fuckers was fucking with my business, and I couldn't not retaliate. Weakness was a disease I had no intention of catching. "Fuck!" I threw the crystal tumbler at the wall, where it smashed. My breath was barreling out of me as I stared at all those shards of glass. I didn't like not being in control. I didn't like the feeling of hopelessness that engulfed me when it happened, so I made sure it didn't happen in every facet of my life.

Wren had been pushing my goddamn buttons with her reluctance to toe the line. My breathing eased as I thought about her, her blonde hair, and those eyes that seemed to miss nothing.

Fuck, I had to see her. I had to touch her. I needed her to ground me.

On the ride down in the elevator, I texted Andy that I needed him. He was waiting for me when I stepped from the foyer of the building. I slid inside the cool interior of the back seat and sat back, waiting for Andy to get this fucking show on the road. Drumming my fingers on the top of my thigh, I tapped my other foot, desperate to get to my Little Bird.

14

Wren

"THANK YOU, MR. BEATTY. I'LL SEE YOU AND CYRIL NEXT week." I waved the older gentleman off, his twelve-year-old beagle hustling beside him. I turned about to go back into the shop when I noticed the town car parked at the curb out in front of my shop. Adrenaline coursed through my veins.

I shouldn't be excited about seeing Bane again. I'd planned on turning his offer down, even though Saturday night had been the most mind-blowing sexual experience of my life. I was going to talk to the bank this afternoon about that loan, to get Hawk the money he needed, then concentrate on working my ass off to pay it all back.

Bane's way would be the easy way out, but I didn't trust myself to walk away from him after two weeks. The longer I gave myself over to him, the more difficult it would become to break the obsession. I didn't know if the obsession was wholly mine or his as well—I simply knew there was this undercurrent that connected us.

But after this was done, Hawk would be on his own.

I refused to bail him out again.

Against my will, a small smile broke out on my face when the rear door of the town car opened and Bane stepped out, looking amazing in a pair of dark jeans and a black T-shirt that sat snuggly against his broad shoulders, the pads of his pecs, and large biceps. The tattoos on his neck were revealed, giving me a tantalizing slice of tanned skin and intricate ink. He walked toward me, his gaze running down my body like he hadn't seen me in years.

"Hi," I said, the butterflies in my stomach feeling like they were the size of a jet. "What are you doing here?"

He wrapped one arm around my waist, the other cradling the base of my skull. "I haven't been able to stop thinking about you," he murmured, dropping a kiss to my lips. I placed my hands on his chest, fisting his shirt in my hands like I was afraid he'd simply evaporate if I weren't holding on. It was only supposed to be one night, but I was already addicted to his touch. What had Bane Rivera done to me?

"I missed you, too," I replied. Immediately, I regretted the words. That was too needy, too fucking personal. I shouldn't have missed him. All he'd given me was an *amazing* night of sex. We weren't in a relationship. We didn't even have a business arrangement.

He stroked my cheek, then directed us inside the salon. "How many more clients do you have?" he asked, turning around to face me as I shut the door behind us.

"None. That was my last one, but I sometimes get drop-ins."

Heat flared in Bane's eyes. He marched to the door and locked it, flipping the plastic sign over before he stalked back to me.

"Bane, what—"

My words were stolen from me when he picked me up, and I immediately wrapped my legs around his waist. For a moment, I let his mouth devour mine before wriggling free of his grip.

"What are you doing?" My words came out as a tortured moan.

He quirked one dark brow at me. "I was going to fuck you until you screamed my name," he replied, coming at me again.

I threw my hands up to stop him where he was. Swallowing hard, I said, "It was only supposed to be one night." Jesus, what was I saying here? Was I turning down the best sex of my life all because of some fucking moral code?

He frowned, the expression only lasting a moment before melting away. He stalked toward me, crowding me against the wall. With his hands on either side of my head, I got a flashback to the private bathroom at Temptation. I was caged there, staring into his dark eyes, wondering what he would do next. Now I knew exactly what he could do, making the urge to resist him even harder.

"I did say it was just one night, didn't I?"

I nodded my head because I was sure my words would come out garbled if I opened my mouth. I was also terrified that if I opened my mouth, I would simply just say, "Fuck it" and let him have his way with me.

With a groan, he stepped away from me, retreating a few steps and perching his ass on the edge of the front counter behind him. I drew deep breaths into my lungs, blinking at him. An erection was straining against his jeans, and my knees went weak with the desire to relieve him.

I watched as he scrubbed a hand over his face, his expression pained. "I'm a fucking idiot," he announced on a harsh bark. His dark eyes were still on my face. "I apologize."

What in the actual fuck? "Accepted," I replied, gripping the wall. We stared at each other, the few feet separating us feeling like a form of torture. I wanted him to fuck me again, but if I let him, he would just keep taking and taking and taking. I didn't agree to the original deal, but it seemed he had enough integrity to stand by that too.

Pushing off the wall, I straightened my fur-covered shirt and walked toward the counter. "Did you just come in here to fuck me?"

He nodded. "It feels like you're in my veins, Little Bird." His admission made my pulse pound in my ear. "I don't know how to get you out of there."

Against my better judgment, I reached for him, running my fingertips along his stubbled jaw. "I feel it, too, Bane. But Jesus, I need to find another way."

"Why?"

"Because giving myself to you for two weeks to pay off my brother's debt is messed up."

Bane looked away at something over my head. My words had affected him.

"I don't know of any other way to do this," he replied roughly. When his eyes returned to my face, there was such anguish in them. "I don't know if I could do it any other way."

I frowned at that statement. "Relationships aren't a transaction. Would you rather I come to you because I want to instead of being forced into it."

He shook his head and pushed off the counter. Putting more

distance between us, he started to pace. "I'd rather you do as I want. Most women would jump at the chance to have access to me for two weeks."

I folded my arms under my breasts, watching him stalk around like a caged tiger. "I'm not most women," I reminded him.

That statement gave him pause. "I know you aren't, Wren. You're something else. I knew it the moment you walked into my club and demanded mercy for your brother."

Slowly, so I didn't frighten him off, I walked toward him. I had a feeling this was a side of Bane Rivera very few people got to see. His vulnerability was bared to me in this moment, a bubble of weakness that wouldn't last beyond the walls of my shop. I opened my mouth, but he stopped me with a finger against my lips.

"Come to dinner with me tonight."

"Why?"

"Because I fucking want you to," he growled. "Jesus, why can't you do as I say?"

I smirked, and it looked like he wanted to bend me over his knee again. "Is this like a date?"

He shook his head. "No. I want to show you something. I need you to see that I'm not some sex-crazed drug dealer without a heart."

"I already know you're not those things."

"Then you need to learn that my word is my bond. Come to dinner at my sister's house tonight, and you'll learn all you need to know. Maybe then, you'll give me two weeks of your life in order to save your brother's."

15

Bane

WHAT IN THE ACTUAL FUCK WAS I SAYING? I WANTED
her to come to dinner with me, but that I had to go and fuck
it up by bringing business into it? I hadn't lied when I said
I didn't know how else to do this. I fucking wanted her like
I needed the air in my lungs, but ever since I was a kid, my
idea of relationships had been fucked up. Somehow Bianca
had survived what very little of our father's lessons in love and
devotion showed us, but I had borne the brunt of his lessons.

Along with patricidal modeling, Wren was in my head too,
scrambling my thoughts and making shit fucked up.

Looking at her now, covered in dog fur, I shouldn't be
attracted to her. I should head back to the club, call some of
my Dolls, and have a fucking orgy off the clock. Screw the
no-fucking rule. I needed some pussy, and I needed it now.
Since Wren couldn't—or *wouldn't*—give it to me, I'd have to go
elsewhere.

But that thought was like a fucking bullet to the chest.

I wanted her and only her.

When the fuck did I become such a pussy?

"Will you come?" I asked harshly.

She nodded, clasping her hands in front of her. "I will."

Relief flooded me. "Good. I'll pick you up at six."

With that, I unlocked the door and strode from her shop. Andy was waiting at the open rear door. I slid inside the car and let out a breath once the door was shut. I turned to find Wren standing just outside her shop, her brows drawn down like she was trying to figure out a problem. Well, good luck to her because even I didn't know what the fuck was wrong with me.

Shit. I have to get my head on straight. I was Bane-fucking-Rivera. I never let pussy dictate to me. I never let pussy interfere with my business. What I needed to do was remember who the fuck I was and how I'd gotten here. Mooning over Wren had made me soft.

"Back to the club, sir?" Andy asked.

"Yeah," I snarled, shifting my raging erection in my pants. I needed a fucking release. Otherwise, I would lose it the next time I laid eyes on Wren. I wouldn't stop myself, I wouldn't give a fuck about our stupid one-night-only agreement. I would simply take what I wanted and force her to see things my way. Once I was in *her* blood, she wouldn't walk away so easily.

Ten minutes later, we pulled up outside the club, and I got out without waiting for Andy. I opened the door and stepped into the cool darkness, the velvet-smooth wrap of my Dollhouse. Fuck, I hated Mondays. I hated how empty this place felt when it wasn't filled with women or music. I hated how empty it made me feel too.

Where had that thought come from?

I wasn't empty. I was fucking fulfilled.

With a growl, I stalked up to my office and poured myself a drink. I didn't know what the fuck I was going to do now. I couldn't get a release. I was fucking wired, and nothing was going how it was supposed to. My head jerked up when there was a knock at the door.

Dagger stepped into the room, his blank expression looking tight—if that were even possible. I took one look at his face and shook my head.

"No," I hissed, slamming back another shot of whisky.

"Two more hits. Simultaneous."

I curled my free hand into a fist. "Who this time?"

"Rabbit and Red."

"Fuck." They were my two best sellers. "Same MO, cash taken, drugs left?"

Dagger grunted. "We need to retaliate, boss. Sitting here with our hands on our dicks is sending the wrong message."

I moved before I even realized I was doing it. I slammed Dagger against the wall, my forearm against his throat. Pushing my face into his, I hissed, "You think I don't know that? You think I like sitting here waiting for the next dealer to go down?"

He stared at me with his dead eyes but said nothing that I needed to hear. "Goddammit!" I wrenched myself away from him and began to pace. My fingers turned to claws as they raked through my hair. Could this day seriously get any fucking worse?

"I have a guy we can use," Dagger said in a low voice. "He'll find out what's going on, then dispose of the culprits discreetly."

"Fucking do it," I growled, waving him away. We didn't need to speak of my outburst. Dagger knew what kind of stress I was under. I knew he would understand. He left me after that, left me to stew, left me to turn ideas and possibilities over in my head until I was practically spinning with betrayals.

I couldn't leave for my sister's house like this. I was a fucked-up mess. I needed to relax. I needed to fucking calm down. Picking up my phone, I dialed Kandy.

"Hey, boss," she answered, her too-bright voice hurting my ears. It was a good thing she wouldn't be able to talk with my dick in her mouth. "What do you need?"

"You," I replied. "My office. Bring a friend, too." I hung up, went to sit on the leather sofa, and poured myself another drink.

IT WAS TWENTY MINUTES LATER WHEN KANDY STROLLED into the office with Rachel on her heels. Both of them were wearing short sundresses, which was fucking fine by me. Kandy was the one who approached me first, perching on my knee. I let my gaze travel down her, taking in the swell of her breasts and the taut peaks of her nipples. She was already fucking turned on. I looked over at Rachel, spread my legs a little wider, and tilted my chin, indicating what I wanted.

"Sit on my face, Kandy," I commanded. The woman clambered up on the high back of the couch, balancing herself there as she dropped her bare pussy onto my waiting mouth.

Rachel unzipped my pants, springing my straining cock. I sucked in a hiss when she wrapped her lips around it, then proceeded to fucking eat Kandy like she was the pussy I really wanted to be feasting on. Kandy writhed against my face, her hips flexing and retreating as she fucked my chin and mouth. I swallowed her down, realizing I was blowing past a line here. My

Dolls gave me blowjobs only, and I never reciprocated by eating their cunts, but there was this driving need in me.

I wanted this to be Wren.

I wanted this to be Wren's dripping pussy on my face, so for a few minutes, I would pretend that's what it was.

Rachel bobbed up and down on my dick, and I reached out a hand blindly, placing it on the top of her head. On the downstroke, I held her against me, grinding into the back of her throat until she gagged. The sensation made me groan, and I eased up a little on her. But only for a moment. I needed that again. Pushing her back, we continued this sick game of asphyxiation until I felt my balls tighten.

Tapping Kandy on the thigh, I indicated for her to stop. "On your knees with Rachel," I commanded darkly, wiping her juices from my chin. She did as she was told, falling to her knees between my thighs. The pair took turns sucking my dick until I couldn't take it anymore. Sitting back, I wrapped my hand around my cock and began to pump. I thought about Wren perched between my thighs waiting for me to cum all over her face and tits. The taste on my tongue was Wren's champagne. The fingers digging into my thighs were Wren's.

With a roar, I came on the two willing women, who sat with their mouths open and their eyes hungry. I came on them, but in my mind, it was only one woman.

Wren.

When I'd finally wrung the last of my pleasure out, I caressed Rachel's mouth. "You give good head."

"Thank you," she blushed.

"If you ever want to come out from behind the bar, let me know."

16

Wren

"ARE YOU SURE THERE'S NOTHING YOU CAN DO?" I hated how desperate my voice sounded. But I was. Desperate. This was my last chance to help Hawk out, even though the financial ramifications would leave me living hand to mouth for the next decade or two.

The loan manager shook his head and gave me a sad smile. "I'm sorry, Ms. Montana, but I can't approve a loan of that amount." He flicked through the application in front of him, frowning at the dire straits of my finances. "And given the state of your revenue stream with your business, I can't see how I can loan you anything at all."

My heart fell to my feet, although I wasn't truly surprised. I knew getting a loan was going to be near impossible. I nodded. "Of course. Thank you for your time, Mr. Kahn." I stood and walked from the bank, now truly left without another option. As I stepped out into the baking afternoon sun, I began the walk home.

As I dodged people on the clogged sidewalks, I thought about what else Bane was going to cost me. Because I only had one choice now.

When I got back to my apartment, I showered and changed, taking extra time on my makeup and picking out an outfit. I settled on a knee-length navy blue dress and wedges, then piled my hair into a messy bun at the top of my head. I'd just completed putting the finishing touches on my makeup when there was a knock on my apartment door.

I was suddenly breathless.

"Little Bird, I can hear you on the other side of this door." Bane's timbre voice rumbled through the hollow wood. "Let me in."

Unlocking the bolts, I twisted the knob and opened it. I edged back a step when I saw the heated look in his eyes, the hunger that burned there. His gaze drifted down my body, taking in my dress and the heels. When they finally returned to my face, I felt a shift in the air. He took a step toward me, then halted. I looked down to find his hands balled into fists at his sides.

"Are you ready?"

"Yeah. What's wrong with you?"

"You're what's wrong with me." He looked down my body again. "How am I supposed to keep my hands off you tonight?" It seemed strange that he would. At my cocked head, he added, "I won't touch you again until you agree to our arrangement."

Huffing out a laugh, I shook my head. Bane Rivera was a tough man to pigeonhole. Grabbing my purse, I asked, "Are you ready?"

As I walked past him, I felt the heat of his body. It was like my soul prickled with awareness. Shaking myself a little, I stopped just outside the door and locked it behind him. Together, we walked to the bank of elevators.

"What's your sister's name?" I asked a little hesitantly.

"Bianca."

"Is she older or younger?"

He gave me a sideways glance. "Older."

"Who looks after who?"

"I look after her. Always have, even when I was a kid."

For some reason, that answer lit me up on the inside, warming the hollow in my chest. He was just like me, only in reverse.

Clearing my throat, I asked, "Where does she live?"

He spun toward me a moment later, walking me backward until I felt the wall at my back. The hard, unforgiving surface didn't yield as I pressed myself against it. Bane filled my vision, my nose, my ears. The only sense he hadn't tortured yet was touch. And with the heat that filled his eyes, I wanted him to touch me.

He ghosted his fingers over my cheek, his gaze burning. "I don't know why I spill my truths to you all the time." His words were a gruff whisper. "But I do." His entire body tensed right before he pulled himself away. Holding out his hand, he said, "Come."

I let my fingers slip into his, and he pulled me close, wrapping his arm around my waist.

"I can't resist you, Wren," he muttered. "No matter what I do, no matter what I say, you keep drawing me back. I know I said I wouldn't touch you, but if this is going to be the last time I can... goddammit, I'm going to touch you until I erase the touches of every other man before me."

We rode down to the lobby in silence, his arm never

unwrapping from my side. When we stepped out, he hustled me through the vestibule and out to his waiting town car.

"To Bianca's, Andy," he said to the driver, who stared at me like he'd never seen Bane with a woman before. Maybe it was because I was fully clothed that was so shocking. Whatever the reason, I didn't need to worry myself over it now. Sliding into the cool leather interior, I let out a little sigh as Bane closed us in there together. His cologne filled the space, and I turned to look at him. That same hunger from before blazed, and I gasped as he dragged me onto his lap.

A small moan made its way out of my throat as I felt his erection pressing insistently at my ass. One arm was anchored around my waist, his free hand sliding through the hair at my nape. A bolt of lust hit me as he pulled back, creating a sting of pain that I was growing to like.

"I need to be inside you again, Wren. Tonight. If this is it, I need to have you one last time. Tell me I can taste your champagne cunt again." He stroked my bottom lip, pulling it down like he was imagining every single illicit thought running through his head. "I need to experience your pretty mouth on my cock. I want to push to the back of your throat and fuck your face until you choke. Tell me I can fucking worship your body all night, make you scream my fucking name?"

I clutched at his shoulders and bit my lip. Jesus, the filthy words this man says to me will be my undoing. I didn't answer him. I didn't know what the answer was. Instead, I reached down between us and stroked the steel length between his legs. He stopped me with a growl on the third stroke. His eyes were foggy with lust, and I really liked that I'd put him into that state.

He shook his head, pulling my hand free and kissing the tips of my fingers. "If you keep doing that, we won't go to my sister's. I'd have Andy take us to my place, so we could play, and then my sister would chew me out for ditching dinner."

Snuggling back into his chest, I watched the street lights of downtown LA flicker into sporadic bursts. I was pushed back into Bane as the car ascended, making switchbacks up a hill.

"Where does your sister live?" I asked into the darkness.

"Bel Air." His words rumbled in his chest.

Holy *fucking* shit. The entire family must be loaded. I swallowed. "You grew up here?"

He snorted and shook his head but said nothing more. "Maybe I'll tell you the story one day, Little Bird," he said, stroking my arm in a hypnotic wave. "Not tonight, though."

When the car finally pulled to a stop, I began to scramble back to my seat. I didn't want Bane's driver to catch me in such a compromising position, but Bane wasn't having any of that. He held me tightly until the door was opened, then helped me out. I stared up at the mansion in front of me and let out a jagged breath. This place was amazing. I'd barely had a chance to absorb it all when Bane took my hand and urged me up the path.

The door opened before we even got to the doorstep. A willowy dark-haired beauty stood there with a smile on her face.

"Bane!" she squealed.

Bane dropped my hand and scooped up who I was assuming was his sister.

"Bianca," he replied in a soft voice, pressing a kiss to her cheek. "How are you?"

"Better now that you're here," she replied, then looked over his shoulder. "Is this her?"

Damn, talk about being self-conscious. I stood there with my hands clasped in front of me, not sure what to do.

Bane saved me, though, by taking my hand and pulling me closer. "Bianca, this is Wren, the woman I was telling you about."

Bianca held out her hand to me, and we shook. "It is so nice to finally meet one of Bane's girlfriends!"

"I'm not his girlfriend," I replied.

"It's complicated," Bane said at the same time.

Bianca looked between us and smiled. "Come in. I'm just finishing off dinner."

Bane gave me a heated look as he ushered me inside, shutting the door behind me. He toed off his shoes, and I did the same, my bare feet hitting the warm honey blonde hardwood. He led me through to a kitchen in the same color tone as the wood beneath my bare feet, and I stopped dead when I saw the size of it.

"It's bigger than my entire apartment," I whispered to Bane when he asked me what was wrong.

He chuckled. "It's a large house," was all he said.

Well, no fucking shit, Bane.

Bianca was working effortlessly in the kitchen, moving from the marble-topped island counter to the eight-burner stove with ease. Honestly, I would have expected a personal chef.

"Where's my girl?" Bane asked Bianca, and my ears pricked. A surge of jealousy shot through me, but I pushed it down. I had no right to be jealous. He owned a fucking gentlemen's club. He was surrounded by beautiful women—I'd seen them.

"She should be up from her nap by now," his sister told him, pulling some tomatoes from the fridge. "You should go and get her."

Bane kissed me on the cheek and strode from the room, leaving me with Bianca.

"Can I help?" I needed something to do with this nervous energy vibrating through me.

"Sure. You can start tossing the salad for me." She pointed at a large bowl filled with green leaves and red and yellow peppers. "So, how did you meet my little brother?"

I paused, then got with the program again. "At work." That seemed like a safe reply.

Her brows shot up. "You're a Doll?"

"Ah, no. Not one of them." Jesus, even I could hear the disdain in my voice for them. "He and my brother have a working relationship, and I met Bane through him."

She hitched a hand onto her hip. "Younger or older?"

"Younger," I reply with a grin.

"Hells yes. Little brothers are such a headache, right?"

A smile pulled at my lips. I liked Bianca. Where Bane was gruff, she was friendly. Where he was aloof, she was open. She smiled a lot more too. "My brother could win awards with the headaches he's caused me."

She snorted and got back to chopping. "I don't know... Bane caused his fair share for me, too."

"Oh?"

"To say he was wild when he was a kid is an understatement. He was always getting into trouble, but do you know what? He was always there when I needed him, too. He may be younger, but he's protective of me."

"I can see that trait in him," I reply. I looked up when I heard Bane walk back into the room, a little girl cradled in his arms. Fuck, my ovaries may have just exploded because seeing him with a baby made my womb ache. He walked over to us, a smirk on his face. I was trying really hard to connect the man I thought I knew to the man I know, and to the man I was being shown now.

Bianca put down the knife, wiped her hands, and rounded the counter. "There's my beautiful girl," she cooed to her daughter.

"She's gotten big," Bane commented, staring down at the swaddled bundle.

"You would know that if you visited more often," Bianca volleyed back, and I got the distinct impression this was an old argument.

"You know how busy I am."

She stroked the baby's head. "I know."

Bane looked up and locked eyes with me. There was such warmth in them. "This is the other female love of my life," he said. "Valentine."

Wiping my hands, I walked toward him and peeked inside the blankets. The baby girl blinked up at me with dark blue eyes, eyes that were very aware of her surroundings. She had a shock of dark hair and the most perfect nose and cupid mouth.

"She's beautiful," I murmured.

"Yeah, she is," Bane rumbled in reply, and I looked up to find him staring at me. Flushing, I walked back to my salad-tossing station.

"How old is she?"

"Four months," Bianca replied.

"And where does she get her dark hair from, your side or her daddy's?"

"James has blond hair, too, as does all his family, so I think she'll probably have the same hair as Bane."

Bane smiled at that.

"Why don't you two go and sit down. I can take it from here."

"Are you sure?" I asked.

"Absolutely." She made a shooing gesture with her hands. I followed Bane to a set of four armchairs grouped around a glass table. Bane sat in one with Valentine still cradled in his arms while I sat opposite him. As soon as he was comfortable, though, Valentine began to fuss.

"I have to feed her," Bianca said, coming over and taking her daughter. Gesturing to her kitchen, she said, "Just leave that. We've still got time."

She left us together, and Bane patted his knee. Hauling myself out of my chair, I lowered myself onto his knee.

"What are you smiling at?" he asked, rubbing his thumb over my bottom lip.

"You."

"Why?"

"You keep surprising me."

"Don't tell me you had me pegged as a drug dealer and peddler of pussy only. I have many layers."

I played with the hair at the base of his skull. "I'm starting to see that."

The playfulness bled from his eyes, scorching lust filling its space. "Fuck, Wren, this is fucking torture."

"I know," I whispered.

He groaned as he repositioned himself. "I can't handle not knowing. It's fucking driving me crazy. You're driving me to distraction, to the point where I can't even think straight anymore." He caressed my cheek, the side of my neck, the swoop of my collarbones. My heart rate increased two-fold at his reverent touch, at his desperate words.

"Please tell me you'll have an answer by the end of the night."

I nodded. "Yes."

Frowning, he dropped his hand to my waist. "Yes, you'll have an answer or yes, you'll be mine?"

Be his.

Fuck, that sounded amazing…

… except he hadn't mentioned the deal.

It seemed like it was as far from his mind as it was from mine.

"I don't know if I could walk away after two weeks, though," I whispered, touching his stubbled jaw. "What if you're done with me after two weeks? What if you don't want me anymore?"

The muscles under my fingers bulged as he worked his jaw. "You're what I want, Wren. Yes, it started out as just a way to fuck you, but now that I've had you, now that I know more about you, I don't care about the deal. Hawk's debt is wiped as far as I'm concerned as long as I can have you in my bed for however long you'll stay."

I wanted to give him exactly what he needed because I wanted it to. Leaning in, I fused my mouth with his, showing how much I liked that idea. With a groan, he skimmed his hand down over my breasts, my stomach, my thighs until he inched his hand under the hem of my dress. I moaned into his mouth when his expert fingers whispered against my panties, stroking my clit through them. Bane rubbed the seam against my sensitive flesh, making me wetter, making me hotter.

The sound of a door opening and closing gained my attention, though, and I pulled away. He didn't let me get too far, curling his hand around the top of my spine. He held me close to him, his mouth curled into a satisfied smile.

"Someone's coming," I whispered hoarsely.

"It's my brother-in-law." He kissed me again.

"What if he catches us?"

He shrugged. "What if he does. Public sex is a fucking turn-on."

"Bane, Bianca said you were coming over for dinner," a man said behind us. I glanced up and caught sight of a fair-haired man in a blue button-down shirt and tan khaki pants. He smiled at me. "She also told me you were bringing a friend, although it's clear you're more than friends."

I wriggled free of Bane's lap, shooting him a withering glare when he got one last feel of my soaked panties. "Hello, I'm Wren Montana," I said, walking around the couches to hold out my hand to him.

"James Ward," he replied with an easy smile. His gaze ran over my face. "I can see why Bane would want to keep you to himself."

"James," Bane warned, but his brother-in-law only smiled.

"I was just yanking his chain. Bane never brings women here. You're the first, Wren. Congratulations."

I swallowed that information a little roughly. "Well, I'm glad I am."

"Where are my girls?"

Bane replied, "Upstairs. Feeding time."

"Ah." Shooting another smile at me, he said, "I'd best go see my queen, then. See you guys in a few. Oh, and Bane, grab a beer for me, will you?" Then, with a wink, he was gone.

Bane grumbled as he stood and moved to the fridge. "Would you like something to drink?"

"A beer would be fine." I followed him into the blonde

wood kitchen, marveling at the scale-shaped pearly tiles on the backsplash.

"Nice, huh?"

"It's gorgeous." What I really wanted to know was what his sister did in order to afford a house like this. Unless they came from old money?

He handed me my drink, and I took a sip.

"Thanks. She fell in love with it, too. So I bought it for her."

I barely covered my mouth in time to stop beer from spraying everywhere. My eyes bulged as I asked, "You bought it for her?"

He watched me as he took a sip from his bottle. "There's a lot you don't know about me, Wren. This is why I wanted to show you another side of my life. You've only seen the seedy side… the dirty fucking shit I do. I wanted to show you that there is light to my dark."

I liked Bane's flavor of dark, but I was starting to get an appreciation of his light too. "I'm not in the habit of taking people at face value," I replied, taking another sip. "I would've found out about this eventually."

Slowly, he walked toward me. When he was standing in front of me, he put his beer on the counter and his hands on either side of my body, locking me into place between his hard body and the equally hard granite digging into my lower back. When he leaned in and placed a sweet kiss on my shoulder, I sighed.

"I want you to find it all out, but not now. Not tonight. I promise I will tell you every dark secret inside me eventually, if you decide to stick around."

Fisting his shirt in my hands, I didn't let him move away. I loved the feeling of him being so close, but that love was tempered by reality. That what we had could fizzle out in a matter of weeks or months. Bane gave me a bruising kiss before stepping away, taking his beer with him.

I turned in time to see James and Bianca returning to the kitchen, Valentine in her daddy's arms. James went and sat down, and Bane joined him while I stayed in the kitchen with Bianca.

She smiled at me as I leaned against the counter. "You have a beautiful home."

"Thank you. I love it, too." She glanced over at her brother. "Bane is really too much."

"How long have you lived here?"

"It'll be five years in the spring." She began prepping what looked like chicken parmigiana. "But enough about me, tell me all about you, Wren."

HOURS LATER, BANE OPENED THE REAR DOOR OF HIS town car for me. I slid into the leather seat and rested my head back. I'd eaten and drunk way too much but Bianca sure as shit knew how to cook. I'd found out she'd worked as a chef before having Valentine, which explained how she knew her way around a kitchen. Bane closed the door after he slid in beside me, then hauled me into his lap.

His hand was under my skirt a moment later, his lips fused to mine. His kiss was demanding, his tongue sliding into my mouth and claiming me. He stroked my thighs, then my pussy before shoving the scrap of fabric out of the way and sliding his finger into my heat. I cried out at the sweet invasion, then began to moan as he pumped it in and out of me.

All through dinner, he'd kept his hand on my thigh, always inching higher, sweeping my dress out of the way. He'd stroked me through my panties until I was practically panting, and he only stopped when I crossed my legs. He gave me a meaningful look, which I'd ignored.

Bane curled his finger inside me, hitting the sensitive spot and dragging an orgasm from me. I groaned into his mouth as he made me come, his relentless ownership over my body not stopping until I grew still.

He kissed me again. "You're so fucking beautiful when you come. You know that?" he asked roughly into my ear, biting down on my lobe. I sucked in a gasp, the sting shooting straight to my still-throbbing pussy.

Keeping me on his lap the whole way back into town, I wondered where this night would lead us. Was he taking me home? Was he returning to his club? No, not the club. It was closed on Mondays. At least I remembered that.

"Stay with me tonight?"

Yes. God, I wanted to. "At your apartment?" He nodded. "I can't. I have to work in the morning."

He stared at me, his jaw working. I braced myself for his refusal, but he stunned me when he said, "Tomorrow night, then. Can I have you?"

A small smile tugged at my lips before I kissed him. "Yes," I breathed against him.

"Will you close the shop on Wednesday? I want you in my bed all night."

"I'll have to check my bookings."

He nodded. "Do it, but fucking make it happen, Wren."

"You know, this bossing me around thing won't work."

"You love it when I take control."

I did. I fucking loved giving it over, knowing that Bane would take care of my needs for me. But work was something else. This was my livelihood and also the only thing I would have left after Bane was finished with me.

"I'll let you know if I can reschedule my clients for Wednesday," I told him.

We pulled up outside my apartment, and Bane got out of the car, shutting the door behind him. I blinked, slightly confused.

"Good night, Ms. Montana," Andy said, looking at me in the rearview mirror.

"Good night, Andy," I replied hesitantly before Bane opened my door and helped me from the car. He escorted me into the building, where I thought he'd stop and let me go, but he went all the way to my apartment. After I unlocked the door, he strode in after me, slamming the thing shut behind him.

"What are you—"

Bane was on me, his kiss more fevered than before. "If you won't come to me, I'll fucking come to you," he hissed, sliding his hand up under my dress and setting my pussy on fire with his touch. "I'll always come to you."

17

Bane

WREN WAS MINE. SHE WAS FUCKING MINE, AND I HAD to show her what she would be walking away from if she chose to end it after two weeks. I wasn't even fucking sure she'd stay for two weeks since she got what she wanted. I'd fucking caved and waived her brother's debt because I was so desperate to have her. Like a pussy, I'd given her all the power. Now I had to wait and see what she would do with it.

"You want to stay here?" she asked, gasping when I slid a finger into her soft folds. She moaned her next words. "I live in a dump."

Yeah, well, that was something I was going to fix too if she'd let me. Fuck, who was I kidding? Even if she didn't let me, I was going to move her out of this rat-infested shithole and into one of my condos. Wren was *my* queen, and even if she walked away after two weeks, I would make damn sure she was safe.

"All I want is to be inside you, Wren." I kissed her again, pushing my tongue past the barrier of her lips and teeth, gaining entry to her sweet mouth. While I worked her mouth with mine, my fingers worked her cunt. Giving her pleasure while sitting at the dinner table had nearly undone me. I'd felt how wet she'd gotten. I could practically see her desire for me dripping from the heated looks she threw my way. I had a feeling Wren would be all-up for public sex, and I wanted to explore that with her.

Moving into her bedroom, I lowered her onto the bed, our mouths still fused, my fingers still buried, the wet sounds of her arousal surrounding us. When I finally pulled free and stood, Wren's eyes were glazed over with lust.

"Stand up and strip for me, Little Bird," I commanded. Wren scooted to the end of the mattress and stood. Sitting on the bed, I watched as she slid the straps of her dress over her shoulders, torturously peeling the top of her dress down over her breasts, her stomach, her hips, and her thighs. She stood before me in her wedge heels and a matching set of navy lace lingerie. Her stomach was toned and her legs fucking amazing. She had a tattoo of a little blue bird on her ribs that I hadn't noticed before.

Tracing the delicate wing with my fingertip, I asked, "What does this represent?"

"It's an Australian Fairy Wren. My parents were big into ornithology, hence mine and my brother's names." She looked down at the tattoo. "It reminds me of them."

I leaned forward to kiss it.

She shivered, her hands coming to rest in my hair. I drifted my mouth lower down her stomach, kissing her hip bones and the top of her mound. Her hips flexed into my mouth when I did that, and I smiled.

"Take off your bra and panties." She did as I asked, sliding her shoes off when she lowered her panties to the floor. When she was exposed to me, I rubbed my aching cock through my pants. *This woman was going to be the fucking death of me.* "On the bed," I rasped. "Face on the mattress and that ass of yours in the air."

Moving past me, she got into position on the bed, her beautiful ass and weeping pussy on full display. For me. *Only* for me. Kneeling beside her, I stroked the globes of her ass, running a finger down into her weeping sex. She rocked against me when I slid one finger deep inside her channel, a small moan escaping her throat. Replacing my finger with my mouth, I flicked my tongue over her clit, making that moan into a desperate whimper. Unbuckling my pants, I freed my cock and started to stroke it. I tongue-fucked her cunt while getting myself off, the sound of her moans like fucking music to my ears.

I pushed another finger inside her, pumping into her. My breathing was a rasp in the back of my throat, and Wren's breathing was much the same. Her inner walls began to pulse around my fingers. That was the signal I'd been waiting for. I withdrew my fingers, rubbing her arousal over my cock before slamming inside her.

She came instantly, her pussy clamping down on my cock and almost sending me over the edge with her. She screamed my name as I pumped into her, milking every last drop of her orgasm from her. When her entire upper body went loose, I wrapped my arm around her waist and chest, pulling her up. I was still buried inside her, unwilling to come until she had more orgasms under her belt. Remaining connected, I laid down on the bed, positioning her on my hips and facing away from me.

Her perfect ass was all I could see as it throbbed in time to my thrusts.

Clutching the tops of my thighs, Wren rode my cock with wanton abandon, her hair coming loose of the knot and tumbling down her shoulders. I caught the scent of her shampoo as she moved, the vanilla fragrance sending a bolt of unbridled lust through me. Anchoring my hands on her hips, I pumped into her, urging her to find another orgasm before I changed up positions once more.

I WOKE UP AT DAWN TO WREN WRAPPED AROUND ME, her leg over my leg, her arm across my chest, and her head buried in the crook of my neck. Fuck, she was spectacular. I'd fucked her for hours, not relenting until she gave me all of herself. Once I was sure she had nothing but exhaustion left in her, I'd come with a roar, filling her, marking her, owning her like I'd never done before. She'd mumbled something about birth control and being clean, and I cursed when I realized I'd let another one of my hard rules slide.

Fucking a woman bare was never an option. I had no interest in finding out a woman got pregnant by me only to get a fucking hand-out. But Wren...

Fuck. I was in deep, and I'd barely known her a week. Scrubbing a hand through my hair, I stared at the ceiling and wondered what it was about her that made me let go of my rules, the things I'd fucking lived by for over thirty years. But as I stared down at her peaceful face, I knew. I was fucking hooked on her.

I traced the shape of her cock-swollen mouth to her bare breasts and cunt that was hidden from my view. I could feel it, though, warm and wet against my thigh. Slowly, easing her off me, she rolled onto her back with a sigh, putting her in the perfect position. Splitting her thighs, I woke her with my head between her legs, my mouth on her cunt, and my tongue teasing her clit. She came with a strangled moan, her legs scissoring against the sheets until the last of her pleasure ebbed away.

I looked up at her, at the warm smile.

"Good morning," she mumbled.

I kissed her sensitive cunt before saying, "Yes, it is."

She stretched her arms over her head, then bolted upright. "Shit, I have to get ready for work." She tried to scramble off the bed, but I caught her ankle and pulled her back to me.

"See me tonight."

"Are you asking me or telling me?" she asked, quirking an eyebrow at me.

"Asking. Begging, if you want. Let me see you. Let me worship you again."

Cupping my face, she pressed a kiss to my mouth. "Yes." She moved off the bed and walked naked into the bathroom. My dick was fucking hard, but Wren's pussy was shut for the moment. I laid back on the pillows and started to stroke myself, but in my mind it was Wren. Her hand glided over my length, her nails teasing me as she cupped my heavy sac. She lowered her mouth to my cock, and I thrust up into it. My hips flexed into my palm, making me hiss.

I got myself off to the vision of Wren, knowing that I was sliding down a very slippery slope. Soon, I wouldn't be able to let her go. Soon, I would want to keep her forever. I came with a bark, my cum splashing against the plains of my abs and onto my chest. I bit my lip to keep the groaning to a minimum, but my orgasm was long and drawn out and fucking intense. I think my ears stopped working too because when I came back online, I heard a gasp and an appreciative moan. Cracking one eye open, I saw Wren staring at me, her hand clutching the towel around her breasts.

I shouldn't want more. I shouldn't need more, but my cock had other ideas. I was still fucking hard despite just coming all over myself. I palmed my length, sucking in a hiss, and her eyes darkened with lust.

"Want to come and help a guy out?" I asked in a drawl.

She nodded, dropped the towel, and crawled up the bed. Biting her lip, she ran her fingers through my cum, then brought them to her cunt, rubbing it over herself.

"Holy *fuck!* Wren, baby, that's so fucking hot."

With a nod, she slid onto my raging erection, burying herself to the hilt and staying there a moment before she began to move.

BY THE TIME I MADE IT INTO THE CLUB, I WAS WRUNG out. I'd fucked Wren until she'd come again, and I was right there behind her. I wasn't sure I'd ever get tired of her, but then that niggling thought that she was only here for the short term sat in my head and blew all my hopes to fucking pieces.

"Hey, boss," Rachel said from behind her post at the bar. She smiled at me like she was waiting for an invitation to suck my dick again, but I wasn't interested. Especially not now when I had Wren in my life.

I lifted my chin in greeting but kept walking. I found Dagger in my office when I walked in.

"Boss, we have a problem."

Not the words I wanted to hear this morning. I was still riding my fucking high, and this declaration was a fucking shot in the chest. "What is it?" I snarled, stalking to my desk and sitting on the chair.

"The cops are sniffing around. They think we've got something to do with the dealers getting hit."

"They've got nothing on us," I replied. "They're fishing."

He folded his meaty arms over his chest. "They were also asking questions about Sanderson's man who turned up dead."

"Did you wipe all evidence?"

He gave me a flat stare. "This isn't my first fucking rodeo, boss."

Of course, it wasn't. Dagger was ex-military. The government had trained him themselves. I tapped my desk as I thought about options. Since the cops were only fishing, and there was nothing to connect me to the dealers, I decided not to worry about it. "Just keep an eye on things, but I'm fucking confident we're not a serious suspect." When Dagger just stood there for a moment too long, I barked, "What?"

"Detective Cox said she was coming to talk to you this afternoon."

"Jesus-*fucking*-Christ, like I need this right now?" I slammed my fist onto the desk, making everything rattle. Pain hummed through my hand, but it did nothing to soothe the dark beast lurking inside. "Get rid of her."

Slowly, Dagger shook his head. "I've been fobbing her off for over a week now. She's done waiting."

Fuck! "Fine. When?"

"In about fifteen."

Motherfucker. I glared at Dagger like he was personally responsible for the heat from the cops. Working my jaw, I bit down the urge to shoot something, took a few deep breaths, then said calmly, "Fine. Send her in when she gets here. Anything else you want to bring to my *attention* this morning?"

His dark brows drew down over his eyes. "We need another Doll to replace Syndy."

I knew this shit was coming. Opening my laptop, I entered the password and went into the directory I kept of all the women who had applied to work here. "All right." I highlighted three names, then turned my laptop around for Dagger to see. "These three. Vet them again. Who knows how much has changed in the last however long since they applied, then get them in for interviews."

"You got it, boss."

18

Wren

I OPENED MY APARTMENT DOOR TO FIND BANE standing in the hallway, looking seriously out of place in his ten-thousand-dollar suit and black silk shirt. I smiled, then pulled him into my apartment while I finished finding my other shoe.

"What are you doing, Little Bird?" he asked as he watched me checking under furniture and in cupboards.

"I lost a shoe," I tell him, frowning. Which was fucking strange since I always made it a point to put all my shoes away in the closet as soon as I get home. Granted, I was looking for a black pump, and I couldn't remember the last time I'd worn them, so I was even more confused.

I sighed when his arms came around my waist, the feeling of his solid chest against my back a welcome distraction. "Pick another pair." He flexed his hips into my ass. "I need to feed you, so then I can fuck you."

He let me go, and I peered at him over my shoulder. "I'll just grab another pair." Walking back into my room, I pulled out a pair of red pumps. They would clash a little with my dusty-rose colored dress but beggars-choosers and all that. Sliding them onto my feet, I wandered back out to find Bane staring out the window.

"Not much of a view," I tell him.

He turned around, his expression serious. "The lock on your window is broken."

Broken? "Fuck, Hawk must've done it last time he was here. He's all about brute force rather than logic."

Bane's jaw bulged as he ground his teeth. "I hate that you live here."

"I hate it, too," I told him, running my hands up his chest, under the edges of his suit jacket. He felt so warm beneath my fingers. "But it's what I have to work with. And before you ask me to do something insane like move in with you, the answer is no. I make my own way in this world. Plus… what happens when this is over?" I gestured between us.

If I thought his expression was unhappy before, now it was downright murderous.

Snaking his arm around my waist, he took control of my neck and forced me to meet his gaze. The intensity with which he looked at me was a fucking turn-on. I shivered in the wake of his desire. "I hope to fuck this never ends, Wren." He kissed me, pouring all his savage emotions into that one action, his fingers digging in and caging me against his hard body. I sighed, feeling the weight of responsibility bleed from my body.

Only Bane could do this to me.

Only Bane could take over that constant weight, that unrelenting drive to keep all the balls in the air.

And that terrified me.

I was becoming addicted to him—to his power, to his demands. What happens when all of this is over? I knew he said he never wanted it to end, but something bad could happen, right? Something terrible could fuck it all up, and then all I'd be left with was a fucking hole in my chest where Bane had ripped my heart out. I didn't want to think about the day either of us would walk away, but I was a pragmatist at heart.

He broke the kiss and stared down at me. "I want you safe."

"I am safe," I tell him. "I have three deadbolts and a Beretta 92FS in the drawer beside my bed."

"And a broken fucking window lock in Boyle Heights. Anyone could get in here."

Pulling out of his arms, I walked a few steps away. "People could have gotten in a hundred times over in the years I've lived here," I retort. Spinning to face him, I added, "You can't protect me all the time."

His emotions boiled over in his eyes as he marched toward me. I backed up another step, but he caught me easily, his mouth slamming against mine in a kiss that branded me as his. "I fucking can if you let me."

"I appreciate the offer, Bane, really, but this is my home." My words were a whisper, all the fight left in me draining away. I didn't want to argue with him about this shit. "We're going to be late for dinner."

With some reluctance, he let me go, but his hand still lingered on the small of my back. "I'm sorry. I'm a little wound up."

"Bad day at work?"

"Yeah, you could say that," he replied darkly. I wasn't going to push him. I had the distinct impression that Bane Rivera was a closed-off man when it came to the ins and outs of his business.

"So, take me out to dinner, then."

Together, we walked downstairs to the town car waiting at the curb. Andy smiled at me when we came out of the building's door, and I returned the gesture. Bane opened the door for me, and I slid inside.

"Where are we going for dinner?" I asked when we were on our way.

"A place called Rivera. I'm part owner."

Of course, he was. "And was it named after you, too?"

This question made him smile. "Bianca and I own it jointly, although I'm more of a silent partner. She was the head chef there until she went on maternity leave to have Valentine."

The depth of this man was fucking surprising. "What other businesses do you have that I'm not aware of?" I asked, taking his hand and intertwining our fingers. I realized what an intimate gesture it was right away and went to pull away, but Bane covered my hand with his large one.

"Leave it there, Little Bird. Somehow, your touch can soothe me when you're not fucking turning me on."

I let out a breath and peered out the window. The lights of LA were blinding, but I'd lived here all my life. I'd seen what lurked in the shadows of those lights, and it wasn't pretty. Eventually, we pulled up outside a restaurant that was modern and sleek. I smiled at the name die-cut in cursive on the steel sheet above the door. Tinted glass walls lined the front, where I could see the vague silhouettes of diners seated at tables against the window. Bane kissed the back of my hand, then got out to open my door.

My gaze drifted down to the large steel and copper door, a doorman waiting over to the side. The man nodded to Bane, then me before he ushered us in.

"Mr. Rivera," a man said in a cultured British accent.

"How are you, Tommy?"

"Fine, thank you, sir. We have your table ready for you."

Bane intertwined our fingers once more and led me through the restaurant. As we weaved through the tables, I found a lot of women staring at Bane for a beat before their eyes slid to me. *Most eligible bachelor, indeed.* We entered through a tinted-glass door and into a private dining room that had glass on all sides. Bane pulled out a chair for me, but I went to the glass instead. The tint was so dark.

"Can anyone see in here?" I hadn't even noticed the room when we'd approached it.

"It's one-way glass," Bane said into my ear behind me. He touched his lips to my neck and whispered, "Very private. Unless you're into exhibitionism, then I can flip a switch and make it two-way."

A shiver went through me at the thought of what Bane and I could do in a room like this.

"You like that idea, Little Bird?" he rumbled, his hands coming to rest on my waist. Pulling me back against him, I squirmed at the feel of his erection pressing into my ass. "If that's a fantasy of yours, I can make it happen."

I spun around in his arms, looping mine around his neck. "Exhibitionism isn't at the top of my fantasy list," I tell him with a coy smile.

Bane stared at me for a beat before pulling my arms free and walking me to the table. I blinked at him, confused.

"Little Bird, if you keep talking about fantasies, I won't make it through dinner with you, and I want to feed you because I've got the rest of the night planned out in my filthy head, and you'll need your strength."

Fuck. I nodded and placed my napkin on my lap. As soon as Bane had done the same, a waiter breezed into the room from a hidden door with a bottle of champagne and a bucket of ice. Bane poured us each a glass, then we toasted.

"To champagne," he murmured.

I could feel the flush creeping up my cheeks. "To champagne." I took a shallow sip while Bane had a whole mouthful and placed his glass back down.

"So tell me about your other fantasies, Little Bird."

Placing my glass down, I stared at him. "I will if you answer some questions about yourself."

He sat back in his chair and folded his hands in front of him. "Is this a negotiation?"

I mirrored his body language. "Of sorts. I have a lot of fantasies, Bane, only I don't like to tell people what they are without getting something in return." I bit my bottom lip playfully.

He shifted his hips, and I had no doubt he was already hard for me. Kicking off one of my shoes, I dragged my foot up his leg to his thigh and slid it over his erection.

Bane's eyes darkened. He grabbed my ankle. "You like playing with fire, don't you? Pushing my buttons, denying me what I want."

I shivered at his intent but nodded. I did enjoy all those things. I didn't back down from things when shit got real—I ran into them headlong.

He smirked. "All right. I'll tell you something about myself, then you can tell me about one of your fantasies. Do we have a deal?"

"How about I ask you about the things I want to know, then I tell you one of my fantasies?"

"Clever girl. Always ask for specifics." I nodded my thanks. "Deal. But I start first. What's one of your fantasies, Wren?"

Biting my bottom lip, I stared him straight in the face when I said, "Voyeurism. I like to watch other people fuck."

He chuckled darkly, his cock jerking against my foot, where he still held it in his lap. "You'd love my club then. I can already see you dressed in lingerie, watching as another woman is pleasured by a man."

Fuck, this was a dangerous game we were playing. My pussy was already beginning to throb. "Okay, my turn. What was childhood like for Bane Rivera?"

He opened his mouth to answer but closed it when the waiter returned. "The usual, Mr. Rivera."

"Please," he replied, not taking his eyes off me. When the waiter was gone, he said, "My father was an abusive alcoholic who battered and assaulted my mother on an almost daily basis. He gambled, and he lost. And when he lost, he would take that shit out on my mother... sometimes on me when I tried to interfere."

I put a hand to my mouth, thinking about the younger Bane and having to witness all that. "I'm so—"

He shook his head. "No, I don't want your pity, Little Bird. He may have been a monster, but I learned some things from him."

I braced for his next words.

"I learned that women weren't ever to be treated like he treated my mother. Men who beat their women are the fucking scum of the earth. That's why I respect and help any of my Dolls who need it."

I took a sip of my champagne. "And would they need it?"

"A lot of them are in abusive relationships. I can't stand that shit. If they can't get out because they have nowhere else to go, I help them. I have a block of luxury apartments where I always keep half a dozen empty in case they need it."

"Is that where you would've put me?" I asked.

He swallowed the rest of his drink and poured himself another, topping my glass off too. "No. I want you in my penthouse, but I understand your reluctance to move in with me."

His words warmed me. I wasn't the kind of girl to believe in fairy tales. I always had to be the breadwinner, the provider for Hawk and me, but there was something so appealing about letting Bane take care of me if that's what he wanted to do. His protective instincts were ingrained, but he was such a juxtaposition. Here he was, the owner of the largest gentlemen's club in California—probably the entire West Coast—who acted and believed in such a way that was counter-intuitive to his work. He may have women surrounding him in a sexual environment, but in his own way, he was protecting them.

"Have you ever had sex with any of your Dolls?" I ask softly.

"Not penetrative sex, no."

Penetrative? "Oral then?"

He dipped his chin, keeping his eyes on me. "I'm not going to lie to you, Little Bird. Before you came into my life, I often used my Dolls for the pleasure they could give."

I tried really hard to lock down my emotions, but they were powerful and banging on the door of my self-control. "That redhead who interrupted our meeting?"

Bane sighed and took another sip of champagne. "Syndy was

one of the girls I used a few times, yes." He stared at me, his gaze moving over my face like he was looking for something. Jealousy, perhaps. I felt it surging through my body, but it was misplaced. This was before me, so I had no right to be upset. "Wren?"

I waved my hand in front of me, telling him to give me a minute. "Logically, I know you've probably used your girls, but hearing it is another thing."

"You're jealous?"

"Yes." Was I wrong to be jealous?

Standing from the table abruptly, he stalked around, then leaned down to give me a punishing kiss. He slid his hand into the top of my dress, palming one of my breasts. "I fucking love that you're jealous," he rasped out. "But you don't need to be jealous now we're together. I don't see those other women. All I see is you." Giving my nipple one last tweak, he sat back down like nothing had ever happened. "It's your turn."

Blowing out a breath, I centered myself and said, "Threesome."

His brows arch. "With another woman or man joining us?"

I shrugged. "I don't really care, to be honest. I think both ways would suit me just fine."

"I'm filing all this away, just so you know," he said with a devilish smile.

"Okay, my turn. How many buildings, businesses, and homes do you actually own?"

"Enough," he replied evasively. I let it slide. It was in that gray area, and I wasn't going to push him for information relating to his business dealings. I hoped that one day he might trust me enough, though.

"What's another one of your fantasies, Little Bird?"

I cleared my throat. "Sex swing." His eyes sparked with lust. "I want to try a sex swing to see what it's like."

Reaching under the table, he readjusted himself. "I could probably take care of that fantasy tonight."

Lust hit me like a lightning strike, my pussy flooding with warmth. Holy shit. "Okay."

The hidden door opened, and the waiter was back with a few long rectangular plates balanced on his arm. He placed them down, then gestured to the champagne bottle. "Would you like another bottle, sir?" he asked.

"Please."

I stared at all the food, wondering where to start. When I looked up, Bane was typing out a message on his phone.

"Work?"

He smiled in a way that made my pulse pound. "Pleasure. Just arranging something for later on tonight. I want it to be a surprise." Gesturing to the food on the table, he said, "Eat. There are miniature versions of every single dish available on the menu. Please, take what you want."

"What's your favorite? I'll leave that one for you."

"It's this," he said, picking up what looked like a mini burger. "Pulled pork slider. Slaw. Delicious. Take it." He offered it to me, and I blinked.

"But it's your favorite?"

"And I want you to have it. I want to see the pleasure on your face as you eat it."

I'd just finished chewing when the waiter returned with our champagne. He put it on ice, took the other away, and we were left alone once more.

"Have you had any serious relationships before?" I asked.

"No, unless you count my girlfriend in grade school. You?"

I smiled at that. "No. I've never had time for it. I was always having to work or fight for scraps of food when there was no work."

"You had a tough childhood?"

I sat back in my chair, staring at the plates in front of us. "Not my childhood, but adolescence. We were so poor that sometimes I didn't eat so Hawk could." My stomach ached with phantom pain at the memories of those days. It was when it was just my brother and me against the world. I shook my head, dislodging the pathetic history from my mind. "What happened to your dad?" I asked.

His eyes darkened a little as he studied my face, wondering whether I was worthy of such secrets. "By the time I was sixteen, I was stronger than him. One night, he came home drunk and started hitting my mom. I got between them this time and baited him into hitting me. As soon as he did, I proved to him it was the last night he would ever raise a hand to her or me."

I wanted to reach out and take his hand, but I held myself back. Bane was the kind of man to pull away from things like that, so I simply let him talk. "He left?"

"After I broke his arm and a couple of ribs, yeah," he replied darkly. I shifted uncomfortably in my seat. "Does that disgust you, Little Bird?"

"No. No, it doesn't. You just did what you had to do to survive, just like Hawk and I had to do. What about your mom?"

"She passed from cancer while I was in college."

"I'm so sorry."

Waving away my platitudes, he swallowed what was left in his glass and placed it back down deliberately like he was pulling himself back together inside. "What about your parents?"

I swallowed some more champagne and stared sightlessly at the table in front of me. "Our parents died in a car crash when I was sixteen. Hawk was twelve. We ran away from every foster family we ever had because of the abuse we suffered there. I became emancipated at eighteen, and I've been looking after Hawk ever since."

"He relies on you," Bane told me softly.

"Yeah, he does because I'm just as much a mother to him as our parents were."

"Is that why you finally agreed to take me up on my offer?"

Plucking the napkin from my lap, I ran the linen through my fingers a few times. The fabric was thick but still soft, and the motion soothed me just like it did when I was petting the dogs I groomed. "Partly," I admitted. I looked into his watchful eyes. "The other reason was because I wanted you, Bane."

"I fucking wanted you from the moment I laid eyes on you, Little Bird."

The intensity of his stare made my blood warm in my veins. "Take me back to your place." He stood and threw his napkin on the table.

We left an entire table of food behind us, but when I had Bane wrapped around me like he was right now as he escorted me out of the restaurant, I knew I would never hunger for anything ever again.

19

Bane

AS I STEPPED ONTO THE COOL MARBLE FLOOR ON MY foyer, I felt Wren stop. Peering at her over my shoulder, I found her eyes were wide. She was taking in everything, every last detail of the wealth I chose to surround myself with. With a chuckle, I dragged her deeper into my domain. The floor may have been white, but everything else in my apartment was dark gray or black.

The couches were soft leather, big enough for ten people, but it was usually only me. On the wall was a ninety-eight-inch television, which I rarely watched because I was always working, and a copper and glass coffee table I rarely used because I was always too busy to be home and have a beer.

Wren walked into the kitchen, running the tips of her fingers over the dark granite countertop as she walked past it. All the appliances were stainless steel, all pristine. She turned to face me.

"This is stunning."

"Bianca helped me fit it out," I replied with a shrug.

She gave me a small smile and continued her exploration of my penthouse. When she reached the start of the hallway, she quirked an eyebrow at me. I gave her a nod, and she started down there too. Stalking behind her, she first went into the master bathroom, then poked her head into both guest rooms.

"You wouldn't have stayed there," I said into her ear, tracing the shape of her flesh with my tongue. "You would've been staying in here." I showed her into the master suite, wrapping my arms around her waist and pulling her back against me. Her firm ass collided with my aching cock, causing her to wriggle against me.

My bedroom had never felt like home to me. It felt more like a place to sleep in between work. There was nothing personal about it—not like Wren's place. Although hers was messy and everything was falling apart, there was a soul to it that came from all the personal things she had. Mine was merely a room with a bed. Stepping away from me, she walked to the bed and ran her fingers over the black sheets.

"Want to explore the rest of the suite?" I asked.

"There's more?"

I bobbed my head. Taking her hand, I lead her into the ensuite. More of the white marble graced the floors and climbed the walls. The double-sized shower with rain showerheads and a bench was the first thing to catch her attention. Then she spun around and looked at the tub. I suddenly got a flash of her in there, the water lapping at her perfect breasts, teasing her nipples as they cooled in the air.

She walked into the shower and took a seat, then turned to

look at me. "This is a nice edition," she said in a purr.

Fuck, yeah, it was. I cleared my throat. "It's a steam shower, so you can sit and steam for a bit if that's what you want to do. It's good for other things, too, though."

"Oh?" she replied playfully.

I stepped a little closer but was conscious of my limits. If I got too close, I would have her, and I wanted her first orgasm to be on the sex swing. "Yeah. It's also a great place for me to taste that delicious cunt of yours."

Her gaze dropped to my crotch, where I wasn't even bothering to hide how hard my cock was. She stood up abruptly and came toward me. "What else is there to find in this bedroom suite of yours?"

With a grin, I threw her over my shoulder and walked into the sitting room area of my bedroom. With another one of those soft leather couches and an even softer rug in front of it, this was a place I wanted to use more but didn't. I dropped her gently onto the couch, and I liked the way she looked at me. It was part pissed off, but mostly she was fucking ready for me. Dropping to my knees, I nudged her legs apart and slid my hands up her thighs, bunching her dress as I went. Then her perfectly pink cunt was exposed to me. I looked up at her face.

"You don't have any panties," I growled.

She shook her head and bit her lip.

Unable to stop myself, I leaned in and placed my mouth against her glistening folds, dragging my tongue through her pussy and making her shiver with pleasure. Wren's hands found their way into my hair, holding me in place as I tongue-fucked her. With every scrape of her nails on my scalp, it felt like a shot of lust was being dumped into my veins, making me wilder and wilder.

KALLY ASH

I wanted to take her so badly, but not like this. Pulling back, she whimpered a little but didn't voice a complaint.

Taking off my suit jacket, I draped it over the arm of the chair. I unbuttoned my shirt slowly, Wren's beautiful blue eyes tracking the movement. She licked her lips as more of my chest and torso were exposed to her. Fuck, I loved it when she looked at me like that. Quickly, I took the shirt off, then unbuckled my belt. Her chest was rising and falling with each movement of my hand, each removal of clothing. I paused at the button on my slacks, choosing not to remove them just yet.

Gesturing for her to stand, she slid from the couch, her neck and cheeks flushed with color. I stroked her cheekbone and placed a kiss on her mouth. I lifted her dress over her head and let the fabric slide through my fingers until it hit the floor. Wren's breathing was ragged now. Standing before me, naked and so fucking turned-on, I could see her arousal slipping down the inside of her thighs, I wanted to take her rough. I wanted to make her mine, but there was something to be said for denying one's release, and tonight, I wanted to make Wren so frenzied with need that she could never walk away from me.

I took her hand and pulled her toward the sex swing. When I'd heard she wanted to try it, I asked Andy to set one up in my bedroom. The large A-shaped frame had two anchor points at the top where the strips of padded nylon were suspended. Wren turned to look at me, lust shimmering in her gaze. Taking the larger, wide strip in my hand, I showed it to her.

"The seat," I murmured. Then I went to the handholds. "To grip on to." And finally, the stirrups. "For your feet."

I waited for her to nod for her permission. When I had it, I lifted her onto the padded seat where her ass balanced. Sliding my hands down her body, brushing past her pussy then down her legs, I helped her into the stirrups.

"Comfortable?"

She nodded, biting her lip. "It feels strange, but not in a bad way. It's like I'm floating."

I kissed her again until she was moaning, the swing shivering with her desire as her body surged with it. I stepped backward and took off my pants and boxer briefs, then stood in front of her naked and so fucking hard my dick felt like steel. She drank me in, her eyes fixed on my dick as it bobbed.

"Sex swings can be very liberating," I told her, stepping forward and grabbing her feet. I pulled her toward me, her pussy coming so close to my cock I could feel her heat. Easing her back into the neutral position, I stroked her cunt briefly, then went to the strap of the handholds. Pulling it, her arms rose higher into the air until they were above her head. I took a step back to look at her. Her arms were floating above her, her legs spread out in front, her cunt glistening in the middle. Fuck, I couldn't wait to taste her again.

"Keep your hands there," I warned as I got down on my knees. Drifting my fingers along her thighs, I kissed my way closer to her drenched opening. "Under no circumstance do you bring your arms down. If you bring them down before I'm ready, I may have to take my belt to that ass of yours. Understand?"

"Yes," she whispered. I sensed her unease and quickly stood, placing a kiss on her mouth.

"I'm going to make this orgasm so fucking amazing for you, baby, but if you don't want to play anymore, just say *Dollhouse*."

With the reassurance that she could actually get out of there if she wanted to, Wren relaxed into the swing. Taking up my previous position, I positioned one hand on her ass and the other on her thigh, holding her sweet cunt in place. She gasped, and I looked up to find her watching me. She was going to fucking love this.

I attacked her cunt with my mouth, sliding my tongue through her folds over and over. Her champagne taste slid down my throat as I swallowed her, and my cock got even harder. Wren wriggled against me, making these cute little mewling sounds as I ate her out. Flicking my tongue over her clit, I felt her thighs tense as an orgasm was quickly approaching. I knew it wouldn't take too long to get the first one, but it was the fifth and sixth ones I wanted before I fucked her.

I pulled back just as she was about to come, the look of displeasure on her face making me chuckle.

"Bane," she moaned.

"Little Bird," I crooned back, stalling to give us both time to calm the fuck down. Palming my cock, I pumped a few times to take the ache away. I may have been denying her orgasm, but I denied mine too.

"Please."

With a growl, I grabbed her ass and dove back in. Heat and arousal flooded her, coating my mouth and chin. I sucked on her clit, nibbling it ever so slightly. When her thighs began to shake again, I pulled back. Over and over, I did this until on the sixth denial, I growled, "Let go of the fucking handholds, Wren."

She did, her hands automatically going to my head and threading through my hair as she held me against her churning pussy. It only took one more stroke of my tongue, and she was coming, coming, coming against my mouth with a groan that was a direct line to my cock. I didn't let up until she was done, and even then, it lasted a good thirty seconds. When she finally came down from the high, she let go of my head, and I stood, wiping away her arousal with the back of my hand.

I was mad with lust, wild to get inside her. Gripping her thighs, I slammed into her waiting pussy and felt her orgasm again. Her inner walls pulsed around my cock, each wave punching me in the fucking chest.

I made her do that. *Me.*

Once her breathing had eased again, I began to rock her gently, my cock sliding in and out of her heat. In this position, I knew I could hit her G-spot, and I fucking intended to.

I slammed into her until I wrung another orgasm from her, this one leaving her limp. Thank fuck for the swing. Still gripping her thighs, I stopped swinging her and started pumping, nuzzling her neck and biting down gently on her shoulder. She grabbed the handholds again, lifting her perfect breasts and inviting me to take what I wanted from her.

Opening my mouth, I sucked one of her beautiful nipples into my mouth, tonguing the sensitive flesh until it was a taut peak. I switched my attention over to the other side, then alternated as I fucked her.

"Bane, I'm going to come again," she moaned, her entire body shaking as her orgasm crept over her once more. I gritted my teeth and pushed back on my own need for release, but that fucking thing was riding me hard. When I finally did come, I thought I might blackout from the pleasure.

Reaching up, I readjusted the handholds, so they were at a more comfortable height, then told Wren to lean back, so she was flat on her back, the seat of the swing cradling her lower back while the straps kept her upper body supported.

"Bring your legs up, baby."

She brought them up, exposing more of herself to me. In this position, I had access to everything, including her ass. Fuck, I wanted to explore that part of her too, but one new experience tonight was enough. Running my hands through her pussy, I rubbed her clit gently, then lined myself back up.

She screamed when I entered her this time, the change in position making her channel fucking tight. I buried myself in her, then held onto the nylon straps beside her torso and began to pound into her. I alternated between shallow thrusts and ones that shunted her violently forward, rocking her back onto my shaft with a moan.

When her third orgasm rocked her body, I helped her out of the swing, catching her loose body in my arms. Taking her over to the bed, I eased her down, then climbed up beside her. Leaning on my side, I rested my hand on her waist and murmured, "Roll over onto your side, Wren. That's right, baby." I dropped a kiss onto her bare shoulder. "Bring your knees to your chest."

I looked down her body, taking in the curve of her ass as she brought her legs up tight to her torso. Running a hand down her body, I slapped her on the ass before finding her opening. Running my fingers through her folds, she wiggled against me, seeking the friction she needed. Taking my hands away, I filled her with my cock, and the sensation of her body clamping down around me made me hiss out a breath.

"You feel too fucking good, baby," I whispered into her ear. She turned her head to kiss me, sliding her tongue into her mouth as I fucked her. Sliding my arm under hers, I wrapped my hand around the base of her throat, applying the slightest pressure. She groaned, and I chuckled. My Little Bird surprised me sometimes.

She whimpered when her orgasm took her over, giving her body over to the experience. She shuddered in my arms, but I didn't slow. My hips were pistoning against her, drawing out her pleasure and torturing the shit out of me.

"I want you to come," she moaned, her breath feathering over my hand. Letting go of her neck, I cupped one of her breasts, rubbing my thumb over her nipple.

"I need just one more out of you," I grunted, slowing my thrusts. "I want you on top of me, riding my hard cock when you come."

Rolling over, Wren clambered on top of me, impaling herself without waiting. My blood ignited when she began to move, rolling her hips against mine, her breasts bouncing with every single movement. Reaching up, I captured them both, teasing her nipples.

"Touch yourself," I commanded. "Then I'll come with you this one last time."

Wren's eyes were half-crazed with lust, her unbound hair falling over her shoulders in lush waves. I imagined what that hair would look like covering my thighs and lower stomach as she sucked my dick, and a low groan escaped me. *Fuck, I was in trouble with this woman.* She rubbed her clit, tipping her head back as she did. I felt her thighs ripple the moment before she gasped, "I'm coming."

Digging my fingers into her waist, I hissed, "Yes, baby, come for me. Come all over my hard cock while you ride it."

She screamed my name, tumbling over the edge and dragging me with her.

20

Wren

"OH MY GOD, BABE, I FEEL LIKE I HAVEN'T SEEN YOU in forever!" Darcy pulled me into a hug, squeezing the air from my lungs. When she let me go, I grinned at her, settling myself back onto the stool at the bar. I was meeting her at The Nightingale after she threatened to blow up my phone every day until I agreed to get drunk with her.

"It has been a while," I admit, crossing my legs and holding back the moan when the ache Bane had left me with reared its head.

Darcy placed her purse on the bar top and pulled herself into the stool beside me. When the bartender walked over—a beautiful blonde woman with breasts that were overflowing the V in her shirt—Darcy ordered us both a drink, then turned back to me.

"What's happening? What happened with Hawk? I need to know everything."

I laughed, then finish off my whisky. "So much has happened, Dee."

She pursed her lips and gave me the once-over. "Okay, why are you smiling like that?"

"Smiling like what?" I asked, knowing I was screwed. I couldn't keep the happiness from my face—happiness that Bane had put there.

"Like you got the best sex of your life last night." I gave her a meaningful look. "Fuck me, you *did* get the best sex of your life last night."

The bartender placed our drinks down, but I waited for her to leave again before I said, "Bane is... something else."

"Okay, I want to know all the details, Wren. The last time I spoke to you, he'd only given you a couple of orgasms. When did we graduate into dirty sex? And what about the deal? And what about—"

"If you shut up, I'll tell you," I said, cutting her off.

She folded her arms over her chest. "Fine. I'm listening."

Sucking in a breath, I let it out, then leveled my gaze on her. "You know how I said Hawk would fuck up again, I just had to wait for it?" At her nod, I said, "Well, Hawk did fuck up again. After I got off the phone with you, he told me he was going to get the money by betting on the horses. I got home from work, and there he was... the little shit had lost the bet and owed a bookie the money."

"Ho-ly *shit*." Darcy threw back what was left of her drink and motioned for two more. "Then what happened?"

I shrugged. "I called Bane."

"*What?*"

"He's the only person I could think of to help," I replied,

picking up my glass and swallowing the rest of my drink as another replaced its fallen brother.

Darcy thumped her chest. "Me. I would've lent you the money, babe."

I shook my head. "No, Dee. You're my friend, and I love you, but money always messes up friendships. Besides, you and Baron are going to start IVF soon. You guys need the cash. Plus, I wouldn't want you to give up having kids to save my punk-ass brother's butt. Anyway, I called Bane. He came over, more than happy to pay the bookie on Hawk's behalf, then add that total to the overall owing amount without adding interest."

"What do you know, a mobster with a conscience," she shot back.

"Anyway, we had sex that night. It was supposed to be only the one night, a free pass because we were both desperate for each other." I took a sip of whisky, wondering how much I was going to tell her.

"Ah… you're going to tell me every single fucking detail, Wren Montana," Darcy demanded. When I looked at her, she added, "I can tell by the look on your face that you were wondering how much to spill. I want it all. Every. Illicit. Dirty. Detail." She punctuated every word by thumping the bar, drawing the attention of some guys standing nearby. Whether it was the noise or her words, I realized we were gaining some attention.

Scooping up my drink, I slid from the stool. "Come on. If you're going to be demanding, let's go somewhere more private."

Darcy strutted past the men, giving them a wink as she went. She was such a shameless flirt. Despite that, she was one hundred percent faithful to Baron.

I found an empty booth and slid into it. "He gave me twelve

throughout the night."

"Shut. Up!" she shouted, drawing everyone's attention that time.

"Fuck, Dee, keep your shit together," I hissed, shooting anyone still staring a look. "Yes, twelve. He only came once, right at the end."

"Fuck, that man has some stamina."

Didn't I know it. "Yeah. He's a fucking savage in bed. It's amazing, don't get me wrong, but I was exhausted when we were finally done."

"Were you walking funny the next day?"

I stared at her. "Seriously? Are we in grade school again?"

Dee shrugged and gave me a coy smile. "I need to live vicariously through you, Wren. Baron is the only fucking man I want, but marriage has worn our sex life down to a grind—a boring, monotonous grind. Add the attempts at baby-making and romance and passion have fucking left the building. I need these dirty stories to get me through."

"I'm pretty sure this is why they make porn," I told her, slowly turning my glass around on the table, each revolution like a loosening of my tongue. "On Monday night, he took me to dinner at his sister's place." I would've laughed at the expression on Dee's face if I didn't feel the same way. "I know... I was shocked. She's really nice, actually, and I saw a side of Bane I didn't think existed."

Darcy threw back her drink and put the glass down with a thump. "What side?"

"He has a baby niece, and he's smitten with her. You should've seen him..."

Reaching under the table, she prods my abdomen. "Did your

ovaries just explode?"

I batted away her hands but was unable to wipe the grin from my face. "It was pretty fucking amazing."

"And? What happened next?"

"He took me home, and we had more amazing sex."

She raised one manicured brow at me. "What happened to the one free pass only?"

I shrugged. I'd like to see her resist Bane when he gets that look in his eye. "I made a decision when we were at dinner. I told him I accepted his offer of two weeks with me, and in exchange Hawk's debt is gone."

"Just like that?"

"Just like that." I let out a sigh. "Last night, we went to dinner, and afterward, he brought one of my fantasies to life."

"Threesome?"

"Sex swing," I corrected. "And it was fucking amazing. Seriously, Dee, you and Baron have to get one."

She tapped her chin in thought. "I'll just get one and surprise him," she said with a chuckle. "His poor uptight accountant pants wouldn't know what hit them."

She looked around the bar for a moment. "What's going to happen at the end of two weeks? Will you be able to walk away from him?"

"Honestly? I don't know. I feel like the more time I spend with him, the more I get to know him, the more I want to stay. Is that messed up? I mean, he's a drug dealer and runs a strip club. How can I move past that? It's hardly an honest living."

"The drug dealing is definitely not an honest living, but the club is legit. Men love sex, and if women can get paid to dance for them, I say more power to them. Do you know if he's slept with any of them?"

"I asked him last night."

"What did he say?"

Smoothing my hair back with my fingers. "He said he didn't have penetrative sex with any of them."

"Penetrative?" She screwed up her face. "So, that means…"

"Oral. I guess he gets blowjobs?"

My best friend pursed her lips. "And this is something he'll continue to do while he has you in his bed?" I could hear every single ounce of disapproval in her tone.

"No. He said he won't see any other woman while I'm sleeping with him."

"Well, at least he's not a complete asshole," she muttered. "Fuck, I love you, Wren, and want to hang out longer, but I need to go home to Baron. All this sex-deal talk has got me all hot and bothered. Want to share an Uber?"

I laughed at my friend's impulsivity but nodded. "I'm sure Baron will be very happy to hear that. I should probably go too… work tomorrow and everything."

Darcy navigated her way through the rideshare app, booking us a lift. "When do you see Bane again?"

"Probably tomorrow night."

With a nod, she glanced at her phone. "Our ride is around the corner," she announced, turning off her phone and sliding it back into her purse. Darcy slid from the seat, and I followed her out, and together we walked out of The Nightingale. As we stepped onto the sidewalk, a car pulled up. "This is us."

We both got in, declining the offer of water and mints.

"How's the baby-making going?" I asked once we're on our way.

She was silent for a moment, then said, "Our first round of IVF is next week."

Reaching across the dark back seat, I took her hand in mine. I didn't need to ask her how she felt about that because I knew. She was terrified. She was terrified of it not working. She was terrified that whatever reason she's unable to have children naturally will interfere with the artificial process too.

"Have you spoken to Baron about how you're feeling?"

She tightened her grip on my hand. "A bit. He wants this so badly, but... what if—"

"It'll take. I know it."

Bobbing her head, she sucked in a breath, then let it out. "We only have enough cash for two rounds. If this doesn't happen, I don't know what we'll do."

"You could adopt? There are loads of children out there who need loving parents. Or you could foster?" If I'd had a mom like her when Hawk and I were going through the foster system, I wouldn't have run away as much. I would've been happy to stay. Been happy to have the love of someone who loved me back, instead of the government check they received for the inconvenience.

Darcy sniffled, wiping the tears from her cheeks. I opened my mouth to say something more, but the car slowed to a stop at the curb. Peering out of my window, I saw we were at my apartment.

"Stay safe, babe," Darcy told me with a smile. "I'm looking forward to hearing more of your sexcapades with Bane."

I huffed as I opened my door. "We don't have sexscapades."

"Um, yeah, you do. You guys are having that hot, dirty sex I wish I were having." Kissing my cheek, Darcy waved goodbye, and I got out, walking inside my building.

As I unlocked my apartment door, I paused when I stepped inside. I didn't know how else to explain it other than it felt like the hairs on the back of my neck were standing on end. Moving quickly and quietly, I went into my bedroom and grabbed my nine-millimeter, taking off the safety and holding it down by my thigh.

After checking all the windows and the locks on the front door, I began looking around. But I found nothing.

There was nothing missing, but Bane's angry words from earlier bounced around my head. Anyone could get into my apartment at any time. I'd never felt unsafe, but my instincts never lied.

Picking up the phone, I dialed Bane's number.

"Little Bird," he answered on the second ring. "What's wrong? I thought you were out with Darcy."

"I was. I'm home now, but…"

Was I being crazy here?

Was I overreacting because Bane had pointed out the busted lock on my window?

Was I psychosomatic?

"What is it, Wren?" he demanded in a low voice.

"I'm sure it's nothing—"

"What?" I heard him slam his fist onto the desk.

Swallowing, I said, "I think someone's been in my apartment." I pulled the phone away from my ear when Bane's cursed viciously.

"I'm sending Andy. Keep your gun with you and lock yourself in the bathroom until he gets there."

I wanted to rail against him, scream that I was not a helpless woman who needed the help of a man, but…

… I had called him because I knew he would make everything

all right again.

I nodded, my body already kicking in with adrenaline. "Okay. Okay."

"I'll keep you safe, Little Bird."

21

Bane

FUCK NO, THIS WAS NOT HAPPENING. I CLUTCHED THE phone more tightly against my ear, willing the rage to stay at bay. It was a fucking losing battle. I could feel it curling around my mind, demanding I protect what was mine. It had happened that night I beat my father to within an inch of his life after he'd hit my mom for the final time, and it was happening now too.

"Are you in there yet?" I barked, then cursed myself for yelling. Wren was worried. I heard it in her voice. I was so fucking glad she called me instead of brushing off her suspicions even though I was sure it was a hit to her whole independent woman thing she showed the world. I stood so I could pace.

There was a soft click, then when her voice came back over the line, it was quiet. "Okay, I'm in the bathroom."

"Good. I'm hanging up now and calling Andy. Stay there. Don't let anyone into your apartment until you hear his voice." She said nothing, and I growled, "Tell me you fucking understand, Wren."

"I understand."

"Good girl." I hung up and dialed Andy.

"Mr. Rivera?"

"I need you to go and collect Wren. Take her to my apartment. Keep the Glock in the glovebox with you."

"Yes, sir."

I called Wren back. "He's on his way now."

"Okay."

The call disconnected, and it was a fucking miracle I let go of the phone. Dropping it to the desk like it was on fucking fire, I shut my eyes and tried to draw in calming breaths. My rage was still darkness swirling inside of me, an insidious run of thoughts. Digging my fingers into the back of the leather chair, I bowed my head and counted to ten. When I finally reached that magical double-digit, I felt slightly more in control.

Slightly.

Sending Andy to Wren hadn't been my first choice. Dagger would've been a much deadlier choice, but my Little Bird hadn't met him, didn't know him, and the thought of making her even more scared was a hell-fucking-no for me. Andy could hold his own, though. He was also ex-military, so he knew his way around a weapon and was adept at hand-to-hand combat. As an added bonus, he'd been trained as a field medic.

Not that Wren was hurt, I reminded myself.

Releasing my fingers, I straightened, then swallowed the rest of my whisky. As I drained the last of the glass, there was a knock on my office door.

"Yeah," I snarled, slamming the tumbler back down.

168

I bit back the curse when I saw who it was. Detective Cox strolled in like she owned the damn place. Her blonde hair was slicked back away from her face, held like a hostage on the back of her head in a bun. The black pantsuit she was wearing was well-pressed, her white shirt underneath crisp.

"Fuck, what do you want?" I snapped.

"Nice to see you too, Bane."

I glared at her. Fuck her. I didn't give a fuck if she was a cop. Now was not the time to fucking walk into my office, especially when I was ready to commit goddamn murder. "I don't have time for this shit, Detective, so tell me what you want to say, then we can move this night right along."

Her lips pursed, but it did nothing to take away their appeal. She had a mouth made for fucking. "You know I've been keeping an eye on your club," she began.

"If you wanted a job here, all you had to do was ask," I baited. "You'd be a nice addition to my Dolls." Her face contorted into a mask of disdain. "You know, you shouldn't knock it until you try it. There's something rather thrilling about liberating a man of his hard-earned money." I glanced down at her finger—no wedding band. "And a good-looking, single woman like you would fucking clean up down there," I finished, gesturing to the club below.

"Unlucky for you, I'm married to my job on the force."

"Well, if you change your mind, I'll keep a spot open for you."

Cox folded her arms over her chest. "I didn't come here to discuss job opportunities."

"Oh? Why did you come then?"

A smile tugged at the corners of her mouth, and I got the distinct impression I would not like what she was about to say.

"Did you know Hugo Ramirez was killed today? Shot in cold blood. Two in the chest. One in the head. When we searched his body, he had coke on him. His bedroom was full of coke too... almost five pounds worth. He was only seventeen-years-old."

Keeping my face blank, I shrugged. "What does this seventeen-year-old punk kid have to do with me?"

She slammed her hands onto my desk. "Because he was one of your dealers, Bane."

"I'm not sure what you're talking about. I don't have any dealers unless you count my Dolls? They deal in sex, but it's one hundred percent legal as you're well aware."

Her expression darkened, her gray eyes turning to steel. "You know, I hate men like you."

"Men like me?"

With a huff, she pushed away from my desk and turned to face the wall of glass. "Men who exploit women for their own gain. Men who think everyone should be on your payroll." When she turned back to face me, utter hatred flashed in her eyes. "Men who break the law repeatedly but are so squeaky clean that shit won't stick."

My chest puffed up a little at that. "You say the sweetest things." It was so fucking hard to keep up this act. Learning of Hugo's demise was a fucking kick to the balls. I was down another dealer, and my hold on the drug trade in No Man's Land was fucking slipping away. But that was something to deal with once Cox was gone.

"One day you'll slip up, Rivera, and I'll be there when you do."

"If that's what helps you sleep at night, then, by all means, you think that, Detective Cox. But I have no idea why you keep bringing me news like this. I'm just a businessman... a

11111111111221121111121112211

businessman who pays his taxes, treats his employees fairly, and who goes to church on Sunday."

She sneered. "I'll be in touch."

"I can't wait. And if you do want to get out of the law enforcement game, my doors are wide open."

She left in a huff, and I collapsed back into my chair. Swiping up my phone, I dialed Dagger.

"Boss?"

"Got eyes on Cox?"

"Yeah, she's making her way to the exit now, but she's giving out her business card to some of the Dolls."

That fucking cunt.

"My girls won't talk, but make sure she leaves the premises. She brought news of another one of my guys going down."

"Who?"

"Hugo. Same MO from what I can tell."

"She's got nothing on us, boss," he told me, making me grind my teeth.

"I fucking know that, but it doesn't help that our guys are showing up with one less heartbeat." I ran a hand through my hair. "Fuck!"

"We're tight, boss," Dagger repeated, and I hung the fuck up on him.

Under normal circumstances, if Dagger were happy we were locked down tight, I would simply leave it, but this business with Wren was coaxing out the beast in me. Dialing Andy, I barked, "Are you there yet?"

"Just walking inside the building now," he replied. "Is there anything I need to know?"

"She just said she thought someone had been in her apartment.

The window in the living room has a broken lock. If they got in, that's how. Check it out, then knock twice on the bathroom door. I'll let her know that's her signal."

"Yes, sir."

Hanging up, I dialed Wren again.

"Hello?" she whispered.

"Andy is almost there. He'll knock twice on the bathroom door. Let him in, then pack a bag because you're going to my place."

"Bane, I don't think—"

"Little Bird, honestly? I don't give a fuck what you think right now. You're not safe there, and until I can get you set up in a new, safer apartment, you will stay with me."

I braced myself for the backlash, but Wren simply said tightly, "We'll discuss this later. I'll go with Andy now, but I'm not staying at one of your apartments."

Curling my hands into fists, I drew in a couple of deep breaths. "If you didn't want my help, why the fuck did you call me?"

"You make me feel safe," she replied without a whisper of doubt. "Somehow, you've broken past my years of shit-fight-thickened skin and breached my walls. I had no choice but to call you."

And didn't that make me feel like a fucking man. "Go with Andy. I'll be home as soon as I can."

Hanging up the phone, I let out a deep breath, then got to work.

IT WAS A LITTLE AFTER MIDNIGHT WHEN I FINALLY GOT away from the club. Andy met me at the curb outside, the heat of the day still lingering in the air.

"How is she?"

"Pissed off, sir," he replied.

"Did she give you any trouble?"

He shook his head and opened the rear door. "No, she came quietly, but I've known women like her before. She's keeping all that rage pent up just for you."

"Don't I fucking know it," I replied, unable to keep the smile from my face. Wren could be angry at me all she liked. In fact, that anger would make the sex fucking mind-blowing. I got into the car, and a few moments later, we were off.

"Did you see anything in the apartment that set the alarm bells ringing?" I asked.

"Nothing that I could see, but I don't live there normally. You get a sense of when things are right or not in the place where you sleep."

Such a military reply.

"Did she pack a lot?"

"Just one set of clothes and her toothbrush."

Which meant she wasn't intending on staying long. My smile intensified. I was so going to enjoy breaking her.

By the time we arrived back at my building, I barely greeted the doorman as I strode to the bank of elevators. Punching in the passcode on the keypad, the elevator rose quickly to the penthouse level. Stepping out into my marble foyer, I looked around. The place was dark except for the lights from the buildings around me seeping in through the wall of glass. Turning my head, I saw the faint glow of buttery yellow light coming out from under my closed bedroom door.

I slipped out of my jacket, draping it on the couch as I passed.

When I got to the door, I paused. Listening. "Shit," I muttered, pushing into the room and surprising Wren, who was curled up on my bed crying. She sat up, wiping the tears from her face.

"Bane."

Fuck, seeing her upset was like getting a fucking shard of glass pushed through my still-beating heart. I went over and wrapped myself around her. It hit me then that I'd never felt this strongly about a woman before. Bianca was my blood, so she automatically received this kind of love from me, but Wren...

"I've got you, Little Bird," I said into her hair. "I've got you."

She sobbed a little harder, but all I could do was let her get these feelings out. I rubbed circles on her back, holding her tightly against me.

"I don't know why I called you," she whispered against my neck. "I don't know why I felt the need to have you rescue me."

I did. "You trust me to keep you safe."

She reared away. "Yes, but when the fuck have I called a man to rescue me?" Her cheeks were stained red, matching her puffy eyes. She saw her needing me as a weakness when, in fact, it was the bravest fucking thing she could've done. I pulled her back into my arms, burying my face in her hair.

"You don't need me," I crooned. "You wanted me. There's a difference."

She froze in my arms. "Fuck."

I chuckled. "Come on, baby, there's nothing wrong with that. In fact, I like that you wanted me to make you feel safe. Do you know how much of a turn-on that is?"

Shoving weakly against my chest to let her go, she sat back, running her sleeve under her nose. She had a frown on her face, one that I wanted to erase. "I shouldn't want you to come to my rescue, either."

"You don't have to fight through life on your own anymore, Wren." I reached for her again, but she slid away and off the bed. I groaned when I saw she was wearing short shorts and a tight tank.

"I don't want to come to rely on you. What we have, it has an expiration date."

"Not if you don't want it to."

"Jesus, Bane, you're a fucking drug dealer."

"And?" I shot back. "What I do for money and the kind of man I am are not the same. Not even fucking close."

She spun around to face the window, staring out at the city. "What happens when you walk away from me?"

Jesus fuck, is that what this was about? I got off the bed and pressed myself against her back. Placing my hands on the glass on either side of her body, I flexed my hips into her ass and bit down on her earlobe. She gasped, then moaned as I sucked the sting away. "I could never walk away from you, Little Bird. Fuck our original two-week deal if that's what makes you feel better. I already told you Hawk was off the fucking hook whether you stayed with me or not." I ground my aching cock into her ass, enjoying the way her eyes fluttered shut in the reflection. "I'm not letting you go, Wren. When will you get that through your beautiful, stubborn, sexy-as-fuck head of yours?"

She moaned, pressing back against me. Dropping one more kiss on her shoulder, I said, "Place your hands on the glass in front of you and don't move."

She did as I asked, and to reward her, I skimmed my fingers along her arms, down her ribs, and onto her waist. She was wearing too many clothes as far as I could see, so I slid the thin fabric of her sleep shorts down her fucking amazing legs until they were pooled around her feet. When I met her gaze in the window, I smirked at the way her blue eyes were molten, at how the rise and fall of her chest were increasing with every passing moment.

I divested her of her panties too, leaving them at her feet. Feathering my fingertips up her legs, I let them linger on her bare ass. She had an amazing ass. Leaning down, I kissed one cheek, then the other, making her gasp. Moving higher, I trailed my lips up her spine, licking and biting my way to the hem of her shirt. I pulled that off too, exposing her to me.

I stepped away for a moment to just stare at the beautiful creature who was mine for however long she'd have me. I'd seen beautiful women before. Hell, I worked with them every day, but there was something tainted about my Dolls. I never noticed it until now, but seeing Wren standing submissively in my bedroom, waiting for me, I realized that I'd been staring at incredibly bad imitations of beauty every damn day.

My fingers flew down the front of my shirt, unbuttoning it and shrugging it off. The sound of my belt buckle coming unclasped sent a shiver of anticipation down Wren's spine.

"Do you want what only I can give you?" I asked, my voice dark and smoky with lust. She nodded meekly, her eyes on mine through the glass. I got rid of my dress slacks and underwear, then walked back to her—close but not quite touching yet. I wanted her to feel the heat coming off me, to know I was nearby but she couldn't touch me yet.

After making her wait for an agonizing minute, I cupped her cunt and nuzzled the side of her neck. "Open a little wider for me, Little Bird."

Shuffling her feet out, she gave me the access I needed, moaning when I swept my finger through her folds.

"Are you already wet for me?" I wondered, sliding a finger into her slick heat. With a groan, I leaned my head onto her shoulder. She was wet—so fucking wet. My dick ached with the knowledge. With my free hand, I gave it a few pumps to take the edge off, then concentrated on giving my Little Bird the pleasure she needed to relax.

"Bane," she said on a breathy whisper. She didn't need to say anything more. Everything she needed was in that one desperate sound. I withdrew my fingers from her, bringing them to my mouth so I could suck off her taste. I watched her in the reflection, seeing the desire burning there.

With my hand between her shoulder blades, I urged her closer to the window until her breasts were pressed against the cool glass. The different sensations—my heat behind her and the cold, hard glass in front—would add another layer to her mind. Plus, the idea that people in the building beside mine could see us right now if they looked, made my cock even harder. Exhibitionism isn't something I get to dabble in all that often, given my high-profile status.

Nibbling her lightly on the shoulder, I growled into her ear, "I'm going to fuck you now."

I waited until she nodded, then dropped one last kiss onto her shoulder. Gripping her by the hips, I tilted her ass toward me a little and slammed into her. I sucked back the hiss as I just stayed there a moment, enjoying the way her cunt wrapped around me, holding me in place. Reaching around her, I flicked my fingertips over her clit a few times, making her head fall back onto my shoulder.

Withdrawing from her body a little, I teased her then drove back inside her. Her greedy cunt compressed around me, attempting to hold me in place. Again and again, I teased her, dragging my cock through the sensitive bundle of nerves inside her that would make her come so hard she would probably drag me down the orgasm rabbit hole with her. Her entire body seemed to quake as I hit that spot, working her into a frenzy. When her legs began to shake, I rubbed her clit, sending her over the edge with a long, drawn-out scream.

Keeping us connected, I wrapped one arm around her waist, the other around her chest, and moved us to the floor.

I kissed the base of her spine, dipping my tongue into the seam of her ass. She let out a little moan, and I knew I had to tap that soon.

"On your hands and knees, baby."

As she got into position, I anchored my hands on her hip bones and began the relentless pounding into her pussy that would make me come if I didn't control myself. Stamina was key sometimes, but tonight, I just wanted my Little Bird to relax, to give over her control, and let me take care of her anxiety and stress.

"I'm coming," she whispered, right before her inner muscles clamped down on my dick, catching me by surprise. My balls drew up, and I came inside her, marking her as mine. Fuck, even the idea that another man could have access to her sweet cunt made me see red. I shoved the violent thoughts out of my head and withdrew from her body. Before she could move, I scooped her up and took her into the bathroom. Shower first, then I was going to fuck her again in the comfort of my bed.

22

Wren

I WOKE UP SLOWLY TO FIND MYSELF WRAPPED IN BANE. He had one arm over my chest and his leg over my thigh. I was too hot—uncomfortably so—but I let out a content sigh. I shouldn't get used to this. I shouldn't want to be here, but he made me feel safe, and that was something I'd been chasing for most of my adolescent and adult life.

After our shower last night, he put me to bed, then spent an hour going down on me. It was heaven and torture wrapped up in one. The man knew how to pleasure a woman, giving me multiple orgasms, ones that chased the one before it. By the time I begged him to stop, he surged up my body, his thick cock sliding between my folds and into my pussy. He'd taken it slow that time. Like when he ate me out, he seemed to be taking his time, making sure I was enjoying every moment of it.

Even though it was foolish, I think Bane made love to me last night. When we came, we came together, and afterward, he'd cleaned me up, then curled around my body and went to sleep. I looked over at his face, smiling at how peaceful he was. I didn't know much about his businesses, but they must be stressful. I wondered how often he slept—really slept that restful, regenerative sleep people need in order to keep functioning.

Beside me on the side table, my phone began to vibrate. Reaching out, I picked it up and saw I had a call from Hawk. Shit, I hadn't even told him about the bookie or Bane and my agreement with him to wipe the debts. Well, now was as good a time as any.

Sliding from the bed, I got a little resistance from Bane, but after I patted his hand, he released me. Scooping up his shirt, I slid into it, then I walked out into the living room.

"Hawk?"

"Wren!" he said happily. "How are you, big sister?"

"I'm great, actually."

"Yeah? That's amazing. Everything is amazing."

Pulling the phone from my ear, I stared at the screen. This was my brother, right? "What's so amazing on your end?" I asked.

"I got the money!" He announced it proudly like this was the first time he'd managed to solve one of his problems on his own. Honestly, I think it may have been. "I'm going to take it to Bane today."

My stomach dropped. "Where did you get the money from?"

"Don't worry about where I got it from, Wren. You should just be happy that I got it."

No, no, no. My legs gave out, and I crumpled onto the couch. If Hawk did something stupid again, I was going to kill him my fucking self. "Hawk, where the fuck did you get the money from?"

"What does it matter?"

I placed a hand to my roiling stomach. "It matters because I already figured out how to get you off the hook."

There was a heavy silence, then, "You did?"

"Yes. It's only just happened, and I've been meaning to tell you—"

"Does Bane have it now? The money? Everything I owe him?"

"Yes."

"How?" His question was small, all trace of bravado now gone.

Sucking in a breath, I curled my legs beneath me, touching the soft leather of the couch. "I made a deal with him."

"You did *what?*"

"You're hardly in a position to be outraged, Hawk," I snapped at him. His reaction to the solution was not what I was expecting. I thought he'd be happy that I'd found a way out just like all those times before. "Anyway, it's done. The debt is gone, and you owe me a lot more fucking gratitude than you're showing."

"Fuck, fuck, *fuck!*" he muttered. "Jesus *fucking* Christ."

"Hawk?" Jesus, I felt sick. "Hawk, what's wrong?"

"Nothing." He hung up, and I pulled the phone from my ear. What in the actual fuck was that about?

"Was that your brother?" Bane asked behind me.

I turned to see him standing a few feet away dressed in a pair of gray sweats that showed off the deep V between his hip bones. Fuck, that was sexy. Or maybe because it was Bane. I didn't know. When I finally looked back at his face, his gaze was heated.

"If you keep looking at me like that, I'm going to take you on the couch and in the kitchen and every other room in my apartment." He readjusted his cock, drawing my eyes there. What was wrong with me? I never got this wrapped up in men.

Keeping my distance was the only way I knew how to navigate relationships, but Bane was resetting all of my methods.

Glancing away, I felt the blush heat my cheeks. Suddenly, Bane was there. He pushed my thighs apart, inserting his big body between them. Framing my face in his hands, he kissed more slowly, thoroughly, and I tasted his toothpaste.

"Who was on the phone?"

"Hawk," I replied. "He says he has the money for you."

Bane frowned. "The debt is gone."

"I know. I don't know where he got the cash from, but knowing him, it's probably not from a legal source."

"He has to give it back, then."

"He wouldn't tell me where he got it from."

Bane's brows drew down over his dark eyes, menace lurking in their depths. "I'll find out where." He stood and walked away, leaving me with an ache in my stomach that had nothing to do with being hungry. I stayed on the couch and overheard the rumble of Bane's voice as he spoke to whoever was on the other end of the phone. Honestly, I'd kind of numbed out. Not knowing where Hawk sourced the money was a gnawing ache in my head. I just hoped he hadn't done something stupid to get it.

When Bane returned, he smiled at me, trying to put me at ease. "I've got someone looking into it right now."

"Do you think they'll find anything?"

Holding out his hands to me, he lifted me from the couch and took me into the kitchen, placing me on the edge of the counter. The marble was cold under my bare ass, but Bane's mouth soon warmed me. His kiss was all-consuming, and I clung to his shoulders, unsure where this was coming from. If he was trying to distract me, he was doing an amazing job of it.

"Are you hungry?" he asked when he finally pulled away.

"Yes," I replied breathlessly, looking down to his hips.

He growled and kissed me again, sliding his tongue into my mouth as his hard cock flexed against my pussy. "Food first, then you can have this," he told me, biting my bottom lip then sucking it into his mouth.

"Are you going to cook?"

"No, I have a housekeeper. She comes in at seven to make breakfast."

Seven? It was almost...

... I heard the elevator ding and someone walk in.

"Good morning, Mr. Rivera," a woman said. I turned to look over my shoulder, then jumped off the counter, tugging down the hem of Bane's shirt. It hit me mid-thigh, but all of a sudden, it didn't seem long enough. The older woman standing before me looked like a grandmother. "And good morning to your guest as well," she added with a warm smile.

"Mrs. Bellinger, this is Wren Montana. You'll probably be seeing a little bit of her around here."

Mrs. Bellinger's smile widened. "I'm glad you've found a nice woman, Mr. Rivera. My husband always used to say that behind every good man is a better woman." She held out her hand to me. "It's lovely to meet you, Ms. Montana."

"Please, call me Wren," I muttered, flushing a little. "Ah, if you could excuse me, I'll just go and throw on some clothes."

Bane's eyes danced with laughter. "What would you like for breakfast?"

"Anything," I replied, dashing back into the bedroom. I searched my bag for some clothes, then thought better of it. I had a quick shower, got dressed, and padded back through to the kitchen. Bane was sitting at the island scrolling through his iPad while Mrs. Bellinger manned the cooktop. Whatever she was making smelled divine.

"Coffee?" Bane asked.

"Please."

He stood and walked around the island, leaving me with a very good view of his muscular back and fine ass as he went. As I watched him, I realized he was showing me another part of him, another facet of his life. Here was domesticated, relaxed Bane, and I found that I liked him like this. Here, dressed in sweats, he was truly comfortable. That's not to say that when he was with his sister he wasn't comfortable, but this was different.

"What are you looking at?" he asked when he caught me staring.

"You," I replied with a shrug. "You surprise me is all."

He walked back with my coffee. "In a good way, I hope." He dropped a kiss to my lips, then sat back down beside me.

I took a sip of coffee and let out a little sigh. I almost didn't want to return to my shitty little box of an apartment, but I knew I had to. Independence and all that.

"What are you thinking about?"

I inhaled deeply, my mouth watering at the smell of the bacon and eggs Mrs. Bellinger was cooking. "I was thinking about how much it's going to suck going back to my apartment."

"So stay here."

"I can't just stay here, Bane. We've been over this."

"I won't want to get rid of you, Wren. Jesus, do you know how amazing it was to know you were in my bed last night, that I was going to wake up beside you?"

"I get that, Bane, but how do you know you'll still want me.

What happens when the gloss wears off, and you're left with a thirty-two-year-old woman with only twelve dollars in her bank account and a failing dog grooming business?"

He was silent for a moment, and I nervously took a shallow sip of my coffee while I waited. "Little Bird, I don't know how else to tell you this, so I'm just going to say it, okay?"

I nodded, suddenly unsure.

"I don't give a fuck about any of that. It's you I want, and if that means I get a thirty-two-year-old woman with twelve dollars in her bank account and failing dog- grooming business, then that's what I get. I want *you*. All of *you*."

Mrs. Bellinger cleared her throat like she's got something caught in there but didn't turn around.

A few minutes later, she placed two plates in front of us. "I'll clean the bedroom while you two eat," she told us, disappearing from the kitchen.

"She's very discreet." I took a bite of my eggs and bit back the groan. They were amazing.

"She is."

"How long has she worked for you?"

He wiped his mouth with a napkin Mrs. Bellinger had placed down onto the counter and took a sip of his coffee. "A few years now."

We finished our breakfast quietly, simply enjoying each other's company.

"What time will you open the shop?"

I glanced at the clock hanging on the wall. "About eight thirty, I think."

"So, we have about an hour before you have to leave."

"I guess so." I narrowed my eyes at him. "Why?"

Pushing away my plate, he scooped me up and kissed me hard. He tasted like bacon and coffee, and I pushed my tongue farther into his mouth. Wrapping my legs around his waist, I groaned when his erection hit my pussy. I rubbed myself against him, earning a slap on my ass.

"Wait," he chided.

"I find it hard to wait with you, Bane," I admitted. Where were we going, anyway?

He walked us into the bathroom, and I got a glimpse of a smiling Mrs. Bellinger as Bane shut the door.

"I've already had a shower," I told him when he started the water.

"Not with me, you haven't. Besides, I plan on tasting your cunt again before you leave." Pulling the sweats down his legs, I appreciated the view of his bobbing cock for a moment. Before he could tell me to get naked, I dropped to my knees in front of him. Wrapping my hands around his cock, I leaned forward, but he pulled away with a hiss.

I looked up at him with a frown.

"No," was all he said.

"No?"

Pulling me up, he held me close. "You're never to be on your knees for me, Wren. Never. It's me who has to worship at your feet."

A thrill went through me at his words, but still, I asked, "Why?"

He shook his head. "It doesn't matter. I never want you on your knees in front of me."

When I simply stared at him, he drifted his fingers down to the hem of my shirt and inched it up my torso. Pulling the fabric up over my head, he teased my puckered nipples through my bra with his mouth before sliding my shorts and panties down my legs. His knuckle rubbed gently over my pussy, making me rock into the touch.

He kissed me until I was breathless, then pulled away to start the shower. I watched him through heavy-lidded eyes, my gaze skating down to his hips, to his cock twitching like a barely contained wild animal. Sinking my teeth into my bottom lip, I started to touch myself.

"Jesus!" he barked, palming his length and giving it a few pumps. Stalking toward me, he lifted and placed me in the shower, backing me against the wall. Strong fingers gripped my thigh, urging me to lift and wrap it around his waist. His fingers found my pussy, gliding through the arousal that was already there.

"I'm going to make you scream yourself hoarse, Little Bird."

23

Bane

SITTING AT MY DESK A FEW HOURS LATER, I THOUGHT back on my morning. Waking up with Wren was a fucking dream. Making her come multiple times in the shower was even better. Even now, just thinking about her convulsing around my fingers buried deep in her cunt made my dick stir.

Any thoughts of getting some manual relief were destroyed when Dagger stepped into the office.

"I've got those three girls for you," he said. I blinked because I couldn't recall telling him to get me more women. "To replace Syndy?" he prompted.

Fuck. That's right. "Send the first one in."

Readjusting my dick, I settled my forearms against the desk and waited for the woman to enter. The last time I'd hired new Dolls, I'd made sure to take them all for a test drive. They'd all offered their services, and who was I to say no to such a generous offer. Today was going to be different, though. I'd *little* BIRD

told Wren I wouldn't even get my dick wet with other women, and to be honest, I didn't want to. Ever since meeting her, my dick has hardly gotten hard without a thought about her first.

I took a sip of my whisky when the first potential Doll walked in. She was teetering on pleasers with a transparent heel and platform, her short skirt flashing her bare cunt at me. Her breasts were contained within a shirt that left absolutely nothing to the imagination.

"Hi, Mr. Rivera. I'm Alyse," she said, holding out her hand to me. After we shook, I motioned for her to take a seat. She took a long fucking time crossing her legs, giving me another look at that pussy of hers.

"Why don't you start by telling me something about yourself?"

"I'm twenty-one and currently working as a waitress."

"Why did you apply to work here?"

She smoothed her hands down her thighs and re-crossed her fucking legs. "The tips are better. Plus, my cousin used to work here, and she told me how good it was."

"Who was your cousin?"

"Bella Andre?" she said, making it a question. Well, if she didn't fucking know who her cousin was, we were in fucking trouble.

I did remember Bella. She played the naughty school girl most of the time. "Can you dance?"

"Bella taught me some moves," she replied, jumping up. "I can give you a lap dance if you like?"

"Sit down, sweetheart," I drawled. "I don't need a demonstration."

This declaration got me a fucking confused look. I guessed my reputation preceded me.

"Do you have a husband or boyfriend?"

"No," she replied with a smile.

"Kids?"

She nodded, her bottle-blonde hair sliding off her shoulders. "I have a son."

"How old is he?"

"Three."

Kids complicated things, but it was a workable situation. "Where is he now?"

"With my mother."

Swallowing the last of my drink, I placed the glass down and twisted it around on the blotter. "Does she know this is where you are?"

"She knows I've gone for a job interview, but she doesn't know where."

"Are you ashamed or something?" I shot back.

"What? No. I just… she wouldn't understand, you know?"

I nodded and sat back in my chair. She was a pretty girl. A little too much on the skinny side, but she would make men give up their cash.

"Do you have a drug habit?"

My question caught her off guard, and she stiffened. "No."

"Don't fucking lie to me, Alyse."

Her shoulders slumped. "I smoke weed sometimes."

"And have you ever dabbled in anything harder than that?"

"No." I gave her a weighted look and waited. And just like a fucking ticking clock inside her head, she snaps. "Okay, look… I may have dropped some Molly a couple of times, too."

"You use it just recreationally?"

She nodded. "Only when I party."

"There's a strict no drugs policy here on the premises. Would that be an issue for you?"

"No, Mr. Rivera."

"All employees must submit to random drug tests."

"That's fine," she replied quickly.

I studied her for a moment more, then dismissed her with a hand. "Thank you. Someone will be in touch to let you know if you've been successful. Send in the next girl on your way out."

Alyse stood and sashayed from my office. When the next one walked in, I went through the whole spiel again. This time I was offered a blowjob, which I declined. The only lips I wanted to be wrapped around my cock were Wren's—she just wouldn't be on her knees when that happened.

By the time the third girl left, I'd had enough.

Enough of the bullshit these women thought I wanted to hear.

Enough lies about whether they were using or not.

Dagger walked in a few minutes after the last girl left, a glass of whisky in his hand.

"Thought you could use this," he said gruffly, handing the drink over.

"How many blowjobs did you get?" I asked over the rim of my glass as I took a sip.

"Two and a hand job."

I made a face. "Who offered the hand job?"

"The first woman."

I snorted. "She wasn't a contender, anyway. I'll take the last woman, Veronica. She seems pretty intelligent."

"No problem," Dagger said, folding his meaty arms and folding them across his chest. "I hate to be the bearer of bad news—"

I held up my hand for him to stop. "Then don't be. For fuck's sake, don't be."

"Cox will be here in ten."

Fuck! "What does she want this time?" I demanded, tipping the rest of my drink down my throat. Fuck, I was so fucking over this bitch looking for things that weren't there.

"She didn't say. What should I do when she gets here?"

Putting a bullet between her eyes wasn't an option, but I could make her uncomfortable as fuck. "I'll take the meeting in the voyeurs' room."

Dagger nodded and disappeared through the door. Standing, I stretched out my back, grabbed my suit jacket off the back of my chair, and walked down into the club. I had half a dozen Dolls dancing on the poles around the club, and I scanned the area for one in particular.

Kym was perched on the lap of a man who owned a Fortune 500 company, dragging her false nails down his chest. When I loomed above her, her green eyes flickered to my face.

"Kym, why don't you show Mr. Franklin here how much you like putting on a show."

Mr. Franklin looked up at me. "I only came for some company, Mr. Rivera."

"I understand, Mr. Franklin, but Kym here knows just what to do to make that loneliness drift away."

Kym took his hand and led him over to one of the rooms at the back of the club. When they disappeared through the first door, I walked over to the wall and clicked a button, parting a curtain from the inside of the room. Kym had Mr. Franklin on the couch in the center of the room, his pants already down near his ankles. She was balanced between his legs, his semi-hard cock in her hand.

Taking a seat on the bench in front of the window, I watched

Kym work her magic and waited for Cox.

"Need some company, boss?" a woman asked. I turned to find Jessika there. She was a stunning woman, covered in colorful tattoos along both arms and her thighs too.

"Why don't you go and help Kym out?" I suggested, gesturing to the voyeur room. Jess sauntered off with her hips kicking out from side to side. She entered the room and shot me a wink.

"Mr. Rivera," I heard Cox say as she approached.

Turning to face her, I gave her a smile. "I'd say it's a pleasure, but I'd be lying."

That was when she noticed where I was sitting. Spinning around to face me, she said, "Let's go and talk somewhere more private."

"If you want to talk to me, Cox, you'll have to talk to me here while I watch my Dolls fuck a man's brains out."

Her mouth puckered, but she took a seat beside me. I kept my eyes on the window but noticed her eyes kept flickering to the scene. "You can watch them. That's what they want."

"It's pornography."

"It's better than pornography," I shot back, widening my legs a little more. "It involves all the senses... sight, smell, taste. Just take a look. You might find you enjoy it."

You uptight cunt.

She cleared her throat, her gaze darting to Kym who was eating out Jessika while Mr. Franklin fucked her from behind. I watched the color rise in Cox's cheeks, the flush breaking out over her cheekbones. She was turned on by this. Was it the dynamic, or was it because of the girl-on-girl action? I wouldn't have fucking pegged her for a pussy diver.

"I know what you're doing," she murmured, her eyes still on the scene. "You think this will make me go away and not ask the questions I need to ask."

"Is that why I'm doing it?" I asked innocently. "Maybe I just like watching people fuck."

She cringed and looked at me. "Your words and actions won't deter me."

I shrugged. You can't please everyone. "What do you want, then?"

"We have a witness."

"Good for you."

"A witness who can place your man, Tony, speaking to Hugo Ramirez."

"He prefers the name Dagger." I glanced at her, feeling the menace leaking from me. I wasn't going to be shutting it down this time. "And you're full of shit."

"He's willing to testify in court to it. Once they nail *Dagger*..." she sneered, "... it's only a matter of time before your ass is nailed to the wall right alongside his."

If she thought Dagger would roll over on me, she had another fucking thing coming. "You have a very active imagination."

Her top lip pulled back from her teeth. "Give it time, Rivera. I will have your ass in jail, then I'll tear down this house of sin."

I faced her, letting the mask slip a little more. The monster who lurked there took stock of her. "Listen here, you fucking zealous little *cunt*, it'll be a cold fucking day in hell when that happens. In fact, I can guarantee it will never happen, so stop fucking sniffing around here like the bitch you are and go solve these murders. And here's a hot fucking tip... I have nothing to do with them. Why would I need to kill drug dealers?"

I sat back, my hands curling into fists on the tops of my thighs. My blood was fucking boiling in my veins.

Cox stood, took one last look at the threesome, then walked away. Before she disappeared from view, she said, "Rivera?"

"What?" I barked.

"Your time will come."

"Fuck you."

24

Wren

I LOCKED UP THE SHOP AND LET OUT A BREATH. TODAY had been hectic, but not as hectic as my thoughts had been. After leaving Bane's apartment this morning, I'd returned to my place to collect a shirt I'd forgotten to pack with Andy as an escort. He'd checked things out for me, reassuring me the place was as secure as it ever was.

"Ms. Montana."

I looked around when I heard my name. I glanced at the car pulling up at the curb.

"Andy," I said with a smile.

"Mr. Rivera wanted me to take you home and to check things out for you." Opening the rear door of the town car, he invited me to get in.

I hesitated, looking down at my fur-covered shirt. "I'm going to get hair everywhere."

"I'll have the interior cleaned after I drop you off."

With a bob of my head, I slid onto the leather seats and let out a groan of relief—I'd been on my feet all day. The ride back to mine was very short, and I would've argued that fact if it weren't for Bane's words to me before I left him after our shower.

Andy pulled up the curb and opened the door for me. "Thank you," I said, staring up at the building.

"Are you ready, Ms. Montana?"

I nodded, and we walked inside. I kept my eyes moving, my senses on high alert. I was still jumpy after last time, but having Andy here helped. I'd even taken my gun with me to work today, something which I'd never done before. I'd found the dogs were unsettled if they could scent the oil and gunpowder.

Andy opened my apartment door, motioning me to stay behind while he did the sweep. A few moments later, he was back. "All clear, Ms. Montana."

"Please, call me Wren."

"Wren," he corrected. "Mr. Rivera has asked that I stay outside on watch tonight. This is my number." He handed me a card. "Call me if you need me."

He strode away, his steps confident and commanding, and I retreated back into my apartment. Walking around, I made sure all the windows were locked, finding that the broken catch had been repaired, then triple-checked the front-door locks. Once I was confident nobody was getting in without my knowing about it, I stripped out of my shirt and leggings, kicking my panties off and dumping my bra on top as I walked into the bathroom to start the shower. I shut the door behind me, not willing to let all that amazing steam disappear.

When the water was hot, I stepped inside and let out a groan of relief. Taking my time, I washed my hair, putting in a treatment while I shaved my legs. After I washed everything out, I stood under the spray for what must have been fifteen minutes, letting the spray pound at the muscles of my shoulders and neck.

When I stepped from the shower stall, I wrapped one towel around my head and the other around my body. I took a minute to look at myself in the mirror. For the first time in what felt like forever, I looked moderately well-rested.

I reached for the handle of the door but recoiled when a warning flashed in my brain. Looking down, I tried to figure out why my hand was red and beginning to blister. I looked back to the door, then noticed the smoke creeping in underneath the bottom of it. Snatching the hand towel from the side of the basin, I turned the knob on the bathroom door...

"Fuck!"

My apartment was on fire. Not just a small little kitchen fire but blazing. The heat and smoke assaulted my senses right away, and I recoiled as I turned away from the living room slowly catching on fire. Smoke and flames filled the hallway down to my bedroom and the kitchen. The only part of my apartment that wasn't fully ablaze was the living room.

Ducking back into the bathroom, I grabbed the extra towel hanging on the back of the door and soaked it, along with the other one around my body, in the shower. Once it was dripping wet, I wrapped one around my chest and the other over my shoulders.

The heavy terry cloth felt suffocating, but it would save my life. Stepping back out into the hall, I shielded my face from the ferocious flames that had grown in the time I was wetting the towels, the glowing red beast feeding off all my shitty old furniture, consuming it and looking for more. I took one step toward the living room, the floor beneath me creaking with the weight. Panicked, I looked down. How long had the fire been burning? And what about the rest of the people in my building?

Looking up, I focused on where I wanted to be. I needed to get over to the living room window so I could get down the fire escape. Coughing, I drew the towel over my nose and began to run. I was halfway through the room when I tripped and fell, hitting my head on the edge of the coffee table. The smell of blood flooded my nose, warring with the smell of smoke. Around me, the air seemed to crackle, the bones of the building groaning around me as the flames consumed it. Racked with coughs, I got onto my hands and knees, clutching at the towel over my shoulders as I crawled toward the window, but no matter how much I moved, I hardly seemed to advance.

Collapsing onto the floor, I peered up at the window, almost tasting the fresh air. There was a slow groan and then a crack.

And then the darkness took me.

I WOKE TO THE SOUND OF BEEPING—AN INCESSANT beeping that seems to be in time with my heart. The violent cough that forced its way out of my body took me by surprise. It led to a fit of coughs that made my already sore throat raw.

"Drink this," a man said gently, shoving a straw near my mouth. I gulped down the cool water I was offered, my eyes finally focusing on the hand holding the bottle. Bane studied me with heart-crushing concern, the seriousness on his face making my already strained heart thump faster. When I finally had my fill of water, I let go of the straw and sat back in the bed—the hospital bed.

He placed the bottle back down onto a table, then dragged his seat even closer to the side of the bed.

"Bane."

He stood, wrapping his arms around me. I clutched at his arm around my chest, the tears streaming down my face taking me by surprise.

"What happened?" I asked.

He pulled away, his eyes darkening with rage. "Someone set fire to your apartment."

I remembered the flames. I remembered the smoke. Even now, I could still smell it. "Why?" I croaked.

His hands curled into fists. "I have no idea, but I will goddamn find out why," he vowed.

A knock on the door drew my attention. "Ms. Montana, I'm glad to see you're awake," a woman with blonde hair pulled back into a severe bun said as she walked into my room. Her gaze darted to Bane for a moment before returning to my face. "My name's Detective Cox. I'm investigating the fire at your apartment."

"What the fuck are you doing here?" Bane snarled at the detective. I looked between the pair, seeing the antagonism simmering there.

"Bane, do you know her?"

He turned his eyes back to me, the anger bleeding out. "We've met before, yes, Little Bird. Although I have no idea why she's here now," he ground out.

"Like I said, I'm investigating the fire." Detective Cox dragged the other chair that was against the wall over to the side of the bed and settled into it. "I have some questions for you, Ms. Montana."

"Call me Wren," I mumbled. "Do you think someone set that fire on purpose?"

"I'm sure of it," she replied, holding out her phone to me. She scrolled through about half a dozen pictures of the burnt remains of my place. "See how there are scorch marks here and here?" She pointed at something in the photograph, but I couldn't see it. "This indicates an accelerant was used... most likely gasoline. That's why it burned as fiercely as it did. That, plus that building wasn't to code, so it had no fire protection or prevention methods in place."

She switched off her phone and placed it back on her lap, looking at me like I was a naughty child who had to confess to something that had happened.

"Do you have any enemies, Ms. Montana?"

Enemies? I looked at Bane, but his eyes were firmly fixed on Cox. "No. No enemies."

"Nobody at work who's threatened you?"

"No. I'm self-employed."

"Where do you work?"

"Bubbly Paws."

She nodded. "That grooming place on Trade Street?"

"Yeah."

"Your brother, Ms. Montana, has he pissed anyone off recently?"

I resisted looking at Bane. "There was a bookie," I replied. "But I don't know the particulars. You'd have to speak to him."

"Maybe I'll just do that," she murmured, looking at Bane. I glanced between them, wondering what was going on. He had a death grip on my hand now, and I flexed my fingers to let him know he was holding me too tightly.

Cox's shrewd gray eyes darted down to our joined hands. "And what's your relationship to Mr. Rivera?"

"None of your goddamn business," Bane snarled while standing. "Get out of here, Cox. Wren is off-limits for you."

The detective got up from her chair smoothly and smiled at him. "You don't get to tell me how to do my job, Mr. Rivera." She looked back at me. "We'll be in touch, Ms. Montana."

As soon as she left, Bane barked, "*Cunt!*"

"Bane, what's going on?"

He ran a hand through his hair then over his stubbled jaw. "Nothing, baby."

Anger at being dismissed surged. "Fuck you, Bane, it's not nothing. Something's going on between you two."

"Wren, leave it alone," he warned.

"No, Bane, I won't leave it alone. Are you fucking her, too? Is that why she's pissed off with you?"

His mouth popped open in surprise. "What?"

"Are you fucking her? After you told me you wouldn't look at other women while I was in your bed?"

"No, baby."

"Then what the fuck was that about?"

He began to pace, then turned to me and blew out a breath. "She's been coming to the club. She thinks she's got evidence she can pin on me regarding dealers getting hit."

My heart thumped at his words. "Does she?"

"Fuck, no, she doesn't. She's just fishing to see what we'll give her."

I looked down at my ash-covered hands folded in my lap. "Did the fire have something to do with you?"

"What?" he hissed.

I cocked my head to the side, studying him. He looked sick at the thought that perhaps he could've been responsible. "Do you think the fire is somehow connected?"

Taking three large strides, he was by my side again. Taking my hand in his, he brushed his lips against my knuckles. "No, I don't think so. My business hasn't crossed over into my personal life." Even as he said the words, I could see there was doubt there. He wasn't sure about that.

"And if it has?"

"Fuck, I don't know, Wren. What if it has?"

"It would mean that you've brought a shit-ton of attention to me."

He spread his arms out wide. "This is my life. This is the shit that happens to me."

I was starting to see that. What else was Bane keeping from me? "What else is happening with you and the club?"

My question caught him off guard because he just blinked at me. "What?"

"What else is happening? Dealers are getting killed. What else?"

"Nothing," he replied. "Cox is fucking breathing down my neck about these hits, and I have no explanation for them. I don't know who's taking my guys out. I just know I've been left with a huge hole in my operation." He turned his head to look at me. "Do you think the fire could have something to do with Hawk?"

I recoiled, physically jerking away even though it hurt. "Why would it have anything to do with him?"

He shrugged. "I don't know. I'm just speculating here."

I thought about his question, ready to deny it, but then I

remembered what Hawk had told me, that he'd gotten the money for Bane but hadn't told me *where* he'd gotten it from. Could this have something to do with him? "Hawk had more money to pay you back. When I told him I'd settled the debt, he'd seemed really upset. Like *really* upset. I didn't know why he'd reacted that way, but maybe…"

"You need to speak to him."

Numb. I felt so numb. I looked around for my phone, then remembered I must've lost it in the fire.

"Here." Bane handed me his phone, and I dialed Hawk's number.

"Bane," he answered half a dozen rings in.

"It's me," I replied, coughing a little to clear my ravaged throat.

"Wren? Why do you have Bane's phone?"

I shook my head. "It doesn't matter why I have his phone. I need to know something, and you're going to tell me." When he remained quiet, I inhaled deeply and let it out. "Where did you get that money? The money you were going to pay Bane back with?"

"Fuck, I can't say."

"You can say, Hawk, because my apartment was set on fire, and I'm in the hospital, so if it has something to do with that, then you better tell me or so help me God, I will flay the skin from your body."

"Jesus, *fuck*, Wren. Are you okay?"

"I'm still breathing. I haven't seen the doctor yet, though. I'm sure they'll have some more information for me."

"When did this happen?"

I looked at the clock hanging on the wall opposite my bed. "Maybe around six last night?"

"Oh shit, shit, *shit*," he mumbled.

"What have you done, Hawk? Tell me you haven't done anything stupid."

"What hospital are you in? I'll come to you."

Putting my hand over the mouthpiece, I asked, "Which hospital am I in?"

"Cedars-Sinai."

I relayed the information to my brother, hung up, and passed the phone back to Bane.

"What did he say?"

"He was shocked. He's coming down here, although whether or not we'll get any information out of him is a different story."

"Ms. Montana, is now a good time?"

I look up to see who'd spoken. There was a young man standing in the doorway. "Ah, sure."

With a confident nod, he strolled in. "Ms. Montana, my name's Doctor Watts. I treated you in the ER."

"Oh, hello."

"Do you remember what happened to you last night?"

I flexed my hands into weak fists, the motion pulling at the skin under the bandages on my forearms. "I'd taken a shower, and when I went to leave the bathroom, the door handle was red-hot. I managed to get out and saw that my building was on fire. I soaked some towels to wrap around myself, so I could try and escape." I sucked in a breath and looked at Bane, but his eyes were on the floor, and the muscle in his jaw was jumping with barely contained rage.

"The only place that wasn't completely engulfed was the living room, so I went in that direction. I…" I touched the side of my head where a throbbing suddenly made itself known.

"You fell and hit your head?" Doctor Watts provided gently.

I squeezed my eyes shut. "The path was clear. I couldn't have tripped."

"Being in a fire is scary stuff. There's a lot of smoke, and the heat plays tricks on your mind."

"I must've blacked out when I fell."

He nodded. "There are some minor burns to your forearms where the towel slipped off, but for the most part, your body was protected by the wet material. You have a bump on your head, too, which we've been monitoring but so far, so good."

"When can she get out of here?" Bane asked.

"This afternoon, I think. That'll give us enough time to make sure she's one hundred percent on her way to recovery." Watts glanced back at me and smiled. "You're very lucky. Ten other residents of your building were not."

"People died? What happened to the building?"

"The fire ripped through it," Bane told me. "It's gone."

I swallowed, mourning the loss of that shitty little apartment that I'd called home for a little over a decade.

"Well, I'll leave you to it. I'll let the orderly know you can have some ice cream to help soothe that voice of yours."

I touched the column of my throat as I watched him leave. I could've died in that fire. Ten people *had* died in that fire. I looked at Bane, who was studying me. I wasn't sure I wanted to know what was going through his head. Judging from his expression, they were murderous thoughts.

"How did I survive? How did I get out?"

"Andy pulled you out. He was in his car down on the street watching your building, remember?"

I did remember that. Thank Christ he was there. I shivered

thinking about what could've happened if he wasn't. I broke out in shivers—I was clearly suffering from delayed shock or something. Bane's arms wrapped around me, holding me tightly against his chest. Burying my face in his neck, I breathed in his cologne and clung to him. The tears leaked from my eyes without permission, but I gave myself over to them. He held me like that for as long as I needed, finally letting me go but not letting go of my hand.

"Where is he now?"

"At home. He got treated for some first-degree burns on his arms and hands, but he'll be just fine."

I nodded, settling back into the pillows.

"Want to watch some TV?" Bane asked.

"Only if you come and lay beside me on the bed." I patted the mattress, and Bane heaved himself onto it. The bed dipped under his weight, making me roll a little toward him.

"Are you comfortable?" he asked after settling me against his chest.

"Very." I yawned.

"Get some rest. I'll wake you when Hawk gets here."

25

Bane

WREN WAS FINALLY SLEEPING. SHE NEEDED TO REST IN order to recover. Those burns on her arms, although minor in the grand scheme of things, needed time to heal. She'd be sore, and the fact that she was hurt at all ate at me. I was supposed to protect her. She was mine to fucking protect.

My eyes had finally slid shut when I heard the door to Wren's room open. I cracked one eye open to see whether it was the doctor again or whether Hawk had finally had the balls to show. It was Hawk, and by the look on his face, he was about to fucking puke his guts up.

Good.

The fucker took Wren for granted. There wasn't a damn thing she wouldn't do for him, including getting into bed with a drug dealer, literally, to wipe his debts. Gently moving her from my chest, I stood up to my full height, grabbed Hawk by the front of his shirt, and hauled him outside. There was no way in hell I was letting him wake Wren right now.

The hallway was busy, nurses and doctors walking the halls. Looking around, I saw a public restroom across the way, one of those big ones meant to fit wheelchairs through the door. Stalking in there with Hawk, I shut and locked the door, then slammed him against the thick wood. The bastard still looked a little too comfortable, though, so I pinned him in place with my forearm, making sure breathing got a little tricky for him.

Hawk clawed at my arm, trying to break my hold, but he had no fucking chance. Enraged had just met its match, and I was so fucking beyond enraged that I didn't know what the fuck to do with that anger.

"What the fuck did you do?"

Hawk's mouth popped open, moving but no sound coming out. With a growl, I eased back a little, loosening his vocal cords.

"Is she okay?" he rasped.

I bared my teeth at him. "Did she fucking look okay?" I shouted the words into his face.

"Fuck, Bane." He clutched more tightly at the arm holding him up, tears beginning to pool in his eyes.

"Please tell me you aren't fucking crying like a little bitch right now."

"She's my sister."

"Yeah, well, you don't fucking treat her like you should. A man's job is to protect his sister, not put her in the fucking firing line."

"I know. I fucked up. I always fuck up."

Fuck me. If I couldn't handle blubbering women, I have no fucking chance in hell of handling a blubbering man. I broke our connection, stepping back and watching Hawk crumple to the floor.

"She could've died. She could've died. She could've died."
On and on he went. I wanted to tell him to shut the fuck up,
but those thoughts had run through my head too. Right now, I
could've been mourning her rather than helping her chase the
demons away.

"You're so fucking lucky she didn't die, Hawk," I barked. "I
swear on my fucking life if she had, you wouldn't be breathing
right now."

He blinked at my words. "You think this is my fault?"

"Who else's fucking fault would it be? You're the one who
makes deals with bookies you can't fucking pay, and do I need
to remind you what happened between us?" Raking my fingers
through my hair, I planted my hands on the edge of the sink and
bowed my head.

"Why are you with Wren right now?" he asked. I looked at
him in the reflection of the mirror.

I turned. "What?"

"Why are you with Wren right now?"

"Because she's mine for two weeks," I shot back, enjoying the
look on his face. The bastard didn't know what his sister had
done for him.

He swallowed, but his eyes—the same color as Wren's—
burned with rage. "What was the deal she agreed to?" Surging
to his feet, he came at me, grasping onto the front of my shirt.
"What the fuck did you make her do?"

"I didn't make her do anything. You did when you stole from
me. You did when you made a bet you couldn't cover. You did
by being in her life and laying your fucking kills at her door like
some proud goddamn Tomcat."

My words lashed at him, and he loosened his fingers. Stepping away, he bowed his head and asked, "What did she do to wipe my debts?"

"What do you think she did?" I wanted to hurt him. I wanted him to feel the pain I was feeling. I wanted him to feel the anguish that had coursed through my body when Andy told me Wren had been in a fire. I wanted him to emotionally bleed out in front of me.

"She's one of your whores?" he whispered.

I wanted to throw that in his face, but I held my tongue. "She's mine," I ground out. "She agreed to do whatever I want with her for two weeks to wipe your debt. She agreed to this because she fucking loves you, Hawk. She would do anything for you, and you fucking know it." Pushing off the edge of the sink, I straightened my shirt from where he'd wrinkled the shit out of it. "And now it's time for you to own your own shit. Where did you get the money to pay me back?"

All the color leached from his face. I expected him to shut down on me, but when he looked up, there was pure torture in his eyes. On a sigh, he said, "I went to Sanderson. He gave me the money."

Mother*fuck!* Without thought, I punched him in the face, the force of the strike spinning him around and leaving him sprawled on the floor, bleeding from the nose. Leaning down, I hissed, "You dumb fucking cunt. You have no idea what you've done, do you?"

Unlocking the door, I yanked it open and stalked back into Wren's hospital room.

WREN WAS DISCHARGED A FEW HOURS LATER. SHE
didn't ask whether Hawk had shown up, but she couldn't hide
the disappointment in her eyes. She wanted him there if only
to find out the truth. I'd already taken care of that for her, and
the thought of causing her any more pain was tearing me apart.
Getting shot point-blank in the chest was a more palatable way
to experience that kind of trauma.

An orderly wheeled her out to the car I had waiting, Dagger
behind the wheel this time. I slid in beside her, smiling when she
rested her head on my shoulder.

"Where are we going?"

"My place." When she opened her mouth to argue, I placed my
finger against her lips. "No arguing. Your place is condemned.
I can get you set up in an apartment, but I want you in my bed
with me for the next couple of days."

"Why?" she whispered.

"So I know you're safe. If I can touch you, smell you, taste
you, then I'll know you're okay."

I braced for the argument that always seemed to come right
after a declaration like that, but she was quiet. Thank fuck for
that.

"Have you heard from Hawk?"

"No," I replied darkly.

"I should call him to find out what happened to him."

I handed her my phone. "Call him now."

She did, dialing his number and pressing the device to her
ear. It rang out on the first attempt, and on the second, it went
straight to voicemail. Handing it back to me, she mumbled,
"He's not answering. I hope he's okay."

"He's probably just trying to come to terms with your

accident." I left it at that. I would tell her we'd had words, but I didn't want her to worry about him right now.

When Dagger pulled the car up to my building, we got out, and I took Wren up to the penthouse where I settled her in bed. Although she protested, I could see how tired she was. By the time I returned with a glass of water for her to take her medication, she was already asleep. I stood there for a moment just looking at her, wondering when I'd become such a fucking pussy.

I never watched women sleep.

Women never slept in my bed.

Except for Wren.

Fuck, she looked perfect in it too.

I just hoped she'd finally seen that I wasn't going to let her walk away from me. She kept throwing the two-week timeline at me like a shield she could use against her heart, but I knew she wouldn't walk away—she *couldn't* walk away—just like I couldn't walk away from her.

Sitting in the living room, I opened my laptop and started to work on the roster system for my Dolls. Since I wouldn't be returning to the office for a few days, I figured I had to get some shit done. The new Doll, Veronica, was starting tonight. Normally, I was there for every new employee's first shift, but with Wren still recovering, I didn't want to leave her. Dagger had everything in hand, though.

Beside me, my phone began to ring. "Yeah?"

"Mr. Rivera," Detective Cox drawled, the sound of her smug voice sending my blood pressure soaring.

"What do you want now, you useless cunt?"

"Such a way with words," she purred. "I was just calling to let you know we've secured that witness. Got their testimony, too. It's only a matter of time before we'll be taking Tony…" she paused and laughed, "… my apologies, *Dagger*, in for questioning. Your days are numbered, Mr. Rivera. I'd enjoy your girlfriend now while you can."

"You don't have shit on me, Cox, so why don't you go and try this shit on someone else. Dagger won't say a word to you even if you do haul him in for questioning."

"We'll see," she shot back cryptically and hung up. Dropping my phone to the couch cushion beside me, I glared at it then swiped it up again.

"Boss?" Dagger answered when I called him.

"Cox is threatening to bring you in for questioning."

"Want me to get rid of her?"

Read: Do you want me to put a bullet in her skull and dispose of the body where nobody would ever find it?

"No. If she goes missing, they'll know something is up. I think this witness thing is bullshit but look into it."

"You got it. Anything else?"

"Just tell me we're locked down tight on this."

"We are."

Running a hand through my hair, I blew out a breath. "Okay. Call me if you need me. I can be down at the club in ten if I'm needed."

"We're all good, boss." Dagger hung up, and I stared at the glowing screen of my phone. Fuck. I hated feeling out of control like this. Cox wasn't playing ball. She was my loose cannon, and having one of them was never a good fucking thing.

26

Wren

I STRETCHED OUT IN BANE'S BED, BLINKING AT THE warm light filtering through the large floor-to-ceiling windows in his bedroom. My arms were still sore, but nowhere near as sore as my pounding head. Rolling over, I looked for Bane, but his side of the bed was empty.

"Good morning," a dark voice rumbled. "I didn't want to wake you."

He strolled into the room in those gray sweats again. I let my eyes drift down his naked torso, biting my bottom lip.

"Don't look at me like that, Little Bird. I'm not going to be fucking you for a few days." He chuckled at my pout, then reached out and brushed the hair from my face as he sat on the edge of the bed. "How are you feeling?"

"Still a little sore." I touched my head, so he knew where.

Holding out his hand to me, he dropped a couple of white pills, then reached for the glass of water on the table beside the bed. "These should help. The doctor said if the pain got any worse to take you back in again."

"It's not getting worse." I washed the pills down my throat with a mouthful of water and handed him back the glass.

"Breakfast, or not feeling up to it? Mrs. Bellinger is already in the kitchen."

"Maybe something small?"

He nodded. "You got it. I'll tell her to ease off with the full spread, then." With a boyish grin, he left me alone with my thoughts.

I had to get a hold of Hawk to let him know I was okay and that I was staying with Bane for a little while. Jesus, this entire thing was fucked up. My apartment was gone, everything I'd ever owned destroyed by a fire. Hawk was still up to his eyeballs in the shit he consistently got himself into. My life was spiraling out of control on me here, and I had no fucking idea how to get off the ride.

The first tear that tracked down my cheek took me by surprise. The second soon followed, and I wiped at those traitorous things with the back of my hand. I didn't cry. Crying was for the weak when they had nothing left to do. I wasn't beaten, though. I wasn't giving up, I was just giving in at the moment.

"Wren, baby?" Bane asked when he caught me sniffling in bed.

I looked at him through tear-soaked lashes and cried a little harder. He was the only thing in my life that was going right. He came to me quickly, placing the cup of coffee he was holding down to wrap me in his arms. I clung to him, burying my face in his shoulder and letting out the tears that I had no hope of stopping anyway.

"I'm here for you."

I tightened my fingers around his bicep. His warmth leached into me, grounding me. "It's all gone."

"I know."

I looked up at him. "What am I supposed to do now?"

"You'll stay with me, or in one of my apartments," he added.

I began shaking my head. I didn't want to be alone right now. Being in a strange apartment, alone, even if it was supposed to be my new home, wasn't something I wanted to do. "Can I stay here with you instead?" I held my breath, wondering whether he would still want that.

"Thank fuck," he breathed, kissing the top of my head. "Yeah, you can stay here. I was prepared to fight you on going to one of my apartments. Wren, baby, I fucking need you here in my bed with me."

"I'll stay out of your way. You won't even know I'm here."

His dark eyes swallowed shadows. "What's mine is yours. If you want to fill my apartment with whatever the hell you want, go ahead."

My smile was weak, but my heart was bursting. "Thank you."

"Anything for you, Little Bird." He kissed me, the slow burn turning into something more. I clung to his shoulders, but he pulled away. "You need to rest." Reaching over, he grabbed the coffee. "Here. Drink this, and I'll get you some toast."

"Thank you." I took a sip of coffee and let out a sigh. "I might take a shower first if that's okay?"

"Of course, it's okay."

I slid out of bed and padded to the bathroom. I was in one of Bane's shirts, the hem hitting me mid-thigh. I closed the door and took off the shirt, standing in front of the mirror to see how bad the damage was. I was exhausted from everything, so I hadn't had a shower like I'd intended to last night. Both forearms were covered in waterproof dressings, the skin around the edges raw and red. I had soot on the side of my neck and some on my face that looked like it had been wiped away very quickly. The rest of my body was fine, and given what I learned about the fire, I was lucky to have survived with just some minor burns on my arms.

Starting up the shower, I got in and slowly began to wash myself, washing my hair at the same time. It smelled of smoke, and the reminder wasn't a pleasant one. Standing under the powerful spray for a while longer, I tipped my face up and shut my eyes. The perfectly temperature-controlled surge of water pounded against my skin, washing away every last trace of the fire.

"Wren?" Bane called from the door. I turned to face him, staring at him through the glass shower door.

His molten gaze traveled down my naked body, his jaw tightening when they reached my dressings. He stepped into the room and slowly began to strip out of his sweats. His cock sprang free, bobbing as he walked. Liquid heat pooled between my thighs. I shouldn't want him right now, not after everything my poor body had been through, but I couldn't deny it.

Prowling forward, he stepped into the shower with me, his broad shoulders filling the space. I braced myself for the same intensity I was used to with him, so when he framed my face gently with his hands, I let out a breathy sigh. He drifted his hands down my neck, over my shoulders, brushing the underside of my breasts on his way around my ribcage. When they got to my hips, my stomach began to flutter with anticipation.

"Sit down on the bench."

When I was in position, he dropped to his knees and spread my thighs. He stared hungrily at my pussy before his eyes roamed everywhere else. I sucked in a gasp when he leaned in and placed his mouth against my heated flesh, drawing another gasp when he parted my folds with his tongue.

Seeing this larger-than-life man between my legs and his broad shoulders pushing the limits of my flexibility did something to me on a primal level. A moan reverberated through the bathroom when he slid a finger inside me, pumping it in and out slowly. He lapped at me but never got close to the place where I wanted him. Each sweep of his tongue diverted at the last moment, each suck was not where I needed him.

Running my hands through his soaked hair, I held him in place, hoping that this time he would give me what I wanted. He slid another finger inside me, brushing against my G-spot and making my entire body quake. He continued to torture me like this for what felt like a lifetime until I was begging him for my orgasm. As soon as the word 'please' fell from my lips, he flicked his tongue over my clit, sending me down a spiral of pleasure that only intensified with the thrust of his fingers and the flick of his tongue. My hands tightened in his hair, making him groan as he lapped at me.

When my body finally stopped pouring pleasure into my blood, I looked at him. His mouth was curved into a small smile, one that told me just how much he liked that.

"I love your cunt."

"I love that you love it," I mumbled. My eyes tracked his body as he stood, his cock jutting out from his hips. It was a beautiful cock. Reaching forward, I wrapped my hand around it, tightening my grip a little when he tried to step back.

"Baby, no. You're still recovering. I didn't eat your irresistible pussy so I could get a blowjob."

"I know. I want to do this."

He seemed torn for a moment, then reclaimed the step he'd taken away. I held his gaze for a few moments, then dropped my eyes to his straining cock. Leaning forward, I ran my tongue over the head, tasting him. Bane threaded his fingers through my hair, holding me in place. I did this again and again, just a small flicker of sensation before finally sinking his shaft into my mouth.

He groaned, his eyes fluttering shut for a moment. Working my way back up, I hollowed out my cheeks and created the suction he needed. Placing my other hand around his cock, I pumped him while still sucking the crown, running the tip of my tongue through the slit at the top.

He hissed, a tumble of words falling from his lips that I couldn't decipher. I was too lost in him, in his taste, in his reaction to me.

"Hands behind you, Little Bird. I want to fuck your mouth."

A whimper escaped me, and I did as I was told. His grip on my head tightened, holding me steady as he slid his cock in and out of my mouth. He hit the back of my throat, my gag reflex kicking in. Each time I choked on his cock, he hissed out his pleasure.

"Yes, baby. Each time you choke, your throat tightens, and it feels fucking amazing."

Tears began to leak from the corners of my eyes, a stupid side effect of the gag reflex. I hoped he didn't stop. I didn't want him to stop. He continued to fuck my mouth until I tasted the saltiness of his pre-cum.

"Can I come down the back of your throat?" he asked.

I looked up at him and nodded. He grazed his knuckle over my cheek. "Good girl."

Saliva dripped from my mouth, increasing the ease with which he could glide into me. I swallowed, that same constriction in my throat making him groan.

"I love watching my cock disappear into your mouth. It's not as good as it being swallowed by your cunt, but it's a close second." I blinked at him, and he smiled. "You like it when I fuck your mouth?"

I nodded.

"Then touch yourself while I do it."

I snaked a hand down between my thighs, finding my pussy wet and wanton. Sliding my fingers over my clit, I detonated with the second touch, the combination of Bane's cock and dominating ways combining with my own ministrations, a heady mix. Bane thrust once more, hitting me deep at the back of my throat before coming. I waited until he withdrew a little before swallowing him down and cleaning him up.

"Fuck, Wren." He angled his hips away from me, and I pouted. With a chuckle, he brushed his fingers over my bottom lip. "This mouth is fucking amazing."

He helped me to stand and shut off the water. Wrapping me in a towel, he set me on the bathmat first before following behind me. I started to dry off, but Bane stopped me.

"Can I please do that?"

I looked at him and nodded. He took his time rubbing the terry cloth over my body, making sure everything was dry before drying my hair too.

"I don't have a hairdryer, but I'll send Mrs. Bellinger to get one for you today along with some new clothes."

"You don't have to do that," I said weakly.

He smirked. "As much as I would love to have you walking around naked the entire time, it's not really going to work with Mrs. B wandering around here, too. Let her buy you some clothes. You can even tell her what kind of things you like."

I relented with a kiss. "Okay."

Picking up the shirt I'd been wearing, he tossed it in the laundry hamper along with his sweats, then scooped me up in his arms and took me into his closet. I looked around in awe. It was fucking amazing in here. One side was filled with those expensive suits he wore, and the other was filled with casual clothes I'd never seen him wear.

"Pick whatever you'd like to put on," he said as he pulled open a drawer and removed a pair of sweats—blue this time. I took a moment to enjoy the show, then went straight to his business shirts. I took a black one off the hanger and drew it over my arms. Bane eased my hands out of the way when I began with the buttons, taking over the job for me.

"You can wear some of my boxer shorts while you wait for underwear."

I stepped into them, feeling completely unsexy. I turned around to say as much to Bane, but he kissed me before the words could come out.

"You are so fucking irresistible. I want to take another taste of that cunt of yours..." he flexed his hips into mine, and I gasped, "... but Mrs. B is waiting for us." He kissed my lips, then my nose, then my cheeks. I stared at the man who kept showing me these different sides of him. He was hard and unyielding, but there was such tenderness there too.

Taking my hand, he took us into the kitchen where Mrs. Bellinger was cutting up some fruit. She gave me a warm smile.

"Mr. Rivera told me what happened, sweetheart. I am so happy you're okay."

"Thank you." Having someone care about my well-being was such a new concept.

"Mrs. B, could you please purchase a hairdryer today as well as some essentials for Wren? Her apartment and everything in it was destroyed."

"Of course," she beamed. "You're a size eight?" I nodded. "Just like my Carla, then. I'll have some clothes for you in a few hours." She placed a couple of fruit cups onto the counter in front of us. "Something light for your stomach."

"How's Andy?" I asked, suddenly remembering that he'd rescued me from that fire. "I'd like to thank him."

"He's okay. I've given him a few days off, but the bastard will probably be downstairs waiting for me, anyway."

"You're going to work today?" I asked. *Fuck, that sounded needy and desperate.* "I mean, of course, you're going to work. Why wouldn't you."

Bane tipped my chin up so I would look at him. "I won't go if you need me here. I can still get shit done in my office."

My heart pounded painfully in my chest. I didn't want to be alone. I opened my mouth to tell him as much but then shut it. I was safe here. I was in a building that was secure and had doormen. "No, you should go."

"Are you sure?"

I plastered on a fake smile. "I've never had to rely on a man to keep safe before."

He framed my face in his hands and kissed me hard. "Please

don't talk about other men you've been with," he growled.

I bobbed my head. "You should go to work, though."

"What will you do?"

I looked around his apartment, eyeing the giant TV. "Netflix?"

27

Bane

FUCK. ALL MY FUCKING SENSES WERE ON HIGH ALERT.
My anger had come out full-force, leaving my employees diving
out of my way. Rachel was the first to pick up on my mood as
I strolled into the club.

"Drink, Mr. Rivera?" she asked, already placing a glass of
whisky onto the counter.

I took the glass with a curt nod, then did a lap of the club.
I had six girls on the poles, each of them with a couple of
gentlemen watching the show. It was mid-morning on a
Saturday. Things weren't going to heat up until later tonight,
but I did have a bachelor party coming through the doors at
four. Some rich daddy's boy was tying the knot and wanted to
have one last fling. The guy getting married was a member, so
I had Dagger organize a twelve-hour pass for the rest of his
party.

I wandered through to the private rooms, checking to see

everything was in order. Mostly it was, except for one room which had been used and trashed. The leather chair had been tipped over onto its side and the seat slashed, the cupboard with the floggers, paddles, and whips in disarray. Even the drawer where the condoms and lube were held had been upended. What in the actual fuck had happened?

Palming my phone, I dialed Dagger's number.

"Boss?"

"What the fuck happened in four?"

"Boss?" he replied.

"Get your ass down here." I hung up, letting anger fill my veins. When Dagger finally appeared, he looked a little flustered, which was odd. The guy was made from fucking stone. I gestured to the room, and he stepped inside, looking around.

"It wasn't like this at closing last night."

"So when did it happen?"

He pulled out his phone, clicking into the club's log system. All the Dolls had access cards to get into the rooms. Each time they swiped to gain entry, it got logged with a time stamp.

"This morning," Dagger replied. "According to the system, the room was accessed by Veronica at ten o'clock."

"Get her in my office. Now!" I bellowed. "And fucking get this room cleaned up." I stalked off, slamming my empty glass onto the counter as I passed the bar. Jogging up the stairs, I strode into my office, clutching the top of the chair behind my desk, bowing my head and breathing in deeply.

Stalking over to the window, I looked down over my club, watching one of the girls on the pole for a moment. I didn't know how fucking long I had to wait for Veronica to get here, so I sat down and started on some work while I waited.

Not long later, I jerked my head up when there was a soft knock on the door. "Come," I barked, standing and buttoning up my suit jacket. Veronica walked in with her head bowed and a slight limp.

Rounding the desk, I tipped her chin up, so I could see her face properly. "What the fuck happened to you?" I demanded, keeping her face turned up toward me. Tilting it from side to side, I took in the black eye that was already forming and the cut on her lip. Her gaze dropped back to the floor as soon as I let her go.

"I got mugged last night after my shift," she replied in a hoarse voice.

Bunching my hands into fists at my side, I stepped away from her and began to pace. "What happened?"

I fucking hated this. These women were mine to protect.

"About a block away from my place."

"You walked here last night?"

She shrugged, rolling her shoulders forward. "I take the bus, but the stop is about a block from my apartment. That's when it happened."

"Jesus *fuck!*"

Veronica flinched when I raised my voice, and I swallowed down the urge to scream and yell out all my frustrations.

"Are you okay? Any other injuries beside the shiner and the busted lip?" Fuck, she wasn't going to be able to work for a while—not until she healed. Men didn't find bruises pretty.

"Fine, physically."

"What did they take? Did you get a good look at them?"

"My bag was stolen. I tried to snatch it back, and my phone fell out. I grabbed that and dialed 911. They were long gone by the time the cops got to me."

"Was your swipe card in there?"

She bobbed her head. "Yeah, and all the tips I made last night."

Fuck. "How much did you make?" I asked, reaching into my wallet.

She looked at me with wide eyes. "You don't have to do that, Mr. Rivera."

"Don't fucking argue with me, Veronica. How much did you make?"

She bit her bottom lip and winced. "About three hundred."

I pulled five hundred-dollar bills and handed them to her.

"This is too much, Mr. Rivera."

"The extra is to get yourself some makeup or some shit to cover that black eye. I can't have you working here with a split lip, though. You'll have to take some time off to heal. I'll pay you even though you aren't coming in."

"Seriously?"

I nodded. "I look after my Dolls, Veronica."

She stared for a minute, then walked over to me, dropping to her knees and reaching for my belt.

I caught her hands, stopping her. "What are you doing?"

"Thanking you."

Fuck, some of these women were messed-up. Or maybe it was me who was messed-up. Before Wren, I would've sat back and enjoyed the perks of my work, but not now. I'd lost count of the number of women who had thrown themselves at my feet and sucked my cock because they thought this was what I needed to see to ensure their gratitude.

Helping Veronica to stand, I turned her around and shoved her gently toward the door. "You can thank me by getting back here as soon as you can. Call Dagger if you need anything."

The look of absolute shock on her face irritated me. After a moment, she slipped out the door. I turned to watch her leave, seeing some of the other Dolls hugging her or squeezing her hand in encouragement.

"What was that about?" Dagger asked.

"She got mugged last night." I turned to face him. "Her swipe card was stolen along with her tip money."

"*Fuck.*"

"Yeah." Running a hand through my hair, I blew out a breath. "I need you to fucking find out who accessed that room, Dagger." We didn't have surveillance cameras inside the club for obvious reasons, so that only left the half-dozen external cameras around the club. "Go through the footage. And when you find out who fucked me over, I'm going to fuck them over."

"Yes, boss."

With Dagger gone, I sat down again and rested my head back against the headrest of my chair. Why couldn't things go fucking smoothly? At least I had Wren. Everything was right with her. Picking up my phone, I went to dial her number, then remembered she'd lost her phone in the fire. I dialed Dagger's number.

"Yes, boss."

"Can you get me a new phone?"

"Boss?"

"Wren lost hers in the fire. Can you get a replacement and everything else we need to go with it?"

"Yes, boss."

Hanging up, I placed my phone on the desk and opened up my laptop, clicking into the scheduling for the upcoming month. I made a start on it last night, but I still needed to put a little more thought into it. About an hour had gone by when there was a knock on my door.

"Enter."

Keeping my eyes on my work, I didn't acknowledge who was standing there until they cleared their throat. Looking up, I bit back the snarl.

"What the fuck are you doing here, Syndy?" And how the fuck had she gotten past Dagger. Fuck, I sent him out for the phone. "Well?"

"How's your girlfriend?" she sneered. "It's a pity about that fire."

I narrowed my eyes at her. "What do you know about her?"

Syn walked further into the office, her short dress riding up with the movement. She made no attempt to smooth it down, leaving me with an eyeful of her snatch. Hopping up, she perched on the edge of my desk beside me, and I shoved my seat back to keep both eyes on her. She slid her foot onto my chair, the toe of her heel touching my dick.

"I know that you've fucked her. I just don't understand what she has that I don't."

"A lot of things, Syn. A fucking clue for one."

Rage bubbled from her. "I love you, Bane. Why can't you see that? We're perfect for one another."

"How do you figure?"

Sliding off the edge of the desk, she dropped to her knees between my legs. "We're good together, daddy."

"You know what you're good for? Sucking dick."

"Is that what you want, daddy? You want me to suck your dick?"

BIRD

Thankfully, my dick didn't stir. That was because only Wren would satisfy me now. She ran her hands up my thighs, inching her hands closer to my crotch. I watched her through narrowed eyes. "How do you know about Wren?"

She smiled. "I know a lot about your little girlfriend, actually. I know she lived in a shitty little apartment. I know she wears plain cotton underwear. Seriously, Bane, how can you fuck a woman who enjoys wearing plain cotton underwear?"

"It's what's inside that underwear that counts," I replied, my shoulders tightening as she brushed her hands against my cock. Syn seemed to know an awful lot about my Little Bird, and I planned on getting all that information out of her.

"I also know that she was supposed to die in that fire. If it weren't for Andy swooping in like a fucking hero, she'd be dead, and we'd be together."

Anger surged through me, stinging all my nerve endings and making the blood pound in my ears. I grabbed her arm as I stood, the chair rolling back and slamming into the wall. Hauling her backward, I pressed her against the desk, bending her back and grabbing her other arm so I could hold her in place.

"What did you do, you little cunt?"

Syn's eyes widened, so I could see the whites all the way around. "Bane, daddy, what are you doing?"

"You tried to kill Wren."

"I tried to save you from a life of boring sex with her."

I blinked at Syn's words.

Was she seriously so delusional she thought I would want her?

Reaching into my desk drawer, I pulled out my Glock and pointed it at her temple. Syn squeaked at the pressure. I *so* wanted to pull the trigger.

She had put Wren's life in fucking danger.

She could've died in that fire.

I could've lost her.

The dark recesses inside my head, the ones that housed the monster of my rage began to stir. My vision started to blackout, and I had to blink to get it back.

"Don't kill me, Bane," Syn begged. "Please. I'm sorry."

I ground the barrel in a little harder, shouting, "You tried to *kill* her!"

Tears sprang in her eyes, and she said, "I just wanted you to look at me like you look at her. I want you to love me like you love her."

I let the monster come out a little more, inviting it closer with a crooked finger. That oily malevolence filled my veins, stripping the humanity from me and leaving only instincts. And my instincts were telling me to put a fucking bullet in the brain of this woman. She was a threat. She had proved that. Syn tried to fight me off, but I dug my fingers into her arm, shaking her a little to get her to focus.

"What else have you done, Syn?" I asked. "And don't even think about lying to me."

Sweat beaded on her brow, and she swiped her tongue over her lips. "Please. I want you."

"What. Did. You. Do!" I shook her again, knocking the words I needed to hear from her out in a tumble.

"Room number four was our room," she hissed, the tears already drying on her cheeks. "*Ours.* Nobody else should be able to use it."

"You mugged Veronica?"

The smile that pulled up her mouth was venomous. "Is that

the little bitch's name? Yeah, I stole it from her. I needed a way to get in here."

Fuck. Jesus *fucking* Christ, this woman was unhinged.

"Boss, I got that phone for—"

The words died on Dagger's tongue when he saw the scene in front of him. Dropping the bag he was carrying, he pulled out his Glock and held it level with Syndy's head, coming at her from the other side. I guessed my man had a little problem with the woman who sliced open his thigh too.

Her breathing kicked up another notch, the pending violence thickening the air and feeding my monster.

"She set the fire at Wren's apartment. She's also the one who mugged Veronica and stole her access card."

Dagger slid his finger off the guard and onto the trigger. "Want me to get rid of her?"

"Please!" she begged, all the color draining from her face. "I just wanted you to see that we are meant to be together."

"Not here," I replied. "Take her somewhere nobody will *ever* find her." Flipping the safety back into position, I placed my gun back into the desk drawer and sat.

"Please. No. *Please!*" Syn begged as Dagger removed her from the room.

"Shut her up. We don't need people hearing her scream."

With a determined nod, he brought the butt of the gun down on her temple and knocked her the fuck out. When they were gone from my office, I started to pace. My body was being battered by a thousand thoughts of revenge. I balled my hands into fists before releasing them, flexing my fingers.

Fuck, I was strung so tight right now.

She had almost killed my Little Bird.

The need to see her, to know she was all right was like a sledgehammer to my chest. My heart was actually racing as I snatched up my phone and called Mrs. Bellinger's number.

"Mr. Rivera?" she answered.

"Put Wren on." There was a muffled thump, then Wren's voice came over the line.

"Bane?"

"I need you. I need to see you."

"Okay."

"I'm going to send Andy to get you, okay? He'll bring you to the club."

"Okay," she replied.

Fuck, I wondered if she could sense this darkness inside me, the one that lingered and needed to be let out.

"He'll be there in ten minutes."

"Okay."

Hanging up, I dialed Andy.

"Boss?"

"Go and get Wren. Bring her to me at the club."

"Yes, sir."

I sat my ass back down, afraid that if I were on my feet, I would sprint to my apartment to collect her myself. I couldn't leave, though. I couldn't leave my club unmanned on a Saturday night, but I could bring my Little Bird to me.

28

Wren

AS I STEPPED FROM THE CAR, MY NERVES GOT THE better of me. Bane had asked that I come to the club. He'd sounded so strained on the phone, struggling with something I had no idea about.

"Would you like me to walk you in, Wren?" Andy asked through the rearview mirror.

"Thank you, but no." I put my hand on the door handle, hesitating. "I never got to say thank you, Andy."

His brows shot up. "What for?"

"For saving me from that fire. If you hadn't risked your life, I wouldn't be here right now."

He turned around in his seat to look at me. "I should be the one thanking you." I cocked my head to the side, unsure what he was getting at. "I've worked for Bane for near on a decade now. I've never, not once, seen him like this with a woman."

"Like what?"

"He's never been this attentive to one woman before."

I felt a flush of heat creep up my cheeks. "I'm…" I actually had no words. "I…"

"Trust me, Wren, you're a good influence on him. I hope that continues."

Shaking my head, I smiled and got out of the car. The bouncer waved me inside straight away, and I stepped into the luxurious Dollhouse. Bane was standing by the bar, his eyes on me. His gaze was so intense that a shiver tracked down my spine. He took a sip from his glass of whisky and stalked toward me, making my entire body light up.

He claimed my mouth in a kiss, sweeping his tongue into my mouth, pressing himself against me. He tasted like wood smoke and vanilla, the aftertaste of leather hitting me. He ran his hand across my hip before dipping it down between my legs.

With a growl, he stepped away from me, leaving me panting. Wrapping his arm around my waist, I noticed a lot of the women staring at me as he led me past the stripper poles to the back of the club. I wondered how many of them had given him a blowjob, the surge of jealousy taking me by surprise. Shoving that feeling away, I took in the half-dozen doors lining the hallway Bane was leading me down. Each with a number on them, and beside the door was a device that looked like you could swipe a card through the reader located to the left.

Bane stopped at room number five and reached into his pocket. He pulled out a credit card-sized piece of plastic and ran it through the reader. The light blinked green, and he opened the door. I stepped in after him, my eyes bulging when I saw what was in there.

"This is the most intense of the BDSM spaces," he said, his

voice dark and hungry. He started to point at something called a Saint Andrews Cross—a huge X-shaped structure with restraints on each of the four points. I walked toward it, fascinated by the concept. Goosebumps spread over my skin in a fevered rush as I imagined myself up there.

Bane wrapped his hand around the back of my neck, pressing the rest of his hard body against me. "I could imagine you on there, Little Bird. Your pussy glistening for me. Your nipples taut and desperate for my tongue."

I turned my head slightly. "Yes."

Uncurling his fingers, Bane turned me around and kissed me. "We have plenty of time for that. Let me show you what else is in here."

There was a spanking bench, something called a queening chair, bars and stocks suspended from the ceilings, a sex swing, and an array of whips, chains, paddles, and cuffs. The main attraction, though, was a giant four-poster bed with anchor points all over it.

"Want to try anything?" he asked me, running his hand suggestively over my ass. My eyes darted to the spanking bench. Bane had used his belt on me that first time we were together, and although I thought I'd hate it, I'd enjoyed the fuck out of it. Lifting my hand, I pointed at it.

"Good girl," he purred. "Get undressed for me, Little Bird, and I'll give you the best orgasm of your life."

With shaking hands, I unbuttoned my new shorts and took off the shirt Mrs. Bellinger had bought me. Bane sucked in a hiss when he saw the matching navy lace bra and panties set.

With a groan, he said, "I need to give Mrs. B a raise." His hands roamed over my skin, cupping my breasts and tweaking my nipples. I gasped when he twisted one hard.

"Your nipples would look amazing in clamps," he said softly into my ear. Biting down on my earlobe, he walked toward the cupboard hanging on the wall and opened it. Selecting something on a long chain, he brought it back with a smirk. "Take off your bra."

Reaching around the back, I unhooked my bra and let it fall to the floor. Bane growled as he stared at my breasts already aching with need. He held out the clamps to me, letting me see them.

"They'll hurt a little bit, but the good kind of hurt," he said, rubbing his thumb over my already hard nipples. "Do you trust me?" At my nod, he kissed me hard, thrusting his tongue into my mouth and dominating all my senses. I sucked in a hiss when the first clamp went on, the pain only lasting for a moment before becoming a dull throb. He slid the other one in place, then trailed his hand down the length of chain that connected them. The metal was cold against my stomach, the two—the heat in my nipples and the cold of the chain—making me see the pleasure in this.

"Take off your panties while I choose something to spank you with."

Hooking my thumbs into the sides, I shimmied out of the flimsy material and kicked them off to the side. I watched Bane peruse the cupboard once more. His strong fingers skimmed over the leather floggers and whips before finally settling on a leather paddle shaped like a love heart. He brought it over to me.

"Lots of surface area on this one," he told me. "So the pain won't be there. If you want something stronger, let me know."

I gulped, then followed him to the spanking bench. It was shaped like a thin park picnic table, and I wondered how I was supposed to get myself onto it.

"Staddle it," he said, pointing to two lower padded pieces. "Your hands and knees go either side, so you're on all fours."

I got myself into position, the hanging chain from the clamps creating a delicious burn in my breasts. Bane ran his hand over my bare ass, slapping it quickly. I sucked in a gasp, then moaned when he rubbed away the sting.

"You're going to enjoy this, Little Bird," he purred, striking me again with his bare hand. I bit my lip, knowing the moan that was trying to come out would sound too desperate. He took his time touching me, warming up my skin. It relaxed me, so I wasn't expecting the first strike with the paddle. It sounded worse than it felt, but the combination of those two things made me wet. He soothed away the slight pain with his hand, then kissed the base of my spine.

"I think we might need something a little more... fun."

I watched him return to the cupboard and pull out a thinner paddle. He tested it on his hand and smiled when he saw me watching. "I'm going to make you feel so good, baby." Strolling back over to me, I licked my lips when I saw the bulge behind his zipper. Reaching around, he tugged the chain on the clamps a little, making me suck in a surprised breath. Lust shot straight to my pussy. With a wicked smile, he did it again. He kissed me on the mouth, then went back to my ass.

The first strike with the new paddle was intense but oh so good. Bowing my head, Bane kissed the spot he'd just struck, then dragged a finger through my wet folds.

"You like that, Little Bird?"

I nodded. "So much."

"More?"

"Please," I replied on a whimper.

Bane lined up for another hit and another and another until I felt my arousal slipping down the inside of my thigh. With each hit, he would soothe away the sting and prepare me for the next. Given Bane's childhood and his experience with relationships, this darker side to his personality kind of made sense. He craved control like I craved the freedom of submission. Although he seemed to be enjoying this, I didn't think he needed it all the time. Maybe just when things were fucking out of control in his life. I think the fire and me almost dying was the catalyst this time.

The next thing I knew, Bane was helping me off the bench and lowering me onto the bed. I had no idea how many strikes he had delivered or how long I was on the bench, but by the ache in my elbows and knees, it had to have been quite a while.

"You kind of went into a subspace there, Little Bird," he murmured into the crook of my neck as he spooned me from behind. He was naked now, his skin hot against mine, his cock hard between my ass cheeks.

"Where?"

"Think of it like nirvana. You were lost in the pleasure I was giving you."

"Oh…"

"Did you like that?" I nodded. "I liked making your perfect ass pink." He slid his hand between my legs, rubbing that arousal over my pussy. "I need to fuck you, Wren."

I looked around at the other furniture and wondered what he had chosen next. Tipping my face back to him, he shook his head. "Here on the bed. I want to fuck you here. I want to lose myself in you here."

I nodded as Bane curled my legs up to my chest, making me into a ball. He played his fingers through my pussy again, but this time his movements were restricted. I then felt the blunt tip of his cock nudging me. I went to open my legs, but he placed a firm hand on my thigh and pushed it back down. "Leave it there. It'll make your cunt tighter."

I let out a sigh when he pushed all the way into me. The sensation was strange, the desire to open my legs to give him space to thrust was something I had to fight. Bane groaned and bit the back of my neck gently, his free hand coming up to wrap around the base of my neck. And when he began to thrust inside me, I got it. There was more pressure there, more friction. I felt each and every slide of his cock through my entire body, making it hum with pleasure.

Bane tugged at the chain still attached to the clamps, making me gasp. He fucked me harder then, savagely taking from me what he needed.

"Fuck, Bane, harder, please," I begged, already feeling my orgasm coming. He tugged at the chain again, sending me hurtling over the edge. Bane followed me with a roar, his thrusts slowing until he finally stopped. Pulling out of me, he rolled my body onto my back and kissed me as he released the clamps. A moan escaped my mouth as the sensation flooded back, and he rubbed my clit once more, making me come again.

Holy *fuck*. When I finally came back down, I let out a breath, my eyes drifting shut.

"Thank you."

I turned my head toward him. "For what?"

"Handing me control. I needed it tonight."

I touched his face, tracing my thumb across his lips. "What's happening?"

With a frown, he rolled over onto his back and stared up at the ceiling. "Just work shit."

I sat up. "Plus my shit, right?"

"What?"

"I almost died in that fire."

He scrubbed a hand over his jaw, staring at me. "Yeah. Losing you would've broken me, Little Bird. I know this is a limited-time thing, but I don't know how I'm going to be able to let you go if you do decide to end it. You're in my blood now, in my heart."

I shut my eyes and let his words settle over me. "I don't plan on going anywhere, Bane. You've awoken something inside me, something that I'm quickly becoming addicted to, too."

He stared at me for the longest time, feeling him down deep in my soul.

Shit, had I said too much? I didn't think so. He was as consumed by me as I was by him.

Rolling off the bed, he helped me to stand. "There's a bathroom through there," he said, pointing to a door that had been painted the same deep red as the room. "Take a shower. I'll wait for you here."

He caressed my ass gently. "How's this feel?"

"A little tender."

"I love the pink blush on your skin." He kissed one cheek, murmuring, "There's some numbing cream in the top drawer of the vanity. Put some on after the shower. It'll help"

With a nod, I walked into the bathroom and shut the door.

Pulling the drawer open, I found the cream and placed it on the marble vanity, then took a quick shower. After toweling off and applying some of the numbing cream, I got dressed and found Bane sitting on the edge of the bed, back in his suit once more.

"I've asked Andy to take you back to my apartment," he said, putting his phone back into his pocket. "It's going to be a late night here."

"Okay."

"I'll be home as soon as I can, though. I need to be inside you again, Wren. Fuck, it's like I'm an addict, and I need another hit already."

I smoothed the frown away from his face with my fingertips. "I'm not going anywhere."

"I know. You're the one thing I can count on now." Capturing my hand, he kissed my fingers and stood, taking me with him.

I looked around the room. "What about…" I waved at the messed-up bed and the paddles still out.

"We have a cleaning staff. All I have to do is press the button on this side of the wall, and someone will be in here to sanitize everything for the next couple to enjoy."

Hitting the button on the wall as we left, Bane walked me back through the club. A lot of his dancers were looking at me strangely, but I ignored them. I turned my head when I heard shouting, though. There were a bunch of guys enjoying one of the dancers who was simulating a blowjob on one of them.

"Bachelor party," Bane told me. "Things might get a little crazy here tonight."

As he passed the bar, he told the bartender to have a whisky ready for him when he returned. She nodded at him, then smiled at me.

Outside, Andy was waiting for me at the curb.

Bane claimed my mouth in a bruising kiss. "I'll see you tonight, right?"

"I'll be the one in your bed," I whispered back, enjoying the way heat flashed in his eyes.

"Fuck yeah, you will." Giving me one last kiss, he helped me in the car, then stalked back inside.

"Returning to Bane's?" Andy asked me when he was settled back into his seat.

"Please, Andy. Thank you."

He shot me a smile and pulled out into traffic. Given the time and the location, the streets were choked with cars, but Andy moved swiftly through the congestion, finding pockets and spaces to slide into to get us where we needed to go.

I'd just settled back into the chair when the car suddenly swerved into a car parked against the curb. With my pulse pounding in the back of my throat, I pulled myself forward to find Andy slumped over in the driver's seat, blood blooming on the front of his shirt. *What the fuck just happened?* I looked out the window to see if I could see the shooter, then screamed when someone opened the rear door and grabbed me by the back of the shirt. I was yanked from the car, landing heavily on the sidewalk where a man stood over me. With a cold smile that made fear skitter down my spine, he pulled me up and shoved a bag over my head. The last thing I saw before being manhandled into another car was Andy's lips moving slowly and blood bubbling from the corner of his mouth.

29

Bane

I DIALED ANDY'S NUMBER AND PUT THE CALL ON speaker. He hadn't texted me to let me know he'd dropped Wren off at my apartment, and the guy was notorious for following orders to the letter. Hanging up, I tried again, but it simply went to voice mail. Fuck, where the hell was he?

"Everything all right, boss?" Dagger asked as he strolled into my office.

"Yes. No. Fuck." I ran my hands through my hair. "I don't know. I can't get a hold of Andy."

"What was he supposed to be doing?"

"Dropping Wren off, but that was an hour ago."

Dagger pressed his lips together in a tight line. "I'll follow it up." He turned to leave, but I stopped him.

"What happened with Cox? Did she speak to you?"

He peered at me over his shoulder. "No, boss," he replied, leaving me in the room alone with nothing but my fear. If something happened to Wren, I didn't know what I'd do. But this was the risk in getting attached to one woman. They could be used as a weapon against you.

Standing, I began to pace, running my fingers through my hair as a new reality settled over me—one where Wren could be hurt.

Digging into my pocket, I pulled out my phone and dialed Hawk's number. It had almost rung out when he finally picked up.

"Bane," he said softly.

"Have you heard from Wren?"

"No. Why?"

I bit the inside of my cheek, stopping myself from screaming until I was hoarse. "If you hear from her, let me know."

"H-How is she? Is she staying with you?"

"She's fine." I hung up and contemplated throwing the damn phone across the other side of the room. I refrained from the outburst, though. I needed the damn thing to keep in contact with Dagger.

When the phone rang, I punched the green phone icon and put the device to my ear.

"Bane Rivera," a man said.

"Who the fuck are you?"

"I'm the man who's been picking your dealers off one by one. I'm also the one who sent that fucking pitbull of a bitch, Cox, after you."

My hands balled into fists. There was only one man who had that kind of power. "Sanderson," I growled. "What do you want?"

"I wanted to talk about that little piece you're currently fucking.

She's got a fucking nice mouth, doesn't she?"

My shoulders tensed at the mention of Wren. "What do you want?"

"I want you to get the fuck out of the drug trade in No Man's Land."

I bit back a laugh. "Why would I want to do that? You might be killing my guys, but you forget that those fuckers are easily replaced."

"True, but I have a feeling replacing the woman isn't."

I paused, all the air evacuating out of my lungs. "What did you say?"

"You heard me. Replacing her is going to be hard, although maybe not so much for you. You have all those women at your disposal. Surely, having one gone won't make much of a difference."

"Where is she?" The words were ripped forcefully from my mouth. I didn't want to ask the question. I didn't fucking want to know that he had her, my Little Bird.

"She's safe… *for now*. But her well-being really does hinge on your cooperation."

My anger surfaced quickly, the switch of my self-control getting fucking flipped. Picking up the empty tumbler from my desk, I threw it at the wall and watched as the crystal shattered.

"Where the fuck is she?"

"I'm going to text you an address. You are to meet me there tomorrow at nine in the morning. And don't try to go there now. I'm holding her somewhere else until our meeting."

I clenched my jaw. "I want proof of life."

He was silent for a moment, then there was a beep. Pulling the phone away from my ear, I opened the picture that had come through and barked out a curse. Wren was sitting on a chair, a blindfold over her eyes, her wrists and ankles attached to cuffs. Blood was spattered over her shirt, neck, and face. There was blood running from her nose and somewhere near her hairline. She was slumped over, her shoulders and head rolled forward like she was unconscious. Putting the phone back to my ear, I snarled, "If you harm another hair on her head, I will *end* you."

Sanderson chuckled. "Whether or not I harm her again is completely up to you, Rivera. You know what I want. If you want your bitch back, you *will* give me what *I* want." There was a click, the line going dead. I clutched at the phone, resisting the urge to throw it against the wall as well. *Fuck!*

Sanderson wanted me out, but I wasn't getting out of No Man's Land. I clawed my way up in the business. I wasn't going to let some punk-ass bitch like Sanderson dictate what I could and couldn't do. But I also couldn't let him take his fucking rage out on Wren. I unlocked my phone once more, navigating through my call log until I found the number I needed and hit call.

30

Wren

MY ENTIRE FACE WAS THROBBING IN TIME WITH my heartbeat, the steady thump bringing me out of unconsciousness slowly. I tried to open my eyes, but there was something over them, my lashes brushing against the rough material. Next, I tried to move my hands and legs, but I could only move an inch or so. It felt like a rope was wrapped around my wrists and ankles, keeping me bound to the chair.

Licking my lips, I tasted blood and wondered where the hell it had come from. Was it from the sharp pain on my forehead, or was I bleeding somewhere else?

"Wren, stay still," a familiar voice said.

I froze in place, hope settling in my chest with a warmth I wasn't sure I was ready for. "Hawk?" I whispered. "What are you doing here?"

Was he tied up beside me?

Did this have something to do with him and his debts?

"Hawk?" I pushed when he remained quiet.

"I'm so sorry, Wren."

I felt a frown form on my face. "Sorry for what? What have you done now?" My stomach sank when he hesitated. Jesus Christ, what had he done? "Does this have something to do with where you got that cash for Bane from?"

"I'm sorry," was all he said.

Shaking my head, I told him, "It doesn't matter. We'll both get out of this."

Fingers brushed against my cheek, and I jerked back. "Only one of us will get out of this alive," he said, kissing me on the cheek. The heat of his body disappeared just as suddenly as it had appeared, and dread wrapped itself around my heart.

"Hawk?" I screamed. "Hawk!"

My words echoed around a room that sounded as if it was empty, the tears that were sitting unshed in my eyes finally falling free.

What the fuck had he done?

Why was I tied to a chair?

My tears turned into sobs that hurt me right down deep in my soul. Fear was my only friend now, and I did the only thing I could do. I clung to it.

I WAS AWAKENED AGAIN WITH A PUNCH TO THE stomach. Pain made my vision blurry, the sound of my desperate breaths the only thing I could hear. Gasping in large lungfuls of air, I thrashed in my chair, trying to move my body and convince my lungs to get with the fucking program.

"Hold her steady," said a man.

Hands were suddenly on my shoulders, pinning me back to the chair. I tensed, waiting for the next strike. Instead of intense pain, I blinked against the light of the room as my blindfold was removed. My eyes went straight to the man who looked like a poor imitation of Tony Soprano, his large belly tucked into a shirt that was straining against the buttons. His suit pants were loose, the cuffs pooling around a pair of cheap loafers.

My eyes flickered over to who was standing beside him next.

"Hawk?" I asked. What in the actual fuck was happening? He wouldn't look at me. Instead, he kept his gaze locked on the concrete floor under his feet.

"Your brother works for me now," the other man said. "Don't you, Hawk?"

"Yes, sir," he said softly.

Swallowing down on my dry throat, I demanded, "What have you done, you piece of shit?"

My brother finally looked at me, sorrow and regret passing over his face before quickly being replaced by cold indifference I'd never seen before. "I work for Sanderson. It's how I got the money to pay Bane back."

"Your brother has been quite useful, actually. He knew exactly where you'd be."

I frowned. "What's he talking about?"

Sanderson chuckled. "I've been trying to get Bane off my turf for over ten years. The bastard was locked down tight, though. There was nothing I could do to get to him until I started killing his dealers. That tripped him up, but it wasn't enough. Neither was the cop I sent for his throat." He strolled toward me, tipping my chin up so he could look into my eyes. "Until you, Wren. Until Hawk told me all about your arrangement with Rivera.

That's when I knew I had him."

I glanced at my brother. "Bane told you?"

He nodded. "When you were at the hospital. He told me what you'd done to save my ass. He told me you were his to use for two weeks. He told me you agreed to whore yourself out to him. For me."

Anger laced his words, but I think they were more reflective of his own self-loathing. "I couldn't let you die," I replied. "We stick together, right?"

My words brought out a glimpse of the young boy my brother used to be, the one who had looked up to me, who used to turn to me for protection. My role had never changed, but Hawk had grown into a man who managed to fuck up in the same ways he did when he was a dumb kid.

"When Hawk found out what you'd done, he came to me again. He wants to take Rivera down just as much as I do, so with his help, here we are."

I blinked as anger filled my veins. I turned back to Hawk. "You did this."

"I can't have you in his service."

"I chose to go to him, Hawk! I tried, and I tried to find another way out of this bullshit, but in the end, I *chose* him. I want to be with him. Fuck, I love him!"

Hawk's face drained of color as my words reverberated around the room.

Sanderson began to chuckle. "Oh, this is all too perfect. I can't wait to see his face when he finds you, beaten to within an inch of your life."

My pulse began to pound, drowning out nearly every other sound.

"And it will be your brother who will be delivering the punishment."

Hawk looked like he wanted to be sick, and I was right there with him. Sanderson was a fucking monster.

"Boss," Hawk began weakly, but Sanderson waved off whatever he was about to say. "You'll do this unless you want to be tied up right beside her? Maybe I should just let Bane take care of you."

Hawk's jaw bulged as he listened, and I begged him with my eyes, begged him not to do this.

"Bane will be here in an hour. Get to it," Sanderson said, walking out the door of the storage locker.

Hawk came toward me. "Please, little brother, you can't do this."

Balling his hands into fists, he said softly, "I have to, Wren. If I don't, I die."

"So what, you'll kill me to save your own skin?"

When he only stared at me, I knew there was no saving him. My brother was lost, and I wondered what I'd done to make him treat me like this. I'd done everything in my power for him. I loved him when no one else would. I provided for him when we were on our own. I even gave him my share of the food when there was nothing else to eat.

Raising my chin, I stared at him. "Go on then. Beat your own goddamn sister. Beat me until I can't get up again. Beat me to make survival easier for you. Fuck everyone else, is that right?"

He balled his hand into a fist as his side. "I'm sorry, Wren."

I cursed when he raised his hand to me.

Then it was pain.

That was all I could feel.

Breathe.
Taste.
See.
Pain.
And then…
… darkness.

31

Bane

I COULDN'T BELIEVE WHAT I WAS DOING. I'D DRIVEN to the parking garage where Cox told me to meet her and am now sitting in the driver's seat while my knee bounced. Wren had been missing for nine hours, and not knowing whether she was still alive was killing me. Sanderson had given me the proof of life, but I didn't know what condition she'd be in once this was all over.

My gaze flickered to the rearview mirror when I saw another car appear at the top of the ramp. The parking garage was six stories high, and Cox was very specific about the location when I called her. Her blue unmarked car pulled in beside mine, the engine shut off, and she got out. I followed her movement around the back of my car, my finger still on my Glock balanced on my thigh. Dagger knew where I was and had very specific instructions about what to do if I didn't return.

"Mr. Rivera," she said while she slid into the passenger seat.

"I must say… your phone call has me intrigued."

"I hope it's intriguing enough that you'll do everything in your power to ensure Wren Montana's survival."

"It is. But to be sure, tell me everything again."

I ground my molars together. This cunt was enjoying this way too much. "Peter Sanderson has Wren."

"Why?"

I stretched out my neck until I heard a pop, the tension in my body almost debilitating. "She's being used as leverage against me."

"Why?"

I wanted to wipe the smug smile off her face with a bullet. "I've been stepping on Sanderson's toes for ten years. I guess he's had enough."

"Stepping on his toes, how? All you're giving me are cryptic statements, Rivera."

I slammed my hand against the steering wheel. "I don't know what you want me to say."

"You know… I looked up Peter Sanderson. Aside from being an art collector, the guy is squeaky clean."

I turned my head to face her. "Then you need to look a little harder."

"How about you tell me what pies he's got his fingers in, then we'll go from there."

"I'm not a fucking rat, and I'm not about to start now."

She smiled, flashing her straight teeth. "You are a rat, though. The only reason I came here was to get information from you. You mentioned something about those dealers getting killed. Are they yours?"

"I have no comment on that. Even if they were, you don't

have a fucking thing to tie it to me."

"Lying by omission is still lying."

"Lying by omission is the only way to stay breathing," I sneered, cutting her with a sharp glare. "The dealers that have been hit. I can tell you who's been giving the orders."

She shook her head, her tightly bound hair catching the light of the interior lights. "I want more than that. I need proof."

"You'll find the proof waiting for you at this address." I handed over the address Sanderson gave to me. "Nine o'clock tomorrow morning. Be there, and you'll get all the proof you'll need."

Her cool gray eyes studied the piece of paper. "Is this legit, or are you sending me on a wild goose chase here?"

I shrugged. "I guess the only way you'll know is if you go tomorrow. Now get out of my fucking car."

She tipped her head to me. "Always a pleasure, Mr. Rivera."

I bit my tongue, swallowing back the barb I wanted to sling at her. As much as it pained me, I needed her on my side, at least until Wren was safely back in my arms. Cox slammed the door behind her, and I watched the woman get back into her car and drive away. I waited another ten minutes before I started the engine of my car, then left the garage, praying I'd made the right call.

A short time later, I returned to the club, and Dagger was waiting for me.

"What have you got?" I asked as I walked through the mass of people. It was nearing midnight, the peak time for patrons to come in and enjoy the delights my Dolls could offer them.

"Andy was taken to the hospital with a gunshot wound to his chest. It missed his heart but hit a lung. The bastard is going to be okay."

"And Wren? Have you heard anything about where she's being held?" If I could get to her before the meeting, things would be a hell of a lot better.

"Nothing. The streets are quiet, and Sanderson's men aren't talking either."

I eyed his clean clothes and still wet hair. "I take it you were persuasive enough."

"Very, but nobody was flapping their gums."

I jogged up the stairs to my office, and Dagger slammed the door behind him. "We'll get her back, boss."

I spun around to face him. "I know we will, then I will fucking *decimate* every single person who was involved in this. I don't give a shit if it starts a turf war or a goddamn nuclear war. Nobody takes what's mine. *Nobody.*"

He stared at me for a moment.

"Fuck, just say it."

He folded his arms over his meaty chest. "This woman, Wren, she means something to you."

"And what if she does?"

He raised a brow at me. "You've never had this before."

I turned to glare at him. No fucking shit, I hadn't had this before. Loving someone was a fucking headfuck. I thought I only had enough room in my heart for Bianca and our mother. Then little Valentine came along, and that damn organ grew to encompass her in my don't-fucking-mess-with-them bubble. And now, Wren. Wren, who had the largest fucking piece of my heart.

Running my hands through my hair, I barked, "Fuck." I glared at Dagger. Fuck him for bringing this shit up. Fuck him for pointing out the wounds, then prodding them to make them bleed. "I fucking need her in my life, Tony."

Something like shock filtered through his expression, but he shut his emotions down tight before saying, "That's all I need to know." With a nod, he turned around and left me with thoughts spinning at a million miles a minute.

If I didn't get Wren back, I didn't know what I'd do. All I knew was that my chest was hurting with the thought she was in pain right now—pain I had caused her by simply being in her life. Sanderson used my feelings for her against me, and I heard that little voice at the back of my head whispering something about 'this is why we don't fall for a woman no matter how good her cunt is.'

But Wren was different.

She didn't want something from me that I didn't want to give. It was me who wanted everything from her—her attention, her love, her body. I wanted it all, and although that thought should've frightened me to death, it didn't. It made me feel like I was whole for the first time in my life, like there had been a gaping hole in the center of my chest that couldn't be filled no matter how many women I used, or how much coke I pushed, or how many blowjobs I got from my Dolls. Wren filled it with everything good in this world, and hungrily, greedily, I wanted more from her. I wanted it all because she made me feel like I could be a better man.

32

Wren

I COULDN'T OPEN MY EYES, EVEN THOUGH I TRIED. I didn't know how long I'd been unconscious for, but I knew I'd come back around while I was still being beaten. I'd heard my brother's sobs as he slammed his booted foot into my stomach and kidneys over and over again.

Sucking in a breath, I let it out through my mouth. My nose was broken. Everything felt stiff like my blood had dried on my skin, caked-on in thick clumps.

The concept of time was an elusive one. The storage locker didn't have any windows, and the only light coming in was from the slit under the door. I tried to lift my arms, only to find them bound to the chair once more. I checked my legs and discovered the same thing. Although where they thought I'd go in this state, I didn't know.

As I waited for someone to come and get me, I prayed it would be Bane. I needed to hear his voice again. I needed to smell the scent of his cologne, the scent of leather and gunpowder. I knew then he was the safety I'd been chasing all my life. I tilted my head to the side when I heard a distant voice, then began to call for help when the voice got closer. If someone was trying to get something from their locker, they could be my way out of here.

I sat up a little straighter when I heard scraping on the door, then braced myself for the light that would pour in.

"Nice work, Hawk," Sanderson said, praising my brother for his handiwork.

The sick fuck.

"Thanks, boss," my brother mumbled.

"Get her up. We need to move her to a new location."

The ties around my wrists and ankles disappeared, then the pressure of a gun barrel was applied to the back of my head.

"Don't try anything," an unfamiliar man said.

A warm hand hooked under my arm, and I was brought up onto my feet. My knees buckled from disuse, and I fell to the floor.

"Fuck, Hawk, carry her out of here."

Hawk scooped me up into his arms, grunting a little with the effort. Even though I couldn't see his face, I positioned mine where I knew his would be. I wanted him to see what he'd done. I wanted him to know that he'd caused me this pain.

"You might as well just kill me," I whispered, my speech slurred.

Hawk stayed quiet as he walked me through the storage facility and out into the warm night air. I felt the humidity settle over my sensitive skin, the slight pressure making me moan. His unsteady footsteps and the faint rush of traffic were the only sounds I could hear. A van door slid open, and I was placed on the hard metal in the back. I sucked in a hiss as gravity took effect, making my aching bones groan in protest. The door was shut, and I was left in silence for a moment.

I breathed through the pain savagely attacking my body, breathed through my wish to just end it all.

No! I couldn't think like that.

Bane needed me alive.

He needed me breathing, so when he came to decimate these fuckers, he would have a reason to stop. If I died, there was no doubt in my mind he would lose his soul to avenge me. A tear leaked from the corner of my swollen eye. I'd finally found someone who could love me unconditionally, and it turned out to be the one person I least suspected.

The engine rumbled to life beneath me, and one door slammed shut. I moaned with every bump out of that storage facility, breathing easier once we were on the smooth road of the highway. The drone of the engine and the hum of the wheels over asphalt lulled me into a fitful sleep, one where I dreamed I was wrapped in Bane's arms instead of being sucked into this living nightmare.

WHEN I WOKE UP AGAIN, I LIFTED MY HEAVY HEAD AND tried to gain my bearings, even with how blind I was. We weren't in the van anymore. The air was cooler here, and I turned my face into a current that seemed to swirl above my head. Somewhere in the distance, the sound of sea birds fought with the clanging sounds of shipping containers. I knew their cadence because Hawk and I had to sleep rough a few nights in winter one year, and we'd found an old shipping container to stay in.

I tilted my head to the side when I heard muffled voices.

"He'll come," Hawk said. "He won't leave her here to die."

"He fucking better come, Hawk, or *you* won't be leaving this place at all."

A heavy door opened in front of me. I lifted my head. "Ah, she's awake."

I sat up a little straighter in my chair, lifting my chin in defiance. If they thought they could break me, Hawk obviously hadn't told them about my stubborn streak.

"Hello there, Sleeping Beauty," Sanderson cooed, then laughed. "Although a beauty, you aren't anymore."

I turned my face toward Hawk who was shuffling closer, getting a better look at what he'd done. I bared my teeth at him, making Sanderson chuckle.

"Looks like you've pissed off your sister," he said, then ran his finger across my mouth. I tried to bite him, but he jerked his hand away in time. This made him laugh again, the sound of it grating on my ears. "I can see why Bane likes her in his bed. The bitch has spirit."

"I have plenty of other things, too," I snarled, hoping my bravado would work. Deep down, I was terrified. I was terrified of not walking away from this, or if I did, living with the knowledge that my own brother—the only person who shared blood with me on this earth—had done this to me. And for what? Because he didn't like who I had to get in bed with to save *his* fucking life?

"It's almost nine," Hawk said softly.

Sanderson replied, "Let's get in position. I want that motherfucker to give me what I want, and if he doesn't, then he'll be joining your sister at the bottom of the bay."

My heart slammed against my ribs, beating at the bone cage and demanding to be let out. Bane would never give them what they wanted. He was like a dragon guarding his gold. He was relentless in his efforts. Nobody would be allowed to swoop in and take what was his, and I was his.

As they walked away, I listened as the door slammed shut behind them.

I waited, my back ramrod straight, my breathing hoarse and labored. Outside, the world continued on, ignorant of what was happening in here to me. The minutes dripped by, feeling like hours to me.

Eventually, I heard the sound of sirens, nearly drowning out the distinct noise of cars pulling up outside, the tires crunching on the gravel right before the engines cut off.

I lifted my head and looked in the direction of the door when it opened, letting out a sigh of relief when I heard a man say, "LAPD, you're safe."

Tears leaked from my eyes as the officer came closer. He hadn't touched me yet, and the wait was driving me insane.

"We've got EMTs on the way," he eventually said from right beside me. Something cold pressed against my wrists, where they were bound behind my back. "I'm going to cut these ties off you, okay?"

I nodded, the movement sending more tears down my beaten and bloody face.

"Do you know who did this to you?"

Another nod, this time a wary one.

Did I want to push my brother under the bus for his role in this?

Could I?

"Who was it?" the officer asked gently. The knife sliced through the ties, and I brought my arms forward, massaging my wrists gently. The cop began working on the ties on my ankles. "Who was it, ma'am?"

I opened my mouth, and a moan escaped me. Although I couldn't see them, I knew there were at least a few other people in the space with us now. I heard the scrape of their shoes, the distinctive rattle of their weapons belts as they walked around.

"Cox, come and see this," someone called.

The sound of heels clicking over concrete grew louder as she walked into the room. There was a sound like a knife cutting through plastic, then, "Motherfucker. That cock-sucking mother*fucker!*"

"Is it pure?"

"As a virgin Colombian. Fuck!"

"Who does it belong to?"

"I need to get the paperwork on this warehouse. Find out who the fuck owns it!" Cox screamed, her voice ricocheting like a stray bullet. She marched from the room, leaving a couple of the officers muttering about how many pounds they estimated were there and who it could possibly belong to.

I tuned them out when the constriction around my ankles was suddenly gone, the blood flowing back into my feet with an almost painful rush. I moaned again, but this time it was in relief. The officer helping me didn't know that, though, and he shouted, "Where's the goddamn EMT?"

"Two minutes out, Ward," someone said.

"Do you think you've broken any bones?"

I took a moment to listen to my body. Besides the throbbing in my wrists and ankles, the sharp pain in my face from the beating and my fear yanking on my self-control, I didn't think Hawk had broken anything.

I shook my head.

The officer, Ward, helped me stand, wrapping an arm around my waist and holding me up. "Okay, the door is about thirty feet in front of us. Once we step through that, I'm going to sit you down in one of the squad cars, and we'll wait there."

A small whimper threatened to come out of my mouth as we began to move, but I pressed my lips tightly together, refusing to let it out. It was a shuffled pace as we made our way outside.

"The car is another sixty feet away," he told me. "Can you make it?"

I gave him a curt nod.

The sun already had a bite to it, making me sweat immediately. When Hawk had said it was nine, I assumed at night, but clearly I'd been wrong. Ward opened a car door, then eased me inside. The interior was still cool from the air conditioning that had been running, then a moment later, cold air was blowing over my face.

"This should keep you comfortable while we wait," he said. Touching my hand, he placed a bottle of water into it. "I'm just going to go and speak to the detective, then be right back. The EMTs shouldn't be long."

I opened the bottle and took a shallow sip just as an explosion threw me back into my seat.

33

Bane

MY HAND CURLED INTO A FIST AS I WATCHED MY brother-in-law help Wren from the fucking warehouse. I was set up on an adjacent wharf, keeping tabs on everything that was going on. I knew Cox wouldn't have been able to walk away from the tip I'd given her. I also knew it had been a fucking risk to even bring her into this. Sanderson was a vicious man. He would've killed Wren whether I turned up or not. At least this way, my Little Bird was safe, I wasn't implicated, and never would be if Cox was smart. I was sure she wouldn't reveal her source for this. She had too much on the line. Then again, so did I.

I waited until James settled Wren into the back of a squad car with a bottle of water, then hit the proverbial red button of the detonator on my phone screen.

The charges I'd set last night came to the party. The explosion that was connected to my finger-walking thundered through the port, making the seagulls that were steadily circling overhead cry out as they were knocked off course.

The sound echoed around us, flames licking above the roofline of the building already. Black smoke billowed out from the building like a dying beast, my latest shipment of coke going up in smoke with it. I had about two billion dollars' worth in there with a street value of fifty billion.

"Was this absolutely necessary?" Dagger rumbled beside me.

"Nobody fucks with me, Dagger." Jerking my head at the destruction of my own property, I added, "This will be a message to any motherfucker who thinks he can come in and take what's mine." I turned back to the carnage, to the pieces of sheet metal that were strewn across the ground, to the fireball still erupting from the belly of the building, to the black smoke swelling high into the sky. Sanderson may have cost me fifty billion in coke sales, but I made sure I would fuck him up even more.

When the text had come through with the address of one of my buildings as the meeting point, I'd called in some fucking favors. Changing over the deed of ownership from me to Sanderson wasn't fucking hard. All it had cost me was one free year's membership at the Dollhouse, along with free drinks for that period too. I gladly gave that up to fuck up the man who had taken Wren from me.

Cox would've had to have been blind not to see all that coke stacked up in there. The discovery had been made. Now it was time for Sanderson to fucking pay. As my gaze shifted away from my business loss, it settled on Wren. I'd told my brother-in-law to park as far away from the warehouse as he could and to make sure he was out of the blast zone too. He hadn't asked why he'd had to park so far away, but he'd done as he was told, and thank fuck he did because it saved his and Wren's lives.

The EMTs pulled in, their sirens screaming, their lights flashing. James was still on his feet. However, the same couldn't be said for some of his brothers in blue. The blast would've taken out a couple of them, but their deaths would be pinned on Sanderson, not me. Not now. I turned my head when I heard Cox screaming at the EMTs to come and help her men. Soot covered her face, her suit jacket ripped and bloody. Her shoes had come off, leaving her barefoot in the rubble.

"We should go," Dagger said. "Before someone sees us here."

Nodding, I retreated to my car and got in the back seat. Dagger slid into the driver's seat.

"To the hospital?"

I shook my head. "It's too soon. I need to get the call first. I can't be implicated in any of this." And Jesus-fucking-Christ did it kill me. I wanted to go to Wren and hold her close, never let her go, but I couldn't. Not yet, anyway. And until Sanderson was arrested, I had to keep my eyes open.

"Back to the club," I said. "Then, we wait."

IT TOOK FOUR FUCKING HOURS TO GET THE PHONE CALL that Wren was safe.

Four.

Fucking.

Hours.

In that time, I'd driven everyone at the club away from me. Even Dagger left me alone, and that bastard was practically with me twenty-four-seven. When I arrived at the hospital, I went straight into Wren's room. Nobody tried to stop me, and if they had, I wouldn't have been kept away for long.

I sucked in a breath when I saw her in that bed. White sheets were pulled tightly across her body, the color a stark contrast to the bruising on her face. Both her eyes were swollen shut, the mottled purple bruises around the sockets already coming out. She had stitches on her forehead, a busted-up bottom lip, and her neck was in a brace. My hands curled into fists at my sides, rage bubbling over in my veins.

"Bane," she said on a breathy whisper. *Was she awake?* I stepped into the room and waited. "You're here." She tilted her face in my direction. Reaching out a hand, she groped around blindly for me. As soon as my fingers touched hers, she sighed. "You're okay."

I fell to my knees beside the bed, staring at this woman who was more concerned about my own safety than hers. How the fuck could I keep her when my lifestyle and the choices I've been forced to make put her in the crosshairs? "I'm okay, Little Bird," I murmured. "How are you feeling?"

"They've got me on some pretty good drugs right now, so not so bad. I just wish I could see."

"Did they say how long it would be before the swelling goes down?"

She swept her thumb over the back of my hand in a soothing motion. "No, just that it will take time." Her voice was soft—sad even.

"Who beat you, Wren? Was it Sanderson? If it was, I'm going to hunt that fucker down and make him swallow the muzzle of my gun." My free hand tightened with barely contained rage, that familiar feeling making its way through my body like a junkie getting their fix.

One small salty tear fell from the corner of her eye, landing on the pillow and staining it pink. "Hawk did this to me."

"Your fucking brother?"

"Yes."

My gaze darted around the room, trying to fucking put all the pieces together. "Why?"

"He said it was my life or his. He chose his."

I winced as the claws of my raging monster raked at the inside of my head. Her brother. Her own *brother* had done this because he was too much of a fucking pussy to own his shit. No, he'd rather let his sister, the only person in this goddamn world who gave two shits about him, take the fall for his fucked-up decisions.

"I will fucking end that motherfucking *cunt!*"

I braced for Wren's objections, but they never came. "I don't care anymore, Bane. I've given my brother everything, and all he's handed back to me is pain and torment."

Getting back onto my feet, I palmed my phone, drawing it out of my pocket. "I'll be back in a minute, okay?" Placing a gentle kiss on her forehead, I stalked from the room, down the busy hall, and out to the front of the hospital.

Dagger picked up on the first ring. "Boss? How is she?"

"Fine, no thanks to her fucking brother."

"Her brother?" he asked. I laid it all out for him, how Hawk had borrowed money from Sanderson to pay me back. Clearly, the fucker had also negotiated so much more than that because he became Sanderson's attack dog too.

"What do you need from me?" Dagger asked. The bastard always knew when it was time for action and not words.

"I need you to drag Hawk down to our usual spot and keep him conscious until I get there."

He hung up and strolled back into the hospital. When I returned to Wren's room, there was a nurse there checking over her chart. She was a little older, a little rounder, but the compassion on her face was undeniable. She gave me a warm smile as I shuffled over to the visitor's chair and pulled it closer to the bed.

"You must be her boyfriend," the nurse said in a soft whisper. "Your girl is a strong one. She'll pull through this just fine."

"Thank you." I glanced back at the now-sleeping Wren, who had her face turned in my direction. It was killing me not being able to see her blue eyes.

"Do you need anything?" the nurse asked as she turned to leave.

Oh, not much…

… the usual.

Revenge.

To spill Hawk's blood.

To dick fuck the hole I was going to put in his skull.

"I'm fine. Thank you."

"I have a feeling we'll be seeing each other a fair bit. If you or Wren need anything, my name is Patty."

With a nod and another smile, she was gone, and all I was left with was simmering rage that seemed to increase with every single beep of Wren's heart rate monitor.

34

Bane

I LEFT THE HOSPITAL AS SOON AS I GOT THE TEXT FROM
Dagger. He had Hawk. The stupid fuck had been found holed
up at his apartment. The asshole hadn't even fought as Dagger
had dragged him to the warehouse where all the wet work was
done.

Dagger had the guy tied upside down over an old oil drum
like a suckling pig waiting to go to slaughter. He had no idea
just how right that was. Dagger nodded when he saw me walk
in, stepping back to watch the show. Hawk's eyes widened in
terror when he saw me, moving his body spasmodically to get
away from the death that was surely coming his way.

Pulling my Glock out from the holster under my arm, I
shoved it into his mouth when he opened it to scream. Those
blue eyes of his widened so much that I could see the whites
all the way around.

"You signed your death warrant when you agreed to be

Sanderson's bitch," I snarled into his face. With my height and his suspension, we were nose to nose. I liked to watch the spark of life drain from a man's eyes as he died. I removed the gun far enough to speak. "Have anything to say?"

"I did it to protect Wren," he gasped.

I rolled his words around in my head for a moment. "You did it to *protect* Wren?" I wanted to laugh, then get down to that dick fucking in the hole in the side of his head, but I also wanted to hear whatever fucked-up, twisted reasoning he had for doing this to his sister.

"Sanderson was going to kill her outright, then leave her dumped outside the club to remind you who was boss."

I seethed but flicked my fingers to tell him to continue.

"I convinced him that this was a better plan."

"Beating and leaving her in my own goddamn warehouse?" I barked, shoving the muzzle of the gun into his temple this time. My finger hovered over the trigger, the last thread of my self-control threatening to snap.

"He would've killed her and waited for you to find her. I convinced him to kill her in front of you instead, to let you live with those memories."

"Because you're generous like that," I replied, my words with bite.

I glanced over at Dagger, whose expression was much the same. Anyone would've thought he looked bored by what he was hearing if it weren't for the feathering in his jaw that gave him away. Returning my attention to Hawk, I shoved the gun harder into his temple, then withdrew it. Holding the gun down my thigh, I waited for him to spill more of his secrets. Men like Hawk—a hustler and a thief—always had more secrets to spill.

"Why did you go to Sanderson for that money?"

Hawk closed his eyes and took in a deep breath. "Sanderson approached me. He told me he'd give me the money, but I had to work for him. If I didn't, he'd destroy Wren and her business."

"To get to me, right?"

He nodded, the motion making him swing a little. "He wanted you to suffer."

"I wanted *you* to realize what a fucking mistake you'd made," a dark voice said behind us.

I spun around to find Sanderson standing in the doorway of the warehouse. Dagger unfolded his arms and reached for the H&K slung across his body. Sanderson's gaze briefly flickered over to him before returning to me.

"You couldn't have just left shit alone, could you, Rivera?" He strolled casually into the room, coming a little closer. "If you had, none of those kids would've died. They would've been working for me instead of you, but you had to flood No Man's Land with your cheap coke and cash in."

I shrugged. "I'm a businessman, just like you. There was a hole in the market."

The other man ground his teeth. "No Man's Land was something Manzetti and I agreed on. That territory put an end to decades of fighting between us, to bring *peace* back to the community, then you swan in and start dealing, start taking *our* dealers from us."

I barked a laugh. "You're whining to me like I give a shit. I don't, Sanderson. I don't give a shit that I've stepped on your toes. You think I'm some punk-ass bitch who doesn't know what he's doing? I know *exactly* what I'm doing. I'm building a fucking empire, and you and Manzetti are standing in the way."

His lips peeled back from his teeth. "You're a little kid playing in the big boys' sandbox."

I shook my head slowly. No, I wasn't the kid here. I was the goddamn king. "I hope you've got all your affairs in order, Sanderson."

Flinty gray eyes clouded over with rage. "If I don't come back from this meeting, Manzetti has orders to bring you fucking down, to burn your *empire* to the ground."

"I'm not talking about killing you, you egotistical fuck. I'm talking about the cops arresting you for drug possession, intent to distribute, and the murder of three Los Angeles police officers."

"What are you talking about?" He narrowed his eyes. "That was your warehouse. Your coke. Your fucking C4." Laughing, he added, "You fucked yourself up the ass with that stunt today."

I shrugged. "Maybe I lost myself some cash with those drugs going up in smoke, but I'm happy with that decision because it wasn't my name on the deed to that warehouse. It was yours."

I watched as my words hit him, contorting his face into an ugly mask of rage. "You motherfucker, I'll fucking end you."

He reached into his jacket and pulled out his Glock. I dove to the floor, crawling behind the oil drum underneath Hawk. Dagger pulled the trigger too, the sound of bullets ricocheting around the warehouse. Something wet hit me on the face, and I reached up to wipe it away, my fingers coming back red. My gaze traveled up to find two holes in Hawk's body, one in his head, one that had gone through his chest and exited through his back.

Gunshots were still bouncing around the space, and I cursed when even more joined them. It looked like Sanderson's men were here now too. Leaning around the drum, I squeezed off a couple of rounds, hitting one of the three newcomers in the thigh. With any luck, I hit the femoral artery, and he was well on the way to bleeding out. Ducking back, I tried to get a sense of where everyone was and in what kind of condition. I took another look to find Dagger taking cover behind two drums on one side of the warehouse while Sanderson and his two remaining men were on the other.

Silence fell over the warehouse as each man reloaded, the distinct sound of metal sliding on metal piercing my eardrums. I checked my own gun and found that I had at least another five rounds in there. I didn't have another clip, which meant I had to use what I had wisely. While there was a lull, I stood and ran to Dagger, sliding in beside him as a bullet pinged against the drum I'd taken cover behind.

"Are you good?" I asked him.

He grimaced but nodded. "I'll take out the other two," he said in a low rumble. "You focus on Sanderson."

Bringing up my gun, I gave the signal, and we both stepped free of the drums. Dagger's submachine gun's *ratta-tatta-tat* was music to my ears. He easily mowed down one of Sanderson's men whose weapon had jammed on him. He fell to the warehouse floor in a tangle of bloody limbs. The other guy was proving more difficult. They both ran out of ammo at the same time, the men discarding their weapons and slinging fists this time.

I came at Sanderson while he let his soldier fight for him. Zig-zagging toward him, he tried to shoot me, but every shot missed. Leaping on top of the drum he was taking cover behind, I unloaded what was left of my clip into the top of his head. Blood and gray matter sprayed, hitting me in the legs and torso.

222

Sanderson fell to the concrete, his expression set in surprise.

I turned to find Dagger and the other guy rolling around on the floor together, knives in their hands. Bringing out my knife from the sheath on my ankle, I dived into the fray, slashing at Sanderson's man with precision. He was quick, though, and my underestimation of him earned me a slash across my chest. Blood welled, but the cut was shallow and didn't slow me down.

We circled the fucker, feeling like we were in some 1950s gang film. The guy's brown eyes darted around the warehouse, looking for a way out.

"The only way out of here is in a body bag," I growled.

Flipping the dagger in his hand, he changed grip and came at me, slashing. Leaning back, I missed each arc of his blade, giving Dagger the advantage by distracting him. The guy was so focused on me, he didn't see Dagger coming. Dagger sank his knife into the man's throat, driving the steel through the flesh where his shoulder and neck met. Blood spewed from the wound, gushing down to the dusty warehouse floor. He weaved on his feet for a moment, clutching at the wound like that would stem the flow. Staggering toward the door, he reached the handle and pressed it down. Dagger looked at me with his brows raised. I simply shook my head. There was no way this little fucker was walking out of here.

Sanderson's man took a lurching step before falling face-first into the dirt. Blood pumped from his neck, pooling on the ground in a macabre black puddle. Turning around, I looked at the carnage, then at the three corpses that weren't there fifteen minutes ago.

Dagger strolled over to me, holding his stomach.

"Did you get hit?"

He stared at me for a moment, the color draining from his face just before he collapsed. I dove for him, catching him under my arm before he could hit the concrete. Easing him down slowly, I moved his hand out of the way, then lifted his shirt. Blood was pumping from a stomach wound.

"Fuck!" Dagger wasn't going to make it if I didn't do something right now. Wiping my bloody hands on my pants, I pulled out my phone and dialed Andy.

"Boss?"

"I need medical," I barked into the phone.

"On my way." Andy hung up, and I pressed my hand against the hole in Dagger's stomach. I eyed the blood that already soaked through his black shirt, knowing it was too much. He must've been hit in that first wave of shooting before he could take cover. I looked behind me at Hawk, whose blood was draining into the barrel beneath him. His eyes were still open, watching me even in death. I would've killed the bastard eventually, but it would've been much slower and much more painful. The fucker had gotten off easy.

Wren was going to be devastated by this news, though, and the thought of breaking it to her made pain lance through me. I would protect her from everything if I could, but my life was dirty as shit, my business done in the darkness. Long ago, I'd made peace with how I earned a living.

Peddling pussy was great.

It was legal.

It was lucrative.

Drugs, on the other hand, I got a high from selling them. There was so much money to be made, but so many lives got ruined by it too, like those of my dealers.

I shook my head and pressed a little harder into Dagger's torso. It made him moan, but he was still out cold. Before Wren, I was hard, driven, cold-blooded, but my Little Bird had opened my eyes to some shit that I can't ignore now. I couldn't ignore everything that had happened. Her brother was dead because of me. I looked down at Dagger. He might die because of me too.

Dropping my head, I waited for Andy. And then I did something I hadn't done since I was a kid—I prayed. I pleaded with whatever entity out there or up there that Andy would arrive quickly.

I looked toward the entrance when I heard a car pull up. A door opened and shut, then Andy walked in, a jump bag in his hand. He scanned the area efficiently, then came our way.

He stopped on the other side of Dagger and motioned for me to move my hands. As soon as I did, blood gushed.

"I need to stop the bleeding," he said, ripping open the medical bag and rummaging through it. He pulled out an endless mountain of gauze, then proceeded to rip the sterile packs open. I followed his lead, tearing open the plastic and pressing the cloth to Dagger's wound.

"More pressure," Andy barked, reaching one-handed into the jump bag again. Both our hands were slick with blood, and I wondered if this would cause Andy to have flashbacks of his time in Afghanistan.

He pulled out a disposable pre-filled syringe, then jabbed it into Dagger's thigh. I felt his body suddenly go limp beneath my hands.

"It's morphine," Andy said. "It relaxed him."

"How bad is it?" I asked, nodding down to the hole in Dagger's abdomen.

"GSW. Nicked an artery. Once I slow the bleeding, I'll turn him over and look for the exit wound. Just keep that pressure on there."

I did everything Andy asked of me, watching as more and more color drained from Dagger's face. His blood wrapped around him on the floor, creeping in my field of vision on all sides. Once Andy was satisfied the bleeding had slowed enough, I helped turn Dagger's body. Andy inspected his back and swore.

"The bullet didn't come through. He needs surgery, and that is beyond my skills. He has to go to the hospital."

Fuck. I avoided them for my men when I could, especially when their wounds came from fucking shoot-outs with rival drug dealers.

"Let's get him to the car."

Together, we lifted and placed him in the back seat of the town car.

"Go," I told Andy. "I have to take care of this." I gestured to the warehouse. Andy nodded, got into the driver's seat, and peeled out of there. Fuck, I hoped Dagger made it. He'd been with me for years, and his loyalty wasn't something that could be easily replaced.

Stalking back into the warehouse, I pulled Sanderson's guys into the middle of the concrete floor, then dragged Sanderson's corpse out too. The next job was getting Hawk down. After moving the drum out of the way, I strode to the wall where the rope was tied off and began to undo it. As soon as gravity helped me, I stood back and watched Hawk flop to the floor. Picking up his hands, I dragged him into the pile of bodies, then stripped out of my clothes, adding them to what was going to be a spectacular fire.

Back out at the car, I cleaned my face with some pre-moistened towelettes, changed into a spare set of clothes I kept in the town car, then grabbed the red gasoline can and the matches. I spread the accelerant around the building, making sure to soak the bodies the most. They needed to burn so hot that not even dental records could help them. Just for good measure, I ripped out a couple of the henchmen's teeth too.

When the gasoline can was empty, I placed it by my feet and lit a match. Touching it to the line of gas I'd made to the door, I grabbed the can and hauled ass out of there, taking cover behind the car. The fire that erupted from the warehouse burned hot, the heat singeing my face as I watched it engulf another one of my buildings—this one under a false name.

Black smoke drifted up into the sky, the flames licked at the stars. I watched it for as long as I could, making sure every square inch of it was consumed by the fire. Content that nothing could get traced back to me, I got back in the car and drove away.

35

Bane

IT HAD BEEN TWENTY-FOUR HOURS SINCE THE FIRE that consumed the bodies of four people who had every-fucking-thing coming to them. I sat back in my office chair, scrolling through the news story on my iPad, looking for any hints that they were going to start sniffing around me. Absently, I scratched at the bandage taped to my chest, the shallow wound hardly worth fucking fussing over, but I didn't want blood leaking through my shirt.

Andy walked into my office looking like he hadn't slept at all. He ran a hand through his dark hair and took a seat. In all the time he'd been my driver, he'd never set foot in my office, so it was strange to see him in here now. But the bastard deserved to be here. He'd saved Dagger's life. He'd gotten him to the hospital in time. Dagger had gone in for surgery to repair his liver that had been turned into a two-hole sieve with that gunshot wound. That, along with two blood transfusions, meant his injury was a bad one. He wasn't out of the woods yet, but apparently, the worst was over. The first twenty-four hours post-op was the most critical. Dagger was still breathing, so I knew he'd pull through.

"You wanted to see me, boss?" Andy asked.

I gestured to the seat in front of my desk, waiting until his ass was firmly planted before saying to him, "I want to thank you for what you did for Dagger."

The guy shrugged like it was no-big-fucking deal. "He's a brother."

"You served in two different streams."

He shrugged. "Army or Marines, we're both fucking brothers."

I leaned back in my chair and studied him. "How would you like to work for me in a different capacity? Just until Dagger gets back on his feet."

Andy narrowed his eyes at me. "I'm listening."

"I need someone I can trust at my back. You've proved that to me."

"You need a new Dagger."

I nodded. "Yes. With Sanderson gone, Manzetti's a threat. I'm not willing to give up my share of the drug trade to that Italian fuck. I need someone like you, someone who keeps his fucking head in a situation. There's a war coming. I need my soldiers."

Andy thought about it for a moment. "Who's going to drive your ass around town?"

Throwing my head back, I laughed. "I'm sure we can find someone else."

"I have a younger brother. Just discharged. Got wounded in Afghanistan and is trying to adjust to civilian life."

"What's his name?"

"Max, but everyone in his unit called him Fox."

"Get him in here. I want to meet him." Reaching into the top drawer of my desk, I pulled out a wad of cash and slid it across the tabletop. When Andy arched a brow at me, I said, "You risked your life for me. I reward people for their loyalty."

Andy's gaze fell on the money before flickering back to my face. "I don't need your cash for doing my job, Mr. Rivera."

"Take the fucking money, Andy. Donate it to charity. Whatever the fuck you want to do, but take it. You went above and beyond, and I thank you."

After a long while, he reached across the desk and picked up the cash. "Thank you."

I nodded. "When could your brother start?"

"I'll call him today. He should be good to go in the next couple of days."

"Good." I stood and buttoned my suit jacket.

Andy did the same. "How's Wren?"

"I'm going to go and see her now."

"Does she know about…" His question drifted off when I shook my head. I'd told Andy everything that had happened in that warehouse. I'd dragged him into the sitch, so it was only right that he knew who the bodies belonged to.

"I'm going to tell her now."

Andy stared at me a little longer before turning around and walking to the door. "She loves you, you know."

"What?"

"Wren. She loves you. You've never dated. You've just fucked the women you wanted. And then those women turned into fucking basket cases when you said you didn't want more. But you want more with her because Wren isn't anything like those women. Don't do what I did and fuck up a good thing."

I tried to tamp down the hope that lit up my chest. There was no place for love in my life, at least that's what I thought. Wren did more than turn my life upside down when she came storming into my office that day. She fucking lit a match and watched me burn—burn for her.

"Call your brother," I told him gruffly.

Andy left my office, and I grabbed the tumbler of whisky off my desk. His words were still pinging around in my head. Wren and my relationship was based on an agreement—a sneaky-as-shit way to get into her pants. I'd wanted her the moment she set foot in my office, but the more I got to know her, the more I touched her, the more I got lost in her, the more I wanted.

Was it love? Fuck, I didn't know.

I wasn't sure I could love a woman like that. Bianca was different. She was my sister, so the love we shared was familial.

Our father had been incapable of showing real love, and our mother was a shell of the woman she used to be. I'm sure she did love our father at one point, but that love had been beaten down and trodden on until there was nothing left but an emotionally broken woman.

I would never raise a hand to Wren. It would kill me. I needed her safe. I wanted her to be with only me—not because of some fucking agreement—but because she wanted to be with me. To love me. To fucking give me the life I had only ever dreamed about.

Placing the tumbler back on the desk, I grabbed my phone and stalked from the office. Andy was waiting by the car at the curb when I stepped from the club. Wordlessly, like he knew exactly what was going through my head, he opened the rear door, and I slid inside.

WREN WAS AWAKE WHEN I WALKED INTO THE ROOM, smiling at something the nurse said.

"Mr. Rivera, nice to see you again," Patty stated, her eyes crinkling in the corner.

"Nice to see you, too," I replied, my full attention on Wren who was sitting up in bed. Some of the swelling around her eyes had disappeared, but she still couldn't see. Holding out her hand to me, I laced our fingers together as I sat beside her on the bed.

"How are you, my little bird?" I asked, brushing her knuckles against my mouth.

"Okay. Still drugged up, so can't feel much."

Patty said, "I'll come in and check on you a little later, Wren."

And with that same efficiency, she left them alone with the scent of the breakfast Wren had been served a few hours earlier.

I had to tell Wren what had happened to her brother. It was her right to know, but I had no fucking idea how I was supposed to broach this subject with her. I was so far over my fucking head. I'd crossed so many lines—with her, with my own personal life, and my business—with everything that used to be clear-cut black and white now had shades of gray.

I sucked in a breath and let it out. "I found Hawk."

She stiffened. "You did?"

"Yeah." I studied her face, knowing that this could break us. "He's dead."

An anguished sob was torn from her throat, her hands covering her mouth as tears streamed down her bruised and swollen face. I reminded myself that Hawk had been the one to put those bruises there, which helped me to say, "Sanderson shot him after he spilled everything to me."

"Jesus," she whispered.

I brushed the tears from her face with my thumbs, cursing myself out when she winced from the touch.

"What happened?"

I opened my mouth, then shut it. I couldn't lie to her about this. If she was going to stay with me, she needed every single dirty detail. She had to have all the information to figure out whether I was worth the heartache.

"Dagger found him. I went to speak to him, and he told me he'd been working for Sanderson. Sanderson wanted to fuck me up the ass, so he used your brother to do that by getting to you. He said…" I hesitated because the truth could be ugly sometimes, and I knew I never wanted Wren to hear something hurtful but, "… he said Sanderson would destroy you if he didn't work for him. The plan was to kill you in front of me to make me suffer, knowing that my blood was on your hands."

"He said that?"

I rubbed at the spot in the middle of my chest, trying to massage away the pain she was feeling. "Yes. Sanderson eventually showed up and told me it was all to get me out of the drug trade. There was a gunfight."

Wren looked up suddenly, her face twisted in agony. "Are you hurt? Did you get shot?"

I touched the bandage over my chest. "No. I got out okay. Dagger, not so much. He's recovering in another ward."

Her head dropped into her hands, and she began to weep. Rubbing her back, I said softly, "It's okay. It's over now." I hesitated over the words I was about to say to her, though. Any sentiment that I was sorry for Hawk's demise was a fucking lie, but Wren loved him even if he was a fucking asshole.

"I'm sorry about your brother, too."

"Thank you," she whimpered. "I did not like the man he'd become, but I still loved him."

"I know you did." Moving farther up on the bed, I continued to rub her back, hoping the motion would calm her sobs and dry her tears. As I waited, I watched the clock on the wall. The big hand moved a full two revolutions before she was finally silent, and I was pretty sure that was because she'd fallen asleep. She turned her face toward me, her cheek resting on the top of her knees. She was struggling to open her eyes. Leaning forward, I kissed the tender flesh, tasting her tears.

"I have to organize a funeral for him… although where I'll get the money to pay for that, I don't know. Maybe give up the shop?"

"There's no body left to bury," I said, kissing the top of her head, hoping she understood.

"But you said—"

"I said he was shot, yes, but so were three other people… the kind of people that the cops would be very interested in finding." *Please read between the lines, Little Bird.*

"Oh," she eventually said. She took in a shuddering breath and let it out.

"We can still have a memorial for him." Even making the suggestion made my stomach turn. Hawk's actions against his sister made him my enemy number one, and I gave zero fucks to people who liked to fuck over their own family.

She nodded, then turned to look out the window. Fuck, that motion slayed me. She couldn't even fucking look at me right now, and she didn't even know the full truth about how Hawk ended up there in the first place.

"Little Bird?" I murmured. "Are you okay?"

"No." Her reply was a bare whisper, hardly big enough to take notice of, but I did because I fucking loved this woman. I was consumed by her. She fed me life just as much as the blood in my veins did.

"I can't wait to take you home." *To make love to you. To love on you. To fucking marry you.* I didn't say all that to her even though I wanted to. I should've been fucking terrified even to be thinking about marriage, but I knew what I wanted with Wren. I didn't want an agreement for two weeks. I wanted her entire fucking life, and I wanted her to share it with me. If she agreed, she could stay with me forever. I could buy the entire goddamn block where her shop was if she wanted to continue, but mostly, I wanted her at home with her stomach growing with new life—a life we created together.

I realized as I burned the warehouse that my life had always been about instant gratification. The women, the drugs, the fucking power that rode my veins when I got my way. Wren made me work damn hard to get her, and I would work hard every damn day of my life to keep and make her happy. I was willing to give away that instant high for her. She was my high. She was in my veins, and I wanted her to stay there. I needed to wake up beside her, to fuck her dirty when I needed it, to slow things down and make love to her when she needed it.

I just needed her.

"Marry me, Little Bird."

She stiffened at my words, turning her battered face toward me. "Marry you?"

I licked my lips. Was I fucking ruining everything here? "I love you. I need you in my life. I want to protect you, so you'll never have to go through shit like this ever again."

Tears streamed down her cheeks, and I brushed them away. "I—"

I silenced her with a kiss. "You don't have to answer now. Not this second while everything is still so raw. But I want you to be my wife."

Wren deepened the kiss, sliding her tongue against mine as that familiar spark between us flashed to life and sent us careening down a path of desire. I clutched her shoulders, holding her to me because as much as I wanted to wrap my hand around the back of her neck and control her, I couldn't.

With a groan, I pulled away. I didn't want to walk out of here with my dick tenting my fucking pants. Panting, I studied her red mouth, her lips swollen from our bruising kiss. Her breaths were heaving from her too, the passion that tried to consume us not letting go just yet. Pressing my forehead to hers, we stayed like that for a moment.

"Yes," she said softly.

Tilting her face toward me, I asked, "Yes?"

"Yes. I want to marry you, Bane. I fucking love you, too. Even though you're arrogant and cocky, I wouldn't give you up after two weeks. How could I after you owned my heart and soul when you took me in and cared for me after the break-in at my apartment?"

That statement brought reality back down on me with a crash. "That fire at your apartment… it wasn't a random thing. One of my ex-Dolls lit it. She was insanely jealous that you'd managed to catch and keep my attention."

Wren's mouth popped open in a little O. "What did you do when you found out?"

I glanced away from her face. Even though she couldn't see me, I still hated that she knew about this filthy fucking side of me. "She was taken care of."

Before she could withdraw, I kissed her again, drowning out all thoughts of the shit that happened to me daily. All that mattered now was that Wren had agreed to be my wife.

"I don't even have a ring," I mumbled against her lips.

She smiled. "I don't need a ring."

"Yes, you fucking do. I need every man who looks at you from now on to know you're mine, and I'm fucking yours."

Even though she wouldn't listen to my protests, she clambered onto my lap, straddling my waist. Stroking my face, she smiled again. "I love it when you go all alpha on me."

My dick jumped at the implication, making her groan. "I want to fuck you so bad, Wren, but we can't here. Not now."

She winced as I helped her resettle on the bed. "I guess you're right."

I laid beside her, turning onto my side and stroking my fingers down her arm. "Do you know when they'll discharge you?"

"Patty said it might be a couple more days. They're waiting to see if I have any internal bleeding that the swelling is masking, although if I did, surely that would've shown up by now."

I kissed her temple, inhaling her scent. It was faint thanks to the hospital sponge baths she'd been having, but I still fucking drew in her vanilla scent, letting it soothe the monster in me. "I'll let you get some rest, then."

"You're leaving?"

"No, Little Bird. I'll be sitting right beside your bed watching over you."

She relaxed, her breathing evening out a lot more quickly than I would've expected. I moved from the bed and quietly placed the chair beside it, watching her rest and heal. I couldn't wait to bring her home, to lavish all my attention on her. Fuck, maybe she'd let me buy her some furniture she liked to fill my apartment. I wanted Wren to put her mark everywhere in my life.

Folding my arms over my chest, I shut my eyes for a moment. Everything was okay in my world *for now*. Wren was safe. She'd agreed to become my wife. Sanderson and his cocksucking men were dead, and my drug trade could expand into the vacuum his death created. Although the tragedy of Hawk's death had hit Wren hard, she would overcome that because my girl was a fucking fighter. Just like me.

I WOKE UP SUDDENLY, UNSURE WHY. TURNING MY HEAD, I figured it out pretty fucking fast. Someone had draped a thin hospital blanket over me, and I shoved it off as I stood. Cox was standing in the doorway of Wren's room, staring at her with a look of consternation on her face.

Taking her by the elbow, I drew her outside, glancing up and down the empty hallway.

"What the fuck are you doing here?"

"I heard your girlfriend was still here, so I thought I'd drop by for a visit."

The way she watched me was unnerving, but you never showed weakness in front of the enemy. Folding my arms, I demanded, "What do you want?"

"I came to see if you knew anything about a warehouse fire

down by the docks."

"And why would I know anything about that?"

"Because you're a fucking snake, Rivera, and I want to cut the head off the snake."

I wanted to laugh in her face, but I kept my shit together. "How were the funerals for those men who got killed in the explosion?"

Her gray eyes darkened off to a roiling storm. "Three of my finest men were killed in that fucking disaster of a rescue of your woman."

"And for that, I'm sorry. I didn't know what Sanderson was going to do. I'm just glad Wren was pulled out of there before it happened." The lies fell off my tongue so easily. "Speaking of Sanderson, have you arrested him yet? There are some serious charges against him, right? Drug possession, intent to distribute, manslaughter."

"*Murder*," she hissed. "He murdered my men." She worked her jaw like she wanted to say more. "But no, we haven't seen him. Even his ex-wife hasn't heard from him, and he usually takes the kids on the weekend. The bastard didn't show to pick them up."

I shrugged, the smirk on my face hard to wipe away. "What can I say? Some men are fucking useless fathers. You got any kids, Cox?"

She glared at me. "Do I look like I have time for kids?"

"You look like you have time for casual dick," I retorted.

Her cheeks pinked up a little, and I knew I had her. "Fuck you, Rivera."

"You're not my type, sweetheart. Now, if there's nothing else you have to say to me, I'm going to go back in there..." I jabbed at Wren's room, "… and keep watch over my woman."

"I'll be seeing you around, Rivera. I know there's more going on here. Plus, I think we could use someone like you helping behind the scenes."

Anger curled in my gut. "I'm not a fucking informant, and I wouldn't flip anyone for you."

"So why did you approach me to go rescue Wren Montana?"

"Because I couldn't fucking go near that place. Sanderson has a fucking target painted on my back. If I'd gone, Wren would've been killed to spite me. I couldn't risk that."

Her eyes widened a little before a sly smile formed on her lips. "Look at that, Bane Rivera does have a heart."

"Yeah, I do," I spat back. "And it's as black as yours. Fuck off, Cox, and don't approach me again unless it's to beg me for a job at the Dollhouse."

I walked back into the room, angry energy working through my body. The muscles in my shoulders were tense—I could feel them all locking down one after the other after the other. Cox was a fucking cocksucking cunt that I needed out of my fucking hair. Killing her was off the table, but maybe feeding her scraps of information was a middle-ground I hadn't considered. I wasn't going to rat out on any of my associates, but anonymous tips might be enough. Fuck, that was a problem for later.

Right now, all I needed to concentrate on was making sure my Little Bird made it home.

36

Wren

Two Weeks Later…

I SMOOTHED DOWN THE NAVY BLUE PRINCESS DRESS I was wearing, touching the frothy knee-length skirt. The opaque sleeves covered easily the remainder of my bruises, the ones my brother had inflicted on me. Tonight, we were going to Bianca's house for dinner. I hadn't known it at the time, but her husband had been the one to pull me out of that warehouse. He had saved my life, and for that, I was eternally grateful.

I smiled when Bane walked into the bathroom. He looked good in his suit, but he looked even better when he was dressed casually. The sleeves of his tee were pulled tight against his biceps, the fabric skimming down over his toned stomach and ending at the waistband of his jeans.

"Don't look at me like that, Little Bird, unless you want me to spin you around so you can watch me fuck you in the mirror."

Heat flooded my body at his filthy words, and I spun around, tilting my hips in his direction, daring him to do just that. His eyes darkened, then he was on me, one hand under my skirt, the other wrapped around my throat. He tilted my head to the side, exposing my neck to him. Running his nose along the space between my shoulder and behind my ear, he inhaled deeply, his cock pressing into my ass.

Burrowing his hand under the barely-there fabric of my panties, he stroked my pussy before sliding a finger inside me. We both groaned.

"You're so wet for me already."

I pushed back against him, looking for more of what only Bane could give me. "I'm always wet for my fiancé."

"Fuck, I love the way that sounds on your lips." He ripped my panties off and slapped my ass. The shock of the sting turned me on even more. Bane fumbled with the zipper on his jeans, finally lowering it and springing free his cock. Then he brushed the head of it against my pussy, the sensation making my knees buckle.

He slammed into me without any warning, anchoring one hand on my hip and keeping the other one wrapped around my throat. I watched him in the mirror with half-lidded eyes, enjoying the way he let his savage side take over when he fucked me. He was relentless with his thrusts, each one getting him further and further inside me. He marked me as his, and I screamed out his name as I came. Bane roared his own release, both of us left breathing heavily, still connected. When he finally slid free, he took the hand towel off the rack and cleaned me.

I placed my hand on his hand as he held me steady, his steady gaze falling to the engagement ring now on my finger. I hadn't wanted anything ostentatious, but Bane wouldn't hear of anything else. He wanted me to get a rock, one that showed everyone who I belonged to. That was how I ended up with a bright blue sapphire, the same color as the little bird I was named after.

"That looks fucking amazing on you," he said, standing up and catching my mouth in another kiss.

"You look fucking amazing on me," I replied, making him smile.

"Are you ready to go?"

I shook my head. "You ripped my panties. I need to get another pair."

"Go bare," he said as I went to move past him. He sank his fingers into my ass as he spun me into his hips. "I love to know I can have access to you whenever I want."

"Bane, I can't do that." Gesturing to the skirt of the dress, I added, "This thing won't cover a damn thing."

"Fuck," he muttered, pressing our foreheads together. "I guess I'll just have to wait for you again."

Getting up onto my toes, I brushed my mouth against his and sauntered into the walk-in closet. "It didn't stop you last time."

"That's because you had me hooked then. I needed another taste."

"And now?"

"I'm a full-blown junkie now, Little Bird, but I wouldn't change it for all the world. I fucking love how addicted I am to you." He accosted me in the closet, pushing me up against the wall. "I fucking love you."

My fingers curled around the base of his neck. "I fucking

love you, too, Bane." I slipped from his grasp, laughing when he growled. "Bianca will be wondering where we are."

"I'll just tell her I was ravaging my fiancée. She'd totally understand."

Grabbing my clutch, I looked at him, letting my gaze drift down his amazing body. "She wouldn't. Come on. You can get your hands on me after we're done."

Marching toward me, he wrapped his hand under my jaw and held me in place. A thrill of lust shot through me, making me squeeze my thighs together. "I'll never get enough of having my hands on you," he said in a low, rough voice—a voice that came more from the darkness in him that I knew existed. His lips were an all-out assault as he took my mouth, plunging his tongue inside with a barely-restrained rhythm.

Wrapping my legs around his waist, I ground my pussy against the bulge in his jeans, trying to find more friction to work with.

Bane chuckled. "I thought we had to go." Sucking on my neck, I tilted my head to the side to give him better access.

"I need you more." I gasped when he slid his hand between us and brushed a knuckle against my already-soaked pussy.

"I guess you do."

WE WERE OVER AN HOUR LATE FOR DINNER. BIANCA only gave me a knowing smile when we walked in before pulling me into a fierce hug.

"I'm so glad to see you looking and feeling better."

"I do," I replied with a smile.

"Now, show me this rock my brother got you."

I showed her my ring finger, tilting it side to side so the light would catch the blue fire of the stone.

"Damn, Bane, you must really love this woman."

He wrapped an arm around my waist, dropping a kiss onto my shoulder. "More than my own life," he told his sister.

His words made me glow with love. "It's more than I wanted," I told Bianca. "But Bane has a stubborn streak a mile wide."

She chuckled. "Don't I know it. And don't even bother to try and deter him from buying you things." She gestured to her house. "See? I mentioned I really loved this house *once,* and he goes and buys it for me." She shook her head and turned around. "Come into the kitchen. Dinner will take a little while to heat back up."

I grimaced. "I'm sorry we were late. We—"

"I was screwing my fiancée like she deserves to be," Bane cut in. I shot him a glare, and he grinned.

I looked at Bianca helplessly, but she only laughed. "I remember when James and I were like that, always wanting to get naked and fuck."

"Please," Bane said, a little pained. "I do not need to know about you and James fucking."

"And why not?" James said, walking into the kitchen with Valentine in his arms. "If we didn't, we wouldn't have our gorgeous girl here." Passing her to Bane, he added, "Hold her for a bit. She's missed you."

Bane became putty in Valentine's presence, his complete focus on her.

"Congratulations," James said softly.

I spun to face him, feeling a blush creep up my cheeks. "Thank you."

"Would you like some wine?"

"I'd love some." I looked back at Bane to find him deep in a game of peekaboo with his niece. I trailed after James, smiling when he handed me a glass of red wine. "I never got to say thank you, James."

He paused with his bottle of beer almost at his mouth. "Thank you?"

"For saving me that day… from the warehouse."

He took a sip of his drink, then placed the bottle down. "I was just doing my job, Wren."

Shaking my head, I tried to keep the tears at bay, but it was a battle I had no hope of winning. They came, making him step closer and rest a hand on my forearm.

"Hey, it's okay."

"I'm sorry," I whispered, glancing at Bane to see if he'd noticed. He'd become really overprotective since I'd been discharged from the hospital, and if he saw me crying again, he was liable to lose his shit at his brother-in-law. "I can't help but feel so guilty. Three of your colleagues died in that explosion."

James looked over his shoulder at his wife, who was stirring a pot of sauce. When his eyes returned to me, he said, "Hey, don't feel guilty for that. They were just doing their job. Don't get me wrong, I'm going to miss every single one of them, but they knew what they were doing. Every time we go out on a job, we know what we're risking."

I wanted to believe what he was saying but discovered I'd been having these real lows where guilt would crash over me. Bane usually made love to me until the feeling passed, but being with James now brought it all home.

Bianca would've been a widow if things had been different.

Valentine would've lost her father.

I wouldn't be here if things had been different.

I felt the weight and familiarity of Bane's arm around my waist, his scent swirling in the air. "Are you okay?" he asked, his eyes serious.

I nodded. "Yes, just having a low moment."

"You might want to think about getting some therapy," James said. "Some of the guys at work… some that were on that job, are seeing the departmental shrink, and they've all been much happier lately."

It wasn't a terrible idea at all. "Okay. I'll look into it." Shaking myself, I tried to move past the crushing weight I felt in my chest and focused on what was happening now. "And how is Miss Valentine?" I asked, stroking the little girl's cheeks. Her mouth flexed into a small smile.

"Why don't you hold her?" Bane suggested, already positioning her so I could take her. I wasn't really comfortable with kids, with babies even less so. I was always worried I'd drop them. Bane nodded in encouragement when I stared at him with wide-eyes.

"Okay." As I accepted the small bundle, I stared down at her face, waiting for the tears. She stared up at me with her calm midnight-blue eyes, and I wondered what the fuss was all about.

"You look good with a baby," Bianca commented, and I jerked my head up to stare at her.

"No, I don't think so," I replied too quickly. My gaze flickered to Bane who was staring at me, watching me with an intensity that made my breath catch.

Clearing my throat, I handed Valentine back to him. Leaning in, he whispered into my ear, "I can't fucking wait to see your belly swelling with my baby."

I shivered, taking another sip of my wine. Babies were never supposed to be in my future. It wasn't what I wanted, and I think that all stemmed from my childhood. I was terrified of leaving them alone out in the world. Hawk and I had to fight for every scrap, and that was something I never wanted a child of mine to endure. As I looked at Bane, I realized any children we did have wouldn't ever be left wanting. Bane had more than enough money to last him half-dozen lifetimes, and if anything were to happen to us, Bianca and James would be there, of that I was sure.

"So, have you made any wedding plans yet?" Bianca asked me while moving back into the kitchen. She pulled open the oven and brought out a tray of lasagna. The scent of oregano and garlic filled the air.

"No. None yet."

She gave me a warm smile. "You weren't one of those girls who dreamed of their perfect wedding either?"

"God, no. I was focused on surviving."

"I'll help you if you like? I may not have planned it out when I was a kid, but I sure got into the wedding spirit after James proposed."

Taking another sip from my wine, I nodded. "I'd appreciate that. Thank you."

When Valentine began to fuss, James went and took her to bed, leaving Bane and me sitting together in the family room while Bianca prepared some salads. He pulled me down onto his lap, resting one hand on my thigh and the other around my waist.

"Did you want to have children?"

"I hadn't thought about it too much," I replied. "What about you?"

"I didn't until I just saw you with Valentine. You have no idea how much of a turn-on it was to see you holding her." Picking up my hand, he placed it on his cock. I ran my fingers along his hard length, enjoying the way his eyes rolled back in his head. His fingers tightened on my thigh before sweeping higher.

He stared at me when he felt my bare pussy. "You little minx," he whispered roughly, biting down on my earlobe.

Sucking in a gasp, I wiggled in his lap. "You said you wanted access to me tonight."

His knuckle brushed against my pussy, making me bite my lip. Sensations sparked across my skin, but I had to remind myself to stay quiet. Another languid sweep of his hand parted my folds, his finger circling my clit.

"I want you to come," he said, his eyes dark and demanding. "I want to feel you on my fingers." He pushed the digits into my slick heat, and I bit his shoulder to keep the groan in. He pumped his fingers, each time hitting that tight bundle of nerves that would send me over the edge in pleasure. Quickly, I looked over my shoulder to find Bianca had left the kitchen.

"She's gone to help James," Bane said, sucking on my neck. "Come on my fingers, Little Bird."

He crooked his finger inside me, shoving me into bliss. I came apart around his hand, staring in wonder at the man who controlled my body with little more than a touch and filthy words. He slammed his mouth to mine, possessing me with his kiss.

"Good girl, Little Bird."

He continued to kiss me until I was begging for him to make me come again. When I couldn't take it anymore, I broke the kiss and pressed my forehead to his.

"I love you, Bane."

"I love you, too, baby."

"And I can't wait to be your wife. I've had enough heartache in my life to know that you make me happy."

He kissed my eyelids, and I knew he was recalling the time when they'd been swollen shut. He'd told me he'd missed seeing my eyes, staring at me, and never wanted me to suffer like that again. I couldn't have agreed more.

"I can't wait to have a family with you either."

"Me, too," I whispered. Because I knew I'd found my home. After drifting for so long, I'd finally gotten to a place I wanted to be.

And that was with Bane by my side.

EPILOGUE

Wren

One Year Later…

I PRESSED MY HAND TO MY STOMACH, THEN LOOKED back at the plastic applicator wand on the bathroom counter. I never thought two pink lines could mean so much to me, but apparently, they do.

"Wren, are you ready, babe?" Darcy called out from the other side of the bathroom door. We were in a hotel suite getting ready for my wedding to Bane, a day that was already amazing, but with this news too, it was starting to become more than I could've imagined.

I pulled open the door, my eyes darting to Darcy's pregnant belly first before returning to her face.

"Urgh, don't tell me. I look awful. I know. I'm the size of a house, and I'm not even halfway through yet."

"You're gorgeous, Darcy." I sniffled, and that one sound put my best friend on high alert.

"What? What's wrong?"

Pulling the pregnancy test from the pocket of my dressing gown, I held it up in front of me and shrugged. "Looks like we might have kids who'll be best friends, too."

Her eyes widened before a giant smile formed on her mouth. "Yes!" she shouted, pumping the air with her first. "Yes, fucking *yes!*"

I began to laugh, her enthusiasm was infectious. "I've literally just done the test, so you're the first to know."

"What do you think Bane will say?" she asked, sobering a little. She led me to the dining room table in the suite, and we sat down.

"He's going to be ecstatic. He's been threatening to knock me up since we got engaged."

"Ah, so Bane was the clucky one, then."

Fuck, she had no idea. Bane had been relentless in his need to put a baby in me. I did nothing to discourage him, enjoying how much sex we were having. I touched my flat stomach and blinked the tears from my eyes.

Darcy started to shake her head. "Ah, no. Nope. No tears right now." Snapping some tissues from the box on the table, she dabbed them under my eyes. "You've just finished getting your hair and makeup done, so this..." she gestured to my face, "... isn't going to work. No tears. Please."

Fuck, she was so right. "You're right. I'm sorry." I internally pulled myself together, then said, "Better?"

"Yeah." Taking my hand, she squeezed. "I'm so fucking happy right now. When will you tell Bane?"

"I don't know. I kind of want to get a blood test to confirm it first."

"How long since you've had a period?"

"Two months, maybe?"

"Tender breasts? Sensitive to smells? Sense of taste gone whacky?"

I recalled last night when Bane had given a little too much attention to my breasts. They'd been sore then and had been for a little while too. I chalked that up to Bane being relentless in his attention to my body, but maybe it was because of the baby instead. Then I thought a little harder. I had become a lot more sensitive to smells. Bane's cologne, which I loved, now made my stomach turn, and I'd also gone off coffee.

"Shit. All of the above."

Darcy nodded like she was the smartest woman in the room. "Yep, classic case of being knocked-up."

Tears threatened to spill from my eyes, but I carefully brushed them away.

"Are they good tears or bad tears, Wren?" my best friend asked. She knew I didn't ever plan to have children—it was something we constantly debated—so I understood her question.

"They're good, babe. I just…" I let my gaze drift down to the positive pregnancy test between us. "I just wasn't expecting it, I guess. I kind of thought it wouldn't ever happen naturally like you and Baron experienced."

"Oh, Wren, we're a fucking anomaly. It's my polycystic ovaries that fucked us up." She placed a hand on her swelling stomach. "I'm just glad the second round of IVF took, you know? I don't think I could've gone through the stress of waiting and watching for a month only to find out it hadn't taken *again*."

My phone beeped with a message from Bane. I read it once, then read it again, this time unable to fight the tears.

Darcy shoved more tissues at me. "What did he say?"

"He said he can't wait to marry me." I left off the bit where he said he'd make my ass pink tonight before he fucked me in the sex swing.

"Aww." Darcy's smile was whimsical. "I remember when Baron and I got married. He used to send me messages like that. Then life got in the way."

"You could always sext him during the day?"

She stared at me for a beat before a huge grin appeared. "Yes. I'm going to do that right now. Is that eggplant emoji still a thing?" She waved her hand in my face. "Forget it. I'll just talk dirty to him. Lord knows these pregnancy hormones make me want to fuck him six times a day."

I got up from the table, taking the pregnancy test with me, and went into the bedroom. A sense of grief washed over me then. My brother wasn't going to be here to see this—the wedding, his niece or nephew being born. Although a year had passed, and I'd mourned the loss of him, there were moments when Hawk's memory slammed into me with all the finesse of a semi-trailer, and I was left floundering with that aching loss once more.

"Pull it together, Wren," I muttered to myself. This was a happy day, and I knew my brother would be watching from wherever he was. I looked up at the ceiling like he would be floating up there or something. But he wasn't. He'd never magically *poofed* into existence when I thought of him over this last year.

Turning, I looked to my dress hanging on a hook behind the door, the white garment bag swollen with the layers of tulle. Bianca had helped me pick it out, coming to fittings with me when Darcy had had to go to an OBGYN appointment. We'd grown a lot closer over the year, to the point where she actually felt like a sister to me.

"Are you ready to get dressed?" Darcy asked, breezing into my room.

"I think so, yeah."

"Good. Oh, wait, that was a knock on the door."

She came back in with Bianca, who looked amazing in an emerald green gown that hugged her perfect figure. Her dark hair was up in a soft twist with soft tendrils framing her face. Her makeup was done tastefully, enhancing her natural beauty.

"Are you ready?" she asked, clapping her hands excitedly.

I smiled. Ready to spend the rest of my life with her brother? "Yes."

Together, my best friend and future sister-in-law helped me into the Pnina Tornai gown. The top half was a corset with a sweetheart neckline and a few see-through panels along my ribs. The bottom half was a princess skirt with layers of tulle and lace. It was stunning, and I felt beautiful in it. As Bianca moved behind me to lace up the back, I stared at the floor, wondering what I'd look like. Seeing it and trying it on in a shop was one thing, but to see it on with full hair and makeup, that was something else.

I sucked in a breath with the final pull of the corset, placing my hand to my stomach.

"You look amazing, babe," Darcy said, looking at me.

"Yeah?" I ran my hands down the skirt. "You don't think it's too much?"

"Please," Bianca adds. "My brother will love it because it's you in there. He was actually more difficult to deal with planning the wedding."

I laughed at that because I could see how Bane's controlling side would've come out. He'd told me he wanted the start of our lives together to be perfect to make up for the shitty starts we'd both had. I told him I simply wanted to be his wife, which, of course, had led to some of the hottest sex we've had so far.

The girls helped me slip on my shoes, then handed me my bouquet. It was almost go-time. We were meeting the photographer downstairs to take some shots before getting in the car and going to La Venta Inn, where we'd get married overlooking the Pacific Ocean. The ceremony was going to be small—Bianca and James, and, of course, little Valentine, Darcy and Baron, and Bane's colleagues, Dagger and Andy, would be on hand for security.

I didn't mind that it was such an intimate wedding. It was going to be nice to be surrounded by my favorite people, but the only thing that really mattered at the end of the day was that I was going to be Wren Rivera.

FUCK, WHY WAS I SO NERVOUS? AS I WAITED FOR MY future wife to walk down the aisle, I did my best not to shove my hands in my pockets or thrust them through my hair. I was fucking wired, and that nervous energy was there for everyone to see.

"She'll be here," James said into my ear.

I turned to look at my brother-in-law. "I know. I just…" I didn't know what. I was nervous, not because I didn't think she'd come but because I wasn't sure I could control myself long enough to get through the ceremony before I had to take her cunt. We slept apart last night, and it had nearly killed me. After being together every single day for a year, waking up beside her, having showers with her, fucking sinking in between her legs at every opportunity, being apart for that one night had seemed like a death sentence.

Turning around, I looked out at the ocean and breathed in deep. Our ceremony was small compared to most of the Hollywood elites. Neither of us wanted to fill it up with people we hardly spoke to. We weren't even having a huge party afterward. Bianca had been granted access to the La Venta kitchen, and she was going to be cooking us some of our favorites. I couldn't wait to sit down with my wife and my family to celebrate.

"Bianca just arrived," James said, bouncing Valentine on his hip. My niece had grown so much in the past year. She looked a lot like James, but I could see my sister in her too. "Darcy's here, too."

I turned my head quickly to take a look. Bianca gave me a thumbs up before she accepted Valentine onto her lap, and Darcy rested her hand on her expanding stomach and smiled. I nodded at her, a pang of longing shooting through me at seeing that new life inside her. I wanted Wren pregnant. I wanted to see her growing with the life *I* put in there, but I also understood if she wasn't so quick to jump on the baby train with me.

The music started, a piece I didn't recognize, and I turned around, my gaze firmly on the place where Wren would appear. I sucked in a breath when I saw her. She looked like an angel coming toward me, her cream gown making her tits and waist look fucking amazing. Baron was walking her down the aisle, her hand resting on top of his forearm as they made the slow walk toward me.

Everything seemed to disappear. I couldn't see anything, hear anything, other than Wren and the sound of my heart thumping irregularly against my ribs. She was a vision. Baron gave her to me with a smile before taking his place beside his wife.

I leaned in and kissed my Little Bird. Fuck the traditions. Our friends and family laughed before the celebrant cleared her throat and broke us up. Wren blinked at me, then smiled.

I tuned out what the celebrant was saying. We'd opted for the traditional vows. Wren already knew how I felt about her, so she didn't need me to say those words again in front of witnesses. The only people who mattered knew the depth of our love, and I would love the fuck out of her for as long as I drew breath.

Wren was looking at me expectedly, and I turned to the celebrant. She whispered, "This is your line."

"Fuck. I do."

I watched as Wren said her vows to me. We then exchanged rings, and I was kissing my wife. My fucking amazing, beautiful *wife*.

James clapped me on the back when Wren and I broke apart. "I never thought I'd see the day," he said. "Congrats, man."

"Thanks, brother." Turning to Wren, I whispered, "I want to get you alone."

She gave me a sexy smirk that meant she had the same idea. "Let's allow the photographer to get his fill first, then we can sneak off."

Thirty agonizing minutes later, the photos were done, and we were shuffling into the restaurant. I grabbed my wife's hand and tugged her away from the table everyone else was going to sit at, leading her back out the doors and into the garden. It was dusk now, the colors from the setting sun gone, leaving us in a warm twilight.

I took Wren into a secluded spot and pressed her against a wall. My mouth was on hers a moment later, claiming her in the kind of kiss I wanted to give her after we said our vows. My hips flexed into hers. I wanted her to know how much I wanted her.

"This dress is fucking amazing, Little Bird," I said, trailing kisses down her throat. "But it's coming off as soon as we're in our room tonight."

"Yes," she moaned, her hands going to the buckle on my slacks. She flicked open the button and lowered the zipper, springing my cock and wrapping her palm around it. We both sucked in a hiss at the contact.

"Fuck, I love you," I growled into her ear, flexing my hips so I was fucking her palm.

"I love you, too."

Something in her tone made me look at her. I placed a hand against her stomach. "I want a baby in here. Soon."

She squeezed my cock, making my vision spotty for a moment. "I have something to tell you."

"Yeah?"

Holding my hand to her abdomen, she whispered, "You already put a baby in there."

I stared at her, her smile telling me she wasn't yanking my fucking chain. Glancing down at her stomach for a second, I looked back at her face, unable to form the words I knew I needed to say to her.

"You're going to be a daddy."

That's when it hit me. Wren was carrying my child. I was going to be a father, and I was going to be the best damn father ever. I kissed her again, sweeping my tongue into her mouth. She pumped my cock, getting me harder while I swept her underwear out of the way and sank a finger into her wet cunt. We both groaned.

"Just fuck me already," she whispered into my ear, biting down on the lobe. "Fuck me like you're never going to let me go."

"I'm never going to let you go, anyway." But I did as my wife asked. I slid into her slick heat, her cunt welcoming me, squeezing the ever-loving fuck out of me. My thrusts were deep, just like our love was. She came a moment later, and if that's what pregnancy did for my Wren, I was going to be giving her multiple upon multiple orgasms for the entire pregnancy. Then I was going to knock her up again.

She clamped down on my cock once more, the sensation, the feelings, the news that I was going to be a father funneling down into my black heart, making it expand with love. I came with a loud groan, burying my face in her neck. Her heart pounded against mine, our breaths mingling in the cool twilight air.

"I'm going to be a daddy," I said.

"And I'm going be a mommy."

I looked at her, brushing some hair from her face.

Fuck, I loved her.

"We're going to be parents."

ANOTHER EPILOGUE

Dagger

The day after the wedding…

FOLDING MY ARMS BEHIND MY HEAD, I SETTLED MORE deeply into my pillow and stared at the woman getting dressed at the foot of the bed. We'd been fucking for more than a year and I still didn't know a goddam thing about her—nothing of importance anyway—which was the way I liked it. I knew how she sounded when she came, how she dug her nails into my shoulders when I went down on her.

I also knew she was a ball-buster in her job and that no-shit attitude extended into her private life too. She was a woman who was not used to yielding, and I saw that as a personal challenge.

She was concentrating on buttoning up her white blouse, her blonde hair free from the tight bun she usually wore it in. It sheeted across her cheeks, hiding her from my view. It…

softened her usually severe face.

"You should wear your hair down more," I told her.

She jerked her head up, staring at me with eyes the color of smoked glass, her mouth set in a hard line. I hated how she pulled away from me after we'd fucked. It was like she was ashamed of what we were doing.

Fuck, maybe she was.

It had started out as a dirty little deal between us—a deal I'd forced her into.

A deal I didn't regret for one second.

She looked away from me. "We can't do this anymore."

"Can't do what?"

"See each other."

"Seeing each other would imply we had more than a sexual relationship," I replied casually, rubbing my palm over my short hair. "Why should we stop? Bane doesn't suspect a goddam thing."

"He could find out." She perched on the end of the mattress to slide her shoes back onto her feet—feet I had digging into my lower back as I'd fucked her—hard—just thirty minutes ago.

"As long as his business isn't affected, he doesn't care who sucks my dick."

"I'm glad to hear that's all you think I'm good for—sucking your dick." Shaking her head, she added, "It doesn't matter anyway. I won't be in L.A. for much longer."

I sat up, the sheet falling away from my chest. "Why?"

Her cool gray eyes lingered on the linear scars across my pectorals. She'd never asked about how I'd gotten them, but I suspected she'd found out about my time in Afghanistan all on her own. She was a clever little rabbit like that. "That's none of

317

your business."

"Jesus fuck, Chantelle." I ran my hand through my hair again. "Just tell me."

"Why should I? We aren't in a relationship. This is just fucking." She threw the words back at me with a sneer, stepping into her skirt, and reaching behind her to zip it up.

I stalked from the bed, completely naked, and semi-hard because when we sparred verbally, it turned me the fuck on. "Where are you going?"

She leveled me with an arctic stare, the intensity of her gaze ratcheting up my lust another degree. "Detroit."

My hands curled into fists. "Why?"

"That's none of your business," she repeated, pulling on her fitted black jacket.

"Is it for work?"

"That's none of your business."

I narrowed my eyes at her. She didn't want me to know? Fine. I'd find out another way.

Wrapping my hand around my cock, I started to pump it slowly.

Up and down…

Up… And… Down…

Her gray eyes slid to my cock before returning to my face. "We're not doing this."

"Yes, we are," I replied, stepping closer. Curling my hand around the back of her neck, I said softly, "If this is it for us, I want to have your lips wrapped around my dick one last time."

"No."

I squeezed a little harder. "On your knees, cara. Now."

"N—"

I slammed my mouth to hers in a dominating kiss, thrusting my tongue inside her mouth and demanding she give me all of her. I sucked in a hiss when she bit my lip, making me jerk away.

"I hate you," she seethed, wiping my blood from her lips.

"I have no doubt about that."

Her eyes blazed with defiance.

"Tell me," I ground out. "Tell me why you're going to Detroit."

"Personal reasons," she finally said after a long moment of glaring at me.

"How long?"

"You don't own me, Tony. And there's nothing you can do to coerce me into telling you."

I tightened my grip. "If you want to keep your career, I do."

"There are some things more important than a career."

She stepped out of my hold, and I let her go. Grinding my teeth together, I tamped down my rage.

"I can find out, you know?" I told her in a low, dark voice. "You have your methods of getting information and so do I."

Pulling the strap of her bag up onto her shoulder, Chantelle turned on her heel and moved towards the door. "Just leave it, Tony. There's nothing you can do to save me—at least not this time." She took in a deep breath and let it out, wincing like it was painful. "This is just something I have to do."

As she shut the door behind her, I cursed, swiping up my sweats and pulling them on. She said I couldn't save her? Well, that's where she was wrong.

There was something more to this and I was going to fucking find out.

little
BIRD

A DARK MAFIA ROMANCE

USA TODAY BESTSELLING AUTHOR
KALLY ASH